FALLING IN LOVE

"What more do you wish me to say?" Lydia asked.

"Tell me *why* you thought it necessary."

Lydia looked at the rug, at the portrait over the mantel, at the window. "Jasper . . ."

"Jasper has waited a fair number of years," Rafe said on a dry note. "He could have waited another few days if that had been necessary."

"I feared you would feel it more than the estate could afford. There is so much to do, so much *expense,* and you've already bought too many mounts; so I thought if one of the mares . . ."

He had eyed her in a judicious manner as she had spoken, and now interrupted. "Although that may have been part of the reason, I think it is something else. I think you feel I have usurped your place in this family, and that you must prove, again and again, that you are necessary to it. Or something of that sort?"

Lydia's blush had faded. Now it returned. "You would say I am jealous." She sighed. "I will admit that at times I have felt that ignominious emotion and have berated myself for it. I know you've a responsibility here. I have watched you go far beyond what the children's father expected or even desired, miser that he had become." It was her turn to walk to the window and stare out. "I do not like myself very well when I stop to think of my reactions to you. I do not know myself."

Lydia felt Rafe's hands on her shoulders and wondered when he ⬛⬛⬛⬛⬛⬛⬛⬛⬛⬛⬛⬛⬛lso found she liked the g⬛⬛⬛⬛⬛⬛⬛⬛⬛⬛plied . . . and still more ⬛⬛⬛⬛⬛⬛⬛ . .

Books by Jeanne Savery

THE WIDOW AND THE RAKE
THE REFORMED RAKE
A CHRISTMAS TREASURE
A LADY'S DECEPTION
CUPID'S CHALLENGE
LADY STEPHANIE
A TIMELESS LOVE
A LADY'S LESSON
LORD GALVESTON AND THE GHOST
A LADY'S PROPOSAL
THE WIDOWED MISS MORDAUNT
A LOVE FOR LYDIA

Published by Zebra Books

A LOVE FOR LYDIA

Jeanne Savery

ZEBRA BOOKS
Kensington Publishing Corp.
http://www.zebrabooks.com

ZEBRA BOOKS are published by

Kensington Publishing Corp.
850 Third Avenue
New York, NY 10022

Copyright © 1999 by Jeanne Savery Casstevens

Zebra and the Z logo Reg. U.S. Pat. & TM Off.

First Printing: September, 1999
10 9 8 7 6 5 4 3 2 1

Printed in the United States of America

One

Miss Lydia Anne Cottrell opened the door to the schoolroom and peered in. She smiled slightly at the glum looks on the faces of each and every one of the young Easten family. The heavy black clothing, in which even the toddler was shrouded, didn't help their mood, of course. Besides, even when one detested the dead and, on occasion, had actually wished the old tartar would take himself off to an unworldly abode, it was a shock when it actually happened. She moved on into the room, drawing all eyes.

"Well, Sir Jasper," she said to the new and very young baronet, "what is all this gloom and doom? I thought for sure you and James would be dancing hornpipes, and your sisters hand-in-hand in a merry round dance." She smiled at the seven-year-old twins, Felicia and Fenella, who smiled back for an instant and then, equally quickly, sobered. Lydia frowned at the lack of response. Again she looked from one youngster to the next. "Come now. Why such long faces?" No one said a word. "I know he was your father, but surely you cannot wish him back?"

"You know we'd never want that, Liddy." Jasper, a tallish lad, rose awkwardly to his feet. He was fast outgrowing his coat, his knobby wrists revealed and doubled-up fists moving restlessly. He obviously didn't know what to do with them or with the inches he had acquired in the past few months. " 'Tis a far more serious matter about which we worry."

"But what that worry may be remains a mystery to me," said Lydia after another moment's silence. "You'll never again find yourselves called into the study for a beating. And, starting with today's dinner, you'll find the food improves. And you'll be able to run and play and even, perhaps, have proper ponies, each and every one of you. You'll learn to ride as some of you should have done long ago and . . ."

Lydia stopped when *still* no one smiled. Not one child seemed even a jot happier. She moved farther into the room. "All right, then," she said. "What *is* the problem?"

"You," said Sir Jasper and shrugged in the hopes of settling his too tight coat more comfortably.

"Me." Lydia felt a muscle jump in her cheek and consciously relaxed her jaw. It would do no good to tell the children how frightened she was or how utterly unsure of what she would or should or even what she *could* do.

"We can't think . . ." Jasper shrugged again, and then words erupted in the quick, tumbling way of the insecure. "What *are* you to do, Liddy? But more, what are *we* to do? We can't possibly get on without you. We *can't.*"

Lydia moved to the chair occupied by the youngest, a toddler muffled in her blacks, who sat with legs stretched straight in front of her and her finger in her mouth. Lydia picked up Alice and seated herself, hugging the youngster close.

"Oh, Liddy dear, what can we do?" wailed Margaret. "We cannot live without you, but will a guardian chosen by our father allow you . . ."

The girl burst into the easy tears that for reasons Lydia

had never discovered, never turned her eldest half sister's face into the unsightly mess such sobbing would make of anyone else's. Certainly her own infrequent tears resulted in red nose, red eyes, and splotchy skin!

"Now, my dear. All is not so desperate as that, surely," said Lydia brightly. Jasper and Margaret just stared at her, the tears still falling one after another down the girl's cheeks. "Well," added Lydia after a moment when their expressions assured her they would not be put off, "it is true I've not yet decided what to do with myself, but it is not impossible my grandfather will take pity on me and take me in."

"Grandfather?" Twelve-year-old Mary, the next younger after Jasper, got up from her chair and came around the table to lean against Lydia. "Do you *have* a grandfather?"

Lydia felt a faint warmth in her cheeks. "I know Mother and I never spoke of him. He wasn't our favorite topic of conversation," she admitted a trifle defensively. "I wrote him when Mother died, of course. He didn't answer then, but that doesn't mean he won't when he discovers I've no roof over my head." Then she smiled. "He is, perhaps, even more curmudgeonly than *your* papa used to be!"

"Then, that explains why you didn't speak of him," said Mary complacently. "Why would you mention someone like that when we already had one? We certainly didn't need another!"

Lydia felt a true chuckle rise at that bit of twelve-year-old logic. She used the arm not holding the sleepy baby Alice to hug Mary and allowed the laugh release. Everyone relaxed a trifle.

"But, Liddy," said Sir Jasper when he'd stopped grinning, "you cannot wish to go live with still another old skint! And if you do, why, that may take care of you, but what of us? We need you." Then it must have occurred to the boy just how selfish that sounded. "But, of course you must do what is best for you, Liddy. I'm certain our guardian will have his own plans for us."

His voice cracked, boy-fashion, on the last words, and his tone was one of such despair Lydia again found herself wishing to laugh. In this case she feared it would embarrass Jasper too much, and she had no desire to do that to a boy just on the verge of edging into adulthood.

Soothingly, she said, "I assure you, I've no desire to contact my grandfather. In actual fact, he might *not* respond to my missive, of course; but I am family, and it is possible he'd not wish to see me in the workhouse." She spoke with forced cheerfulness. "Of course, there is the fact he told Mother when she eloped with my father that he never wished to see her face again, and although he cannot know it, mine is very like hers; so that alone might put him off. But I'm certain you know I've not the least desire to leave you children. You know very well I think of you all as my very own. I may be nothing more than a sister, a half sister at that, rather than your mother. And at twenty-six, I am not old enough, of course, to have given birth to some of you, but that is, nevertheless, the way I feel."

Lydia hugged the youngest and laid her head on the soft baby hair of the child who had been her mother's last and, it turned out, her bane. Lydia sighed softly. It would tear her heart out to leave this child, who had been most truly hers, and go . . . somewhere. To leave *any* of them would be difficult. She would not be there to soothe their tears or laugh at their pranks or watch them grow into worthwhile adults.

"Liddy, you don't *have* to go, do you?" That was nine-year-old James. "I'll be good, Liddy. I promise I'll never ever again cause you grief. Truly Liddy."

He came around the nursery table to stand at her

other side, but Liddy was out of arms and couldn't give him the hug she knew he needed.

"Don't go." A tear escaped, and James wiped it away with the back of his grubby hand, the tear smearing grime into mud which transferred to his cheek in a streak.

"Jamie, if I go, it will *not* be because you spend so much of your energy getting into mischief! Although I appreciate your thought, I think it better if you don't promise you'll *not* misbehave but, perhaps, that you will *try very hard* not to misbehave." She smiled at the boy, who was shaking his head vigorously. "Jamie," she half scolded, half teased, "the first time you see something which draws your interest, you'll be in the middle of new mischief at once! I *know.*"

"Not if you stay. I'll be . . ." He glanced at his half sister and sighed. "I'll *try* to be good."

"I'd like it better, Jamie, if you'd try whether I'm here or not. It is for your own sake you should promise to reform." Lydia tried to look stern but failed. She sighed softly. "But this is not the time for a religious lesson, is it? Now. All of you. You mustn't worry about me." She looked around the table. *"None* of you. You will be starting a new life which will be fun, will it not? After all," she said a trifle desperately when that roused no cheer in the children, "it cannot possibly be so bad as it was! It *must* be better!"

"But can we expect any such thing?" asked Jasper slowly. "My father . . . Do you not think it likely he'd choose a guardian very much like himself?"

Lydia's smile faded as the other children seemed to diminish in some slight way difficult to define. She firmed her back and directed a look straight at Jasper, a warning which the boy, young as he was, read. "It is not possible," she said and forced a wide smile. "Your father could have searched the length and breadth of

England, and surely he'd have found no one so irrationally stern or so unforgiving or so much a miser."

"But he'll have tried," said Margaret. She rose and rounded the table with the newfound grace of a girl just coming into womanhood. "You *know* he'll have tried." She stood behind the chair and put her arms around Lydia's neck. "Liddy, please don't leave us. You won't, will you? Promise?"

A hint of despair was in the look Lydia cast Jasper's way. "I can't promise, Margaret. How can we predict what your guardian will say about the existence of a pauper half sister who has been left nothing in your father's will? And why should he have left me anything? I'm none of his, you know. From your guardian's point of view, it would very likely be better if I were nothing more than your governess, teaching you your letters and proper posture and how to sew, than that he discover an unwanted spinster dwelling in Sir Jasper's house!"

Jasper, too, rose to his feet, his chair clattering over to land on its back. He ignored it, leaning over the table, his weight on his spread hands. "But, Liddy, that's the answer!"

Lydia blinked. "Answer?"

"The way we'll keep you, Liddy! You *will* be our governess. Our much beloved governess without whom we'll turn into little monsters." He grinned and winked broadly at James, who frowned, not instantly understanding. "But with *you* here, we'll behave like angels. *Won't* we, James?"

Jasper glared at James, whose misery caused him to take in his brother's words more slowly than he would normally have done. A smile grew just as slowly. "And I know who will play the devil if she isn't allowed to stay with us," said the younger boy. "*I* will! I'll throw temper tantrums, and I'll put frogs in our guardian's bed, or, better yet, I'll put them in the maids' beds. If we have maids again. And when they quit he'll be mad as hops!"

"Yes, and he'll punish you for it," objected Lydia. "Don't you dare do any such thing!"

"Besides," said Jasper, after a moment, "it is far more likely he won't object to the extra fees the way our papa did and will send you off to school along with me. So we won't be around except for the hols. It's the girls I'm worried about," he added in an airy voice which fooled no one. "You must stay as their governess, Liddy."

Everyone knew he depended upon Lydia to help him over rough spots and to speak for him when he had needs. Needs best illustrated at this particular moment by the much to be desired new coat, one he could button properly rather than do so only by straining the holes.

"Be your governess . . ." Liddy repeated after a long moment's silence.

"It's what you are, Liddy. Along with all the other things you do, like housekeeper and, while she still lived, lady's maid and nurse to Mother and all that sort of thing." Margaret paused, frowning ever so slightly. "It wouldn't be a lie, exactly, would it?" she asked carefully. "And telling our guardian we need you? That would be truth. We could explain that there have been too many changes in our lives in the last year and we can't survive yet another."

"That last is surely true," said the brand-new Sir Jasper. "First our mother died and that was very bad; but then Father got rid of the servants except for Cook and the kitchen girl and old Herbie out in the barn, and then he made Herbie work in the garden which he hates, because all the horses—excepting that cantankerous old stallion he couldn't sell for a meg if it would save his soul and . . ."

Lydia got lost in all the boy's pronouns as he continued, but thought perhaps she followed well enough she got the gist of it.

". . . You know, Liddy," finished Jasper and tipped his head thoughtfully, "I wonder what he thought he'd ride if he *did* get rid of Devil's Spawn as well as the rest."

"Your father? He didn't think of that, did he, and he *should* have gotten rid of them all, should he not? If he could rid himself of that stallion no other way, he should have *given* him away. If he *had*, he'd be alive today," said Lydia. They all looked at her, and she colored. "Well, it's true."

"True but *not* devoutly to be wished!" said a new voice. They all turned to the door where the children's aunt stood straight as a poker. Her scowl fooled not a one of them.

Excepting Lydia and the youngest, who was napping on her lap, the children, led by the twins, rushed to be held awkwardly to the angular form of Miss Eunice Easten. Miss Eunice lived near the gate in the dower house which her father's will had made available for her use for life along with an annuity which her brother had forked over each quarter with the greatest reluctance.

The children talked all at once until Miss Eunice shushed them, told Margaret to take Baby Alice to the tot's bed and that the rest of them were to go about their business. "You, Sir Jasper," she said sternly, "are needed below stairs. There's a delegation of your tenants awaiting you. They'll likely have all sorts of demands."

Jasper turned a horrified face toward Lydia, who had been relieved of Alice's warm body and now stood looking at her sometimes friend, but often foe.

"Liddy?" he asked on a faintly plaintive note. "Will you come?"

Eunice answered in Lydia's place. "No, Jasper. She will not."

Lydia put a hand on the boy's shoulder and felt a tension so extreme it caused faint shudders. "You need do no more than tell your tenants that although you very much wish you could help them and expect to do so when you are of age, you are unable to do anything yet," she recommended in a soothing voice. "Say that they must direct all requests to Lord Huntingdon, your guardian, who will be responsible until you are old enough to take over. It is that simple, Jasper."

With a sigh and one last quickly fading look of hope that she would come, too, Jasper disappeared around the corner to where narrow stairs led from the nursery floor to the family bedroom wing. From there a better staircase led to the first floor, and from there wide, shallow steps descended to the old-fashioned, slate-floored entry where Jasper would find his tenants.

Even before he could go beyond hearing, Eunice spoke. "You coddle the boy."

"I merely give him guidance, knowledge everyone seems to believe he should somehow know *without* the teaching."

"His father should have taught him. Not you."

"But his father did *not* teach him," retorted Lydia. "As you well know."

Eunice glared. She rarely admitted that her brother was less than perfect, but she did her best, behind the scenes, to mitigate the worst of his excesses.

Those had ranged from the overly severe punishment of his children, sometimes for nonexistent faults, to supplying less than adequate funds for running his house. Then, although the late baronet was never lacking in tirades when things were not done to please him, he could not be brought to see that one could not dress a proper table when one had not paid for meat eaten

long before. He merely thought it intolerable that the
butcher objected to supplying more for no better reason than the baronet's accounts were far in arrears!
There was also their supplier of tea, coffee, wines and
stronger drink. He, too, insisted he must be paid. As
did others.

Lydia, knowing Eunice was aware of all that, wondered that the woman had never been able to bring
herself to castigate the head of her house. Would she
be similarly respectful of Jasper? Somehow Lydia
doubted it. To avoid the smile that idea roused," she
asked, "Did you hear the children's silly notion that I
be presented to their guardian as their governess so
that he'll not summarily throw me out?"

"No, I did not. But why," asked the elderly woman
gruffly, "do you find it silly?"

"But . . ."

"It would be no lie," said the angular woman, echoing Margaret's argument. "You *are* their governess. You
need not even give a false name because I doubt a creature chosen by my brother will have the least interest
in your mother's previous marriage and therefore he'll
not recognize it."

"But . . ."

"Lydia, do you *wish* to find yourself out on the streets?
Not," said Eunice with a ladylike sneer and a quick
glance at Lydia's elegant if exceedingly plainly dressed
figure, "that you'd do badly, not with your looks and
form, but it's not a way of living I'd wish on my worst
enemy. And even when we disagree, Lydia, which, of
course we *do* and on a great many subjects, even then
I'd not call you my worst enemy."

Lydia felt a softening in her feelings toward Eunice.
"I apologize for so often rubbing you up the wrong
way, but we do seem to disagree on just about every-

thing. Unfortunately, I've never been one who can say aye when I believe the answer nay."

Eunice's mouth twitched. "Has it never occurred to you, Lydia, that the solution to our arguments is for me to refrain from expressing my feelings about certain subjects when I *know* you'll find it necessary to contradict me?"

"Refrain from . . ." Lydia blinked. "Surely you cannot be suggesting you actually . . ."

"Can I *not!* I enjoy our arguments and will miss them if you are forced to leave. I believe you should think seriously about introducing yourself as the children's well-beloved governess."

Having revealed the edges of a softness she hated others seeing, Eunice proceeded to redeem herself by glaring at Mary, who, while grinning at her aunt's expression, still shrank back against Lydia's skirts.

"You, missy," said Eunice, "look the complete hoyden. Come with me and I'll rebraid your hair and find you a clean ribbon to say nothing of a fresh sash. We cannot know when your guardian will arrive. It behooves all of you—" She glared in turn at the other children, who had *not* gone off about their business as she had suggested they do. "—to be ready to be presented to him at any instant!"

Reluctantly, having experienced her aunt's mode of hair brushing on several prior occasions, Mary gave her hand to her aunt. The other children immediately checked to see if they, too, needed something done to make themselves more presentable.

James was told he must wash his face, an order he ignored since he couldn't see it himself, but after a quick look at his hands, he shoved them into his pockets to hide them.

And then all cast worried looks from one to another, wondering what would happen next. When no one else spoke, James moved closer and tugged at Lydia's hand, and she glanced down at him.

"Will you?" he asked.

"Will I what?"

"You know." When arched brows were Lydia's only response, the boy scowled and added, "Tell our guardian you're our governess and that we can't do without you. That's what."

Tension had that muscle jumping in Lydia's jaw again. "I am young to be your governess." What she could not say was that she was far too pretty a young woman to be acceptable as governess in any home in which resided a gentleman unrelated to her. "Your guardian may feel you should all be under the tutelage of someone far more mature than I."

"You've been a very good governess," said one of the twins, her features taking on a stubborn expression.

Lydia thought it was Fenella, but wasn't certain. Even the family had difficulty telling the seven-year-old twins apart. "Thank you, child, but you cannot know that, can you? Since I'm the *only* governess you've had, you've no one to whom you might compare me!"

"But," the other twin argued, "you taught us to read before we were five. Vicar's Sarah can barely read *now*, and she's older than we are by a bit."

"See?" The first grinned. "We know you've been a good governess."

"It only proves you are bright little girls who learn easily." Lydia thought of the vicar's Sarah, who, while not stupid exactly, had not been excessively blessed with intelligence. "Not everyone learns with ease. It is not the fault of the child when that is the case, and you must not tease your friend because of it. Instead, girls, you might help her."

"Like you did us?" asked one twin, doubtfully.

"Sitting with her and helping her with the words?" added the other.

"Like that," said Lydia, nodding.

The twins looked at each other. "Maybe, then, we will," said one.

The other twin reached for and held her sister's hand. "Sometime."

"When we've nothing else to do, you know?" added the first.

Hand-in-hand the twins whisked themselves out of the room and off to one of their hidey-hole places where they would giggle and talk and spend endless time enjoying each other's company.

"They are such clunches," said James, disparagingly.

"They are no such thing! James, you *must* not."

"But they are," he insisted. "There they go, running off no one knows where."

"Not even you?" interrupted Lydia, startled. She had always assumed James, the most curious of the children and closest to the twins in age, knew their secrets.

"Not even me."

He scowled, and Lydia smiled. "I see. It is that you do *not* know, that you call them clunches. It is yourself who is the clunch, perhaps?"

James grinned, appreciating her humor to say nothing of the truth of what she said.

"I hate to do this to you, my fine young fellow, but once you've washed your dirty face—" Lydia gave James a stern look he knew well, "—and your hands as well, you must return and finish that translation I set you yesterday. I must insist you do so *before* you go off on your daily ramble."

"Must I?"

"I think you must."

James sighed dramatically, but he disappeared and returned with pink cheeks. He went obediently to his desk where he drew out his Latin text. He wished Latin weren't such a pain. It wasn't that it was difficult. In fact, he suspected he was already beyond poor Lydia's expertise and that she struggled to keep ahead of him. Which was one reason, he thought piously, that he put off his translations: it gave Liddy more time to keep up!

Lydia was well aware of her inadequacy when it came to James's studies and thought it another reason she should not accept the children's solution to her problem: she was not an adequate tutor for James! But, Jasper's notion might be a cure to that particular problem. If James were to be sent to school, something the boy wanted and needed, then she would be a good governess for the girls. Despite her lack of years.

Lydia stared out the rather wide window the room boasted and sighed softly. It was all very well to wonder and worry and, of course, *daydream* about such easy answers to her problem, but should she not, instead, be practical? Should she not sit herself down to write the much dreaded epistle to her grandfather? The one in which she would explain her situation, bend her pride, and beg for his aid?

The fact he had not replied to the letter sent him soon after her mother died was not truly relevant. At that time she had felt responsible for her half siblings and made no mention of need. But now, even though she expected him to ignore her, it was only proper he be informed of her new situation, which must include the information she had been left penniless and, just as soon as the guardian showed his front, very likely homeless.

It behooved her to stop writing variations of The Letter in her head, and sit herself down and put a real pen to real paper. But, oh, it was so very difficult to approach the old man who had disowned his only daughter and had not even had the courtesy to respond to news of her death. Wouldn't being out on the street be better than betraying her mother's memory by asking help of such a man?

Lydia chuckled softly at such dramatics. *Of course* the streets were no solution. To clinch that particular argument, her mother would not approve if her daughter were to parade her wares along the high street!

Still, there was the hope the children's guardian might *not* throw her out to fend for herself. Perhaps he would not wish the bother of finding one, or perhaps he would dislike the *expense* of a real governess for the girls. Perhaps she dared wait until Lord Huntingdon arrived, when she would see which way the wind blew. Then, if he said she must go, Eunice, or perhaps the vicar's wife, would take her in for so long as it took to discover if her grandfather would help or, if he would not, until she found a position.

Lydia nodded. Once. Firmly. She would wait.

A noise caught her attention, and Lydia turned just in time to see James tiptoe out the door before racing off down the hall. She sighed again, more heavily, and went to see if, before taking himself off, he had actually done the translation set him. His sneaking out suggested he had not, but much to her surprise he *had*. Lydia seated herself at his desk. She took the translation and the book and, struggling, did her best to see he had done it correctly.

"When Jasper comes back upstairs," she mumbled to herself, "I'll have him look it over, too, although—" She looked up, speaking more loudly, "—I sometimes wonder just how good *Jasper's* Latin may be! The last report from his school had his father scowling. For days."

Lydia heaved one last sigh and bent her head to her work.

* * *

The newish Lord Huntingdon was known to his friends as Rafe, since his given name, Raphael, had seemed less than appropriate during his wild and willful grass time. Now, nearly a decade beyond all that, he turned his glass in the sun streaming in the high window and squinted through it, admiring the ruby red color which was, by far, the best thing about the wine!

Roger, he thought, *really should stop his experiments with wine making!*

One of Rafe's oldest friends, the Marquis of Maythorn, had yet to produce a drinkable wine. In justification of his continuing attempts, Roger invariably cited the fact that the friars, who in ancient times held the land hereabouts, produced wine. No one could convince him that the good friars might also have produced *very bad* wine!

"I'm sorry, Roger. What did you say?"

"Easten Meadows," repeated Rafe's host with falsely ponderous pomposity, "has had *less* than a groat spent on it since I don't know when." He grinned when Rafe grimaced, and continued in more normal tones. "You've told tales of what you found when you inherited your earldom, my Lord Huntingdon. You've issued long and—" His eyes twinkled, "—I am sorry to be the one to tell you this, *tedious* lectures on the means by which you set your uncle's estate on the road to recovery. Well, Rafe," he continued on a confiding note, "I've a suspicion all that you did for yourself was merely practice for what you'll find must be done at Easten. Poor Sir Jasper is far too young to do it, of course, and besides, if his father was half as odd as I think he was, he didn't raise a finger to put his son in the way of doing things; so the boy wouldn't know how, would he?"

Rafe groaned. "So I've to do it all over again, have I? And the boy to train as well? Is Sir Jasper still at school, then?"

"He is. Or he's supposed to be. I believe my valet quoted my butler, who has a cousin who is one of the boy's tenants, to the effect the lad is home at present." When Rafe raised brows into a questioning arc, he added, "It hasn't been all *that* long since his father died, you know."

"Why do *you* apologize?" Rafe scowled at the wine he had barely tasted and no desire to finish. "My first duty, then, is to get the boy back to school and then to put the estate into the hands of a good agent. I hate letting staff go, but there is no reason to keep the house open when I'll likely need every cent I can scrape together to start his farms on the road to recovery."

"Ah. You mean to throw . . ." Roger paused, doing his best to remember names. "Margaret, James, Mary . . . no, I believe the twins are older. Or are they? I'm not certain. And there is an infant, I believe, as well. But, you mean to throw them all out into the hedgerows?" Roger grinned at the growing horror revealed in his friend's face.

Rafe sat up, his back rigid and eyes staring.

"Oh, yes," added Roger. "I believe there is also a much older girl whom I've seen once or twice in church, and there is an aunt, although I believe you needn't concern yourself about her. If I rightly remember Mother's gossip, the aunt has a life interest in the dower house. Why do you goggle so, Rafe?"

"Because," said the harassed earl, "I was informed of Sir Jasper's existence. Period. No more! There was no mention of any other children."

"By whom?"

"The boy's solicitor wrote me. Or, perhaps I should say, his father's old solicitor, who is now, by default, the boy's. For the moment. Until I see to changing that! Anyone so incompetent he'd not inform me of the extent of my duties would seem far *too* incompetent to retain."

"What exactly were you told, dear one?" asked the basso tones of a new voice. Lord Kenrick Horten's words rumbled from the depths of a chair turned away from the fire.

It was a peculiarity of the baron that he was often far too warm even when friends felt a chill. Since the marquis's butler had seen fit to light a fire in the library's grate against the evening damp of what had been, until sunset, a reasonably warm spring day, he was, as usual, uncomfortable. Also as usual, he had turned his chair so he faced away from the blaze. His friends were used to this foible and treated him as if he were facing them.

"Yes, Rafe," repeated Roger, "what, exactly, did the solicitor tell you? One must believe you were *very* ill informed if you are unaware of the existence of so many children."

"Did I not show you the letter, Kenrick?"

"You did not."

"And you certainly haven't shown it to me, your lordyship."

Rafe, who had been christened Raphael Weston Montgomery Seymour some thirty-odd years earlier, and had, for some years, been known to his troops as Lieutenant Seymour, had, two years earlier, quite unexpectedly inherited the earldom. Since he had not expected to inherit—two cousins had stood in his way—he had put up with a great deal of jesting. His friends could not, it seemed, refrain from teasing him about his honors even yet.

In this case he ignored Roger's less than respectful naming and frowned at his glass, once again turning it against the light. "The letter," he said, finally. "What did I do with the letter? Not that it matters. It was, in fact, quite brief. It did no more than inform me that my uncle had been named guardian of the Easten heir and his estate. Unfortunately, the will was drawn up so that the guardianship was given to the *earldom*, not to a specific *earl*. Thus the responsibility descended from my uncle to me. I was informed, but without explanation, that it might be best if I were to set in motion active guardianship at once." He smiled a trifle wryly. "All very cryptic, you see, but I can take a hint with the best of them when it sounds like a disaster in the making!" He raised the glass in mock salute. "So," he continued, "with our Kenrick tagging along to satisfy his well-known curiosity, I set out with, I'll freely admit, the hope you were in residence and would give us houseroom while I looked into things."

"You are very welcome, as you know. In fact, you might have stayed if I were *not* at home." Roger glanced up. "Surely you are aware of that."

Rafe grinned the rare, mischievous smile for which those who knew him well watched. "Of course I know, but I didn't think it quite the thing to tell you I'd have battened on you even if you *were* off on one of your adventures." The grin faded, and the frown reappeared, deeper than ever. "There was, I repeat, no mention of children or an aunt. How old is the eldest girl, then? Will the aunt chaperon her? At least, I presume she must be of an age to need chaperonage if she's older than the boy who is at school?"

"She is very nearly old enough she's no need of one at all!" The marquis, Roger Littledon, smiled at the thought of the eldest Easten. "I don't know it for a fact, since I've never had anything to do with Easten or his family, but I'd guess she must be a relic of an earlier marriage. In my opinion, she is too old to be one of the current crop. I'd guess there were a good ten years between her and Miss Margaret."

"I am to assume, then, that she's an antidote, since she must have long-ago been presented?"

"Presented!" Roger adopted a shocked expression. "Oh no, Rafe, what can you be thinking? Surely you don't think that old screw, Easten, would cough up the ready in order to give a mere female something so unnecessary as a season? *Particularly* when the female in question is exceptionally useful around the house?" He snapped his fingers. "Which reminds me of another thing, Rafe. You'll have no difficulty with your conscience about servants. If there are any remaining at Easten beyond a cook, it could only be a groom or two." Roger frowned. "Come to that, I think the old pinchpenny got rid of his cattle some time ago, so, with all the horses sold up, there would be no reason for a groom either."

"You cannot mean there are literally no servants."

"Can I not? You'll see."

"Rafe, dear boy," rumbled Kenrick's deep voice, "I do believe I'll remain here with Roger when you go tomorrow to look into the way of things. I do not think my sensitive nature could stand to observe the difficulties those poor, bereft children must have suffered in merely surviving from day to day!"

Roger chuckled when Rafe retorted, "Kenrick, you shouldn't mince your words that way. What you really mean is that you'll not subject your poor, sensitive *self* to the deprivations you foresee." Kenrick's rumbling laugh was answer enough. "Roger, how many children did you say there are? I lost count."

Roger held up one hand and began turning down fingers. "The oldest. Don't know her name. I've only rarely seen her in church and not been introduced, but she's *not* an antidote. On the contrary. Myself, I'd call her a beauty. Old as she is, I don't think you'll have her on your hands for long. If she hasn't a dowry, give her a small one and turn her over to your aunt, assuming her own will not see to her presentation. Then, of course, there is Sir Jasper. He's at that lanky stage so awkward not only for himself but all around him. I remember surviving that period and have pity both for you and for the boy! Miss Margaret Easten promises to be nearly as lovely as her elder sister. The twins . . . or perhaps it is Mary next? Oh. Somewhere in there I forgot James. A scrubby schoolboy of nine or ten. More? Perhaps as much as eleven. Except he was never sent to school, of course." Roger thought for a moment. "I think the baby finishes it."

"Lord!" Kenrick peered around the side of his chair. "That's nine!" He settled back. "If there are nine living, how many do you suppose they lost?"

"I counted eight," said Rafe, frowning, "but that is more than enough."

Roger frowned. "I can't think of any dead. Not that it is something to which I pay attention, but my mother is forever prosing on about such things, and she gets upset when I don't remember. Which is why I recall the Easten children's names. I've learned to tuck such bits away for future reference. But it is unusual, is it not, that they haven't a few in the churchyard?"

"It certainly is. Our vicar has six living and four buried. So sad but he feels blessed it isn't the other way around!" the baron's voice rumbled from around the back of his chair.

"It is the other way for the vicar at the Chase," said Rafe. "Four living and six buried. I wouldn't know," he admitted, "except his wife tells every new acquaintance the circumstances surrounding the birth and death of each and every one! If I'd an inkling she made a habit of it, I'd have found some means of avoiding the duty visit I made to the vicarage, but I did not know and was trapped. I can commiserate with her sad life, but I did *not* appreciate being made privy to the details."

Silence settled over the three. After a moment the gurgle of wine flowing into the marquis's glass was followed by the question of whether the others wanted more. Neither guest answered, and Roger sighed. "I know. It is not very potable, is it? But I swear I'll discover the secret! Maybe this year's crop . . ."

"Give it up, my dear friend," rumbled the disembodied voice.

"Yes! *Please* give it up!" said Rafe, the rare smile again hovering over his lips.

"I will *not* give up." Roger straightened in his chair, raising his glass. "You'll see. One of these years I'll have it sorted out, and you'll beg for a taste of my wine!"

Chuckles of disbelief were the only response. Roger set the bottle down with a snap, settling himself as well, ready for an argument, but the baron, still there only as a voice, asked, "Tomorrow you'll visit Sir Jasper?"

"And the beauty whose name we were not given and Mary and the twins and James and . . . I forget. What," Rafe asked rhetorically, "past sin did I commit that I deserve such a fate?"

The bass voice asked, "Well, what about the time you put a goat in the rector's study, and I might mention—"

Standing, Rafe moved to lean over the back of Kenrick's chair. He poured the wine he had ceased to pretend to drink down over his huge friend's face. Kenrick broke off, sputtering. He rose to his feet.

"I did *not,*" said Rafe when the outraged baron faced him, "require an answer!"

Then, watching the ruby wine run down wide brow, then drip from strong nose and square chin onto a formerly pristine white cravat, Rafe burst into laughter. The marquis, looking up, saw what had occurred and laughed as well.

Faintly outraged, Kenrick stared across the back of the chair straight into Rafe's eyes—dark blue eyes which sparkled with devilment—until they took on an apologetic cast because of the ruined raiment. But the baron could take a joke with the best of them and grinned.

Besides, Kenrick had a trifling suspicion he might have deserved it. The thing he had very nearly mentioned was private, known only to the two of them. At least, he was almost certain that not even Roger was aware of that particular prank-gone-wrong. In any case, he added his growling basso chuckle to Roger's lighter voice.

"In answer to your *unasked* question, my friend," said Rafe, "you may remain here with Roger and discuss his next experiment in wine making!"

Kenrick sobered instantly, blinking his long blond lashes very fast. "Er . . . Rafe, old friend, I've changed my mind. I'm certain you can make use of me. I'm very good at entertaining old ladies, for instance—"

"To say nothing of young beauties," inserted Roger, sotto voce.

"—and I've learned to play with children," he added earnestly, "thanks to all the practice I've had with my nieces and nephews."

Thus far, Kenrick's three elder sisters had produced seven children, all very close in age. The Hortens were a large, happy family which got together often, using any possible excuse. It was a family Rafe envied and one he happily joined whenever he was invited to visit. The first time had been for the Christmas holidays the year he and Roger met at school, but there had been many such occasions since.

Ignoring a paternal aunt and her children and the late earl and his deceased sons, Rafe's own family consisted of himself, his mother, and a younger sister. The small size had done nothing to draw them together.

Instead, very early, they had gotten into the habit of spending no more time in each other's pockets than absolutely necessary. Sometimes, Rafe felt the Hortens were more his family than his own. More, he had often *wished* that were the case.

So now, when Kenrick earnestly outlined all the reasons he should *not* stay to be bored to death by Roger's problems with his wine making, Rafe was happy to invite his friend along . . . with only a minor qualm about the beauty's fate once she and Kenrick met! Kenrick had a very bad habit of flirting dangerously with any pretty face. And if the girl had reached marriageable age so long ago as Roger suggested, she might be ripe to fall desperately in love with the first man to cross her path! So, although Rafe welcomed Kenrick's company on his first visit to Easten Meadows, he also made a mental note to lecture the baron sternly on what was proper behavior toward marriageable chits—even if they looked like angels.

He then forgot that decision in the far-ranging discussion which the three carried on far into the night. They agreed that Napoleon could not possibly continue the war much longer. The debacle in Russia where the winter weather ravaged his army must, surely, have put paid to all future hopes. Later, when the level of brandy in the bottle had lowered more than a trifle, they settled everything from deciding which mature lady would next delight the Prince Regent's eye to whether they would or would not spend time in London during the season which had begun less than a month earlier.

As for that last, since all three were exceedingly eligible parties and none of them looked forward to running the gauntlet of marriageable young ladies, they concluded they might run up to town for a week or two, but that would be *quite* sufficient, thank you just the same!

"No matter how much my mother begs," added the Marquis of Maythorn airily.

His mother, he admitted, had begun hinting, *strongly,* that she wanted grandchildren sometime before she reached her dotage!

Two

"Will you look at *that!*"

James's exclamation brought the children running to his side to peer out the schoolroom window onto the sunlit approach to the manor. Their morning's assignments were nearly finished, and all the children were getting restless. They were happy to have an excuse to leave their desks.

Even Sir Jasper strolled from where he had been idly twirling the globes, stopping them and putting his finger down at random, then stooping to see where it landed. It was a game Lydia had taught each child in turn, and it was quite amazing how much they learned from it. Lydia had, from the beginning, tried to make learning fun. Only with James did she feel she had failed. He was by far the brightest of the children, and all too often, he was bored to tears long before he convinced Lydia he had truly learned the day's lesson.

The children automatically arranged themselves so all could see. The twins were nearest the window, and Jasper at the back, looking over the heads of the others. Baby Alice struggled from Lydia's lap and walked a few steps before dropping to her knees and crawling after her siblings. She reached up and jerked at Jasper's trouser leg. The boy looked down, grinned, and reached for his youngest sister. "Want to see the pretty horses, do you?"

"Horses?" Lydia rose to her feet.

"Hmm. Nicest bit of blood and bone I've seen for many a day. Just a pair, but, from this angle, which is not the best of course, I'd say they are all black except for a white spot on their foreheads. They look to be perfectly matched."

"Is it your guardian, Jasper?"

The boy, to whom the thought had not occurred, tensed, then leaned over James's shoulder, pushing the younger boy aside a bit. Slowly he relaxed. "It can't be, Liddy. Far too young. The both of them."

"Them!"

Lydia gently made a place for herself to the fore of the crowding children but was too late to judge for herself. The men had left the team in the hands of the old groom-made-gardener and moved beneath the colonnaded porch which ran between the angular towers jutting from each end of the house.

"I must go down. Cook will never hear the bell, or if she does, she'll ignore it. Children, I haven't a notion who has come, but most likely a couple of blades who have lost their way and wish directions to Maythorn. Do, please, settle back to work. Jasper, perhaps you should come with me. I doubt if they will be—" she searched for a polite word, "—uncivil, but it is not proper for me to answer the door with no one in attendance."

Jasper struck a pose, his face poker-serious. "I'll pretend to be the footman, shall I?" he said.

Lydia chuckled. "More likely the boot boy, Jasper. You aren't quite old enough to be a footman, are you?"

The children laughed and, although reluctant, moved back to their desks. Except for James. "Let me come, too, Liddy. If they aren't nice men, you may need both of us. I don't suppose we could stop them," he added with that honesty which endeared him to Lydia, "but Jasper and I could hold them long enough so you could escape!"

Liddy kept her desire to smile well hidden. "You, James Easten, have been reading Cook's Gothic romances again, have you not? Very well. I'll admit I'll not object to having the both of you. Come along. Quickly. They'll have been waiting long enough. On second thought," she immediately contradicted herself, "perhaps, if we do not hurry, they will go away."

But James was already clattering down the first flight of stairs. Jasper was not far behind, although, with his newly acquired title weighing on him, he was a trifle more on his dignity than he would have been before his father's death. He reached the hall just as the men, allowed in by James, began removing driving cloaks adorned with multitudinous capes.

The elder boy stopped on the bottom step. "Good day," he said, and hoped his voice would not behave in the embarrassing way it sometimes did.

The taller, although not the broader, of the two men turned to look at him. "Sir Jasper?"

Jasper nodded.

"I am Raphael Seymour, Lord Huntingdon, and have the honor of being your guardian until you come of age."

Jasper cleared his throat, wondering where Liddy had gotten to. He glanced up the stairs and glimpsed just a bit of her black skirt. Why, he wondered, did she not come down? James jerked at his sleeve, and the young baronet realized how long the silence had stretched. A chagrined look crossed the boy's face, but he could think of nothing to say and merely cleared his throat again, shifting his weight from one foot to the other.

"May we come in?" asked Rafe, hiding a smile at the boy's lack of ease.

"Oh! Well, yes, I suppose we should—"

James hissed the word salon.

"—Perhaps the drawing room?" Jasper suggested. He gestured up the stairs, simultaneously giving his brother a surreptitious poke. The younger boy, guessing correctly that Lydia should be warned if she had not heard for herself, whisked himself back upstairs.

Rafe and Kenrick heard whispers but, ignoring them, set themselves to slowly climbing the broad, shallow steps behind their obviously reluctant host. The boy then bowed the two men into the sun-filled but sparsely furnished room he had called a drawing room. Lydia had seated herself on a long, padded settle near the empty fireplace. Now she rose to her feet and waited, hands clasped before her, for the strangers to approach.

"Perhaps you could introduce us?" Rafe suggested, and Jasper's ears turned bright red.

"Liddy . . . I mean, Miss Cottrell," said Jasper, his embarrassment growing, "be pleased to meet Lord Huntingdon and . . . and . . ." The lad gave up, casting a despairing, almost accusing, look from Huntingdon to his friend and back again.

"I'm sorry," said Rafe softly. "That was rude of me, was it not? I forgot you'd no notion of my friend's identity. Miss Cottrell, Sir Jasper, be pleased to make the acquaintance of Lord Kenrick Horten. Lord Horten, my ward, Sir Jasper, and . . . Miss Cottrell?"

"I've been the children's governess for years, my lord." She turned to hold out her hand to Lord Horten. "My lord?"

The huge baron grasped her fingers in a gentle hold. "Very pleased to make your acquaintance, Miss Cottrell."

"Governess?" inserted Rafe. "You appear over young to have been a governess for any length of time."

"I am orphaned, my lord. Lady Easten was . . . very kind."

For a moment Rafe struggled with himself. Why would a daughter of the house pretend to be someone else? But perhaps, he decided, he would let it ride. For the moment. "I understand there are several children. Sir Jasper, would you be kind enough to ring the bell and have the others brought to us?"

The red which had been fading from the lad's complexion returned with interest. He glanced at Lydia, then at his feet, and then, clearing his throat, he turned to James. "Go. Get them. And, James," he called in a harsh whisper, "see they all look right for company!"

"Perhaps it would be best if I were to see to my charges," said Lydia. "James, since his lordship is interested in meeting Jasper's brothers and sisters, perhaps you should stay and be first?"

James recrossed the room to stand before Lord Huntingdon, his hands clasped behind him and his legs sturdily straddled. "Sir!" Belatedly the boy bowed. "Sir! Your horses. Beauties, both! Would you mind if I took them an apple?"

"You may do so . . . *later.*"

The last word bore a distinct emphasis as James was already halfway to the door. The boy sighed and, much more slowly than he had begun his departure, returned. "Yes, sir."

"Now, James," began Rafe with firm kindness, a tone he realized was very nearly that of his favorite tutor from his years at Balliol College at Oxford. He cleared his throat and began again. "James, I've been informed your brother is at school, although I do not yet know where. You look of an age to have joined him. What school do the two of you attend?"

It was James's turn for red ears. "Papa wouldn't fork over the necessary to send me. He said it was bad enough he had to pay for one. Two was out of the question. But he kept trying for still another son, so I don't see why he objected to—"

"James!" Jasper, who had been standing somewhat away from the strangers, came nearer. "You should not say such things, although," he added, his chin rising, "it is nothing but the truth. The way my father went on, you'd think the estate could not bear the cost, but it isn't true. I have been looking at the accounts and, sir, do you think we might do something about Farmer Rolfe's roof which, he swears, leaks like his wife's colander, and my tenant on the Little Farm says there isn't a hedge that doesn't need fixing or a fence that hasn't a break, which is difficult for him, because he has a fine herd of milk cows and . . ."

"I am glad to hear that you have a care for your tenant's needs, but it will have to wait, Sir Jasper," said Rafe. He smiled, more hopeful than he had been since learning of the estate's condition from Maythorn. "We must see what we can do, but not this instant. Once I've had an opportunity to look around and have checked the accounts myself, we will do all we can to right the problems you've mentioned. We cannot, however, make such decisions on the instant, and certainly not *this* instant," he added, raising his head and listening. "I believe I hear your sisters approaching."

Rafe and Kenrick turned to face the door, and although the new guardian had expected it, thanks to Roger's priming him, he was startled by the line of young females. Roger had been correct about the eldest Easten chit. Miss Margaret Easten was set to become the reigning beauty of the London Season in another year or two. The next, Mary, was still too sturdily built to predict just how she would turn out. Twins, hand-in-hand, glared at him from identical pairs of brown eyes, and he wondered what he had done to get in their black books before he had ever been told their names. Then, last in line, Miss Cottrell stood with the youngest in her arms. That was it. There was no other. As he had suspected, Miss Cottrell was actually the eldest sister.

So what game was the young woman playing?

Rafe decided, again, that the solution to that mystery must wait. He had quite enough on his plate with just this lot. His eyes went from one to another and finally to the eldest, this Miss Cottrell, who, despite an attempt to play down her assets, looked very like the rest. He glanced at Jasper and then at James. The whole family had much the same features.

Suddenly the twins stepped forward. "Sir," said the one.

"We want to know . . . ," said the other.

Shushing noises came from a variety of throats.

". . . if . . . ," said the two together, and the first finished, "you mean to make our Liddy go away?"

"Because," said the second, "we'll run away and find her if you do." The girls looked at each other and nodded once, firmly, before turning and glaring at him.

"You like your . . . governess?"

"She is a very good governess," said the one twin.

"She *is,*" said the second as if he had objected. The twins went to stand beside Miss Cottrell as if to protect her.

Rafe looked from one twin to the other. Slowly, he said, "I have told Sir Jasper I can make no decisions until I know more and give the whole some thought. Ah. Good day to you," added Rafe as a tall, angular woman entered the room, her salt-and-pepper hair pulled strictly away from her face, her gown clean but well worn. Was this woman also his responsibility?

"Good day to *you,* whoever you might be." She

scowled. "I think you might have been considerate enough to bring a chaperon if you intended a visit here. When you pulled by the dower house, I assumed you were lost and would be returning soon. I've come to discover why you have not."

Rafe decided he now knew from whom the twins had inherited their scowl which had not abated with the information that their governess was not to be immediately tossed out on her pretty ear. Although, thought Rafe, the girl really was too young. Besides, one would think it unsuitable that a daughter of the house play at being a servant. Even an upper servant . . .

"Aunt Eunice," Sir Jasper said, interrupting Rafe's rampaging thoughts, "may I present our guardian, Lord Huntingdon . . . and Lord Horten," he added as something of an afterthought.

"Lord Huntingdon, is it?" Ignoring the second man, the harridan looked Rafe up and down in such a scornful way the earl felt his ears warming. "I'd have thought my brother would choose an older man."

"I suspect he did," said Rafe, holding on to his temper with some difficulty. "My uncle passed away nearly two years ago. Your brother's will, written prior to that, gave the guardianship of Sir Jasper to the title rather than the man. The responsibility is, therefore, mine."

"I see." She scowled still more harshly.

Rafe wondered just exactly what it was she thought she saw. He turned to the other children. "Now, Sir Jasper, will you introduce your sisters?"

This was soon accomplished, each girl curtsying, including the twins, although they did so only at the urging of their governess.

And that situation, thought Rafe, must be delved into and soon. A young governess—far too young—with very much the look of the family and nary a hair nor nail visible of the eldest sister of whom Roger spoke. Those twins ready to defend her as if she had been threatened when he had certainly done no such thing. And the aunt not so much as glancing toward the chit . . .

One had to assume a plot. It smelled of one.

Why, the thought continued to nag at him, *would a young woman deliberately pretend to be something she is not? Something* less *than she ought to be?*

For a long moment his gaze met that of the tall young woman who, although she was beyond the first blush of womanhood, was still extremely attractive.

You, he thought, a scowl forming, *are a mystery. I do not like mysteries.* He stared fiercely.

The woman's chin rose, and she glared right back. From that moment Rafe found himself intrigued rather than disturbed. She had backbone, this young woman who played the governess. But didn't that only complicate the mystery? A very shy young woman might have wished to remain in the background, might use a position such as governess to avoid social occasions. But this woman wasn't shy. Not if the nicely firmed chin meant what he thought it meant.

"Hmm? Yes?" Rafe looked down at the twin who had come to stand before him. "I'm afraid I was thinking of something else."

"We only want to be certain that you'll not be an old meanie and send Liddy away. You have not said it, you know."

"I'll certainly not send her away any time soon." Rafe heard a faint note that could only be called grim in his tone. He relaxed. "There is far too much to be seen to, to be thinking about a proper governess for you."

"Liddy *is* a proper governess," said the soft voice of the one called Margaret, who appeared to be fourteen, or perhaps fifteen. Then the girl blushed and looked considerably younger.

"I'm certain she's done her best," said Rafe, assuming that would settle things.

"She has not only done her best, but her best is very good indeed," the aunt said, cutting short whatever the children might say next. "You will not find better the length and breadth of England. If you disbelieve me, you will test that young man," she said, pointing at James. "You'll be surprised, I believe, at just how well he is up on his Latin, and try any of them on the globes. Lyd . . . *Miss Cottrell* has insisted they all learn from them. The girls do very well at their needlework, and if they are less well trained on the pianoforte, that is more the fault of the instrument than their teacher or the girls themselves. You will, I hope—" the practiced glare was turned up to full force, "—see that it is tuned?"

"It will be added to a list which even in the few minutes I've been here has burgeoned to grand proportions," said Rafe with a slight sigh.

For half a moment the older woman grinned, a wide smile that showed that she was missing several back teeth. Then the smile disappeared. "It will grow every time you turn around. You will, of course, see to the hiring of servants and will find proper mounts for the children? To say nothing of someone to teach them to ride?" Her eyes narrowed. "Another thing. Get rid of that devil's mount that killed my brother. A bullet to the brain might be kindest."

Rafe rather boggled at that and looked at Kenrick, at Sir Jasper, who nodded several times, and then at James, who frowned very slightly, giving one small disagreeing shake of the head. Ah! Another mystery?

"Come along, girls. His lordship will not wish you distracting him from learning what must be done for the estate. Good day, my lord," added the stiff-spined Miss Eunice Easten. She nodded to Lord Horten and

shooed all the young females from the room, including
the intriguing Miss Cottrell.

"Shoot him?" asked Rafe, deciding the lesser mystery
would be most easily solved.

"A rogue stallion, my lord," explained Sir Jasper.
"Wild to a fault. Father couldn't find a buyer for him
when he sold the rest. The creature's temper is too well
known."

"Jasper, he isn't so bad." James turned red when his
guardian's eyes shifted to stare into his own. "Not really.
Truly! Please don't shoot him!"

Rafe, thinking of his own intrepid behavior at much
the same age, felt cold inside at what the boy might
have been attempting with the horse. "What would you
know of his temperament, my lad?"

"He just don't like men," explained the boy. "He's
gentle enough with Liddy. But he hates Old Herbie and
he killed our father. There's never been a man who
could ride him," he finished with a hint of pride in the
horse's irascibility.

Rafe winced. Then, politely, he asked, "He will, however, allow Miss Cottrell on his back?"

James blushed furiously and dug his toe into the well-
worn carpet. "Don't know that she's ever actually *ridden*
him, do I?" he muttered, his ears fiery red.

Rafe decided he would let pass, for the moment, what
was so obviously a lie, but he was equally determined
that he really must discover more about the young lady.
It appeared this Miss Lydia Cottrell-Easten-whoever was
more a mystery than he had thought.

But she was not a mystery destined to be easily or
soon solved. Instead, Rafe suggested to Sir Jasper that
he be shown the accounts, the bills due, and be given
some sense of the extent of the estate and its problems.
When they left late that afternoon, he felt he and Sir
Jasper had reached something close to an understand-

ing. The boy had gradually relaxed, gradually revealed signs he trusted that Rafe would not simply shove him aside and do all himself.

Because it was late in the current term, it was decided the boy should remain home until Michaelmas term in the fall, when he and James would both be sent to school. But, to prevent Jasper from falling behind, and to assure that James was up to snuff, one of Rafe's first duties must be to find a tutor to work with the boys in the meantime.

And, although the earl did not explain this aspect of his thinking to Sir Jasper, the most important reason the young landowner was to remain at home was the lad's incredible ignorance. Rafe wanted the boy at hand. They would work together to turn the estate around, Sir Jasper learning his role in life as they did so.

One excellent piece of news resulted from his study of the accounts: righting the wrongs he guessed were innumerable would be far more readily accomplished than he had expected. For reasons Rafe did not understand, one problem did *not* exist. There *were* funds with which to ease the way.

Then he had spent half an hour with the tartar-faced aunt, asking politely if she would see to hiring servants for the house and grounds, since he had no knowledge of the local availability of such. He grinned again when he recalled her acid request to be told exactly how many servants he thought she should find and what she could inform them about wages. Wages at Easten Meadows, it seemed, had not been such that they drew panting hordes of willing help that way.

"That Miss Eunice is as acerbic and eccentric as any woman I've ever met," he said, breaking the silence which had settled on the two men as he drove back toward Maythorn. "I can't do without her, but she may drive me mad before we finish!"

"The children like her," rumbled Kenrick. "She can't be all bad. Perhaps it is a case of bark and no bite? Are things as bad as Roger led you to believe? Will you find it possible to deal with the estate without dipping into your own funds?"

"The condition of the estate is about as bad as it could be, but I was astounded, actually, at the healthy state of Sir Jasper's *finances*. Still, the first thing I must do is get a copy of the will to discover what provision was made for the other children. I mustn't use monies which should be set aside for dowries, for instance." He grimaced. "That assumes there *was* provision, of course. From what I've learned today, I have come to the odd suspicion none was made for the children."

"Not even the boy? James, I mean?" Kenrick cast his friend a startled look. "A likely lad, I thought."

"So did I. In fact, although I hope you'll never say I said so, I like that boy far better than I do Sir Jasper, who appears to be afraid of his own shadow."

"James asked if you'd beat them. At first I tried to make a joke of it, but when I saw how pale the other children got, I backtracked quickly enough. If the elder has faced the brunt of such violence as seems to have taken place in the library with great regularity, no wonder he's something of a rabbit."

"You sound a trifle grim, Kenrick."

"The twins talked James into removing his shirt."

"So?"

"So their father has been dead for going on three weeks?"

"Yes."

"The boy is still a trifle scabby where lash marks have nearly healed."

Rafe's jaw tightened painfully. "I'll be less impatient

with Jasper now that I know. And, when I go back to-morrow, I will tell the two boys they need never fear such things again. At least not from me. I can't guarantee the behavior of their tutors at school."

The baron's grumbling laugh rumbled about them. "I hope theirs don't believe in caning one as severely as mine did. But, Rafe, you'll not inform the girls of *their* good luck?"

"The girls, too?"

"Not to the same degree. But they were rarely able to sit to their supper for a day or two after one of their father's rages."

"You seem to have discovered more than I."

"Don't sound rueful. Children talk. At least, they talk to me," Kenrick added, his low-pitched voice sounding smug to the degree such a rumbling tone was capable. "Besides, you were busy with accounts and the estate problems."

"Miss Easten allowed them to talk so freely?"

"Miss Eunice Easten, Miss Margaret Easten, or do you mean *Miss Cottrell?*" asked Kenrick, grinning.

Rafe grimaced.

"Their dearly beloved governess added her encouragement when it came to James removing his shirt. She would not say one word against her father. At least, one assumes he was her father, but she didn't object to a single thing those very outspoken twins said. And, like children that age anywhere, they managed to prattle about a very great number of bits and pieces."

"Including their beloved governess?"

"Oh, yes. A wonder, if they are to be believed. A feeling endorsed by Miss Eunice Easten."

"When I spoke to Miss Eunice, she as much as warned me to leave Miss Cottrell be and not poke my nose into the business of nursery and schoolroom. Her voice held nuances of warning me off. I can't put my finger on it, but something's wrong with the wench. What is it, Kenrick?"

"Not a thing I could see. Not that I saw much. Your dragon sent her off to do something in the kitchens soon after she arrived in the nursery. But, from what I observed, she seems a pleasant enough young woman."

"You got to know the children while I made plans with Sir Jasper?"

"Took the young ones for a walk down into the meadow."

"You and *Miss Cottrell* took them?"

"Did I say that?" He grinned when his friend glowered. "Miss Eunice came with us."

"Good." Rafe wondered at the disturbance he had felt at the thought of Kenrick spending much time with his Mystery Lady. He recalled the warning he had meant to give his friend. "I want none of your usual nonsense where Miss Cottrell is concerned."

"You mean I'm not to flirt with her?"

"Exactly. Especially since your flirting all too often leads to something far more, er, personal."

The big man sighed, and gave his friend a sidelong glance of mixed curiosity and chagrin. "Then, I suppose I must return to London. Life is such a bore if there is nothing with which to entertain myself." He turned a second glance toward Rafe and noticed a deeply furrowed frown.

"How about," asked Rafe, who didn't want Kenrick leaving, "if I find ponies for the children and you take on their education in that respect?"

"Teach all those children to ride?" The instant and instinctive horror faded as Kenrick thought about it. "Did manage to teach my nephew . . . ," he mumbled after a long minute's cogitation.

"So you told me. At greater length than I required,

if you must know! But that's what brought the notion to mind."

"Sorry if I ran on too long, but I seem to remember it was rather fun."

"So, you might set up as riding master, might you not? And having one after the other in your charge should entertain you for most of the day!" Rafe felt satisfaction flow through him; it disappeared at Ken's next words.

"I wonder if Miss Cottrell rides . . ."

"*I* wonder if Miss Cottrell rides that murdering stallion!"

"What?" Kenrick swiveled in his seat, one hand going behind Rafe to hold the back of the curricle's seat. "You jest, of course!"

Rafe grinned. "It sounds odd, does it not? But something young James said . . . I really must look into the situation with that animal. Lord, I cannot keep straight all the things which must be done, and each and every one of them immediately if not sooner! I had thought to come, see what was involved, hire Sir Jasper a good agent, and have all set in motion in a few days. And then I meant to return to my own problems."

"*But*? I did hear a but, did I not?"

Rafe sighed. "From what I learned today, I very much fear I may be here for weeks. Possibly it will run into months. I mean to make the boy learn his role as baronet and landowner by keeping him at my side when I make decisions concerning the estate. To begin with, that is. It will take some time just discovering what must be done. I'll have to poke my nose into every little detail. To oversee that everything is accomplished will take far longer."

"Will financing it all come from your pocket?"

"Did I not say?"

"Only that you were astonished, which didn't sound good."

"You misinterpreted me. That, at least, is *not* a problem. The boy had already done some things, with Miss Cottrell's help. The bills due in the village shops have been paid, for instance. Even so there is plenty of the ready to make a start on turning things around. The late baronet has to have been draining the estate for years and hoarding every penny. I don't understand people like that."

"You mean taking out every cent possible but returning nothing for repairs and equipment?"

"Exactly. The only landowners I know who behave that way are the gamblers who cannot seem to control their wagering and lose every shilling they get their hands on just as quickly as may be. But it appears there was nothing like that here."

"Just good old-fashioned miserliness?"

"It would seem so. The aunt has agreed to hire two parlor maids, a footman, a butler if one can be found, and two maids to help cook and to deal with the laundry. There is, already, a child from the workhouse who has been working for her room and board, and one of the farmers' wives has been coming in to do the heavy work, scrubbing and that sort of thing, but perhaps she has done it out of compassion for those children rather than because she wishes to. Miss Eunice will see if the woman will continue or if someone else must be hired. Among all else, I'm to find grooms and restock the stable. Perhaps I could leave that to you?"

"Ponies?"

"Ponies for the children. A smallish horse, I think, for each of the boys, and at least one strengthy beast which can be hitched to the dogcart, which is the only remaining excuse for a carriage. And that is something else to which I must see! At the moment there is no way for the family to ride into the village which is a longish walk for the young ones. Miss Eunice says it is beyond everything her brother refused to see that they got to church regularly. She said it," reported Rafe, with the first chuckle since he had entered the Easten household earlier that day, "with a look which made it clear I am to rectify *that* particular problem soonest! That, by the way, was the only word of criticism I heard from the lady concerning her brother, which indicates a great deal of self-control on her part. Or so I would say."

"You didn't mention a mount for Miss Cottrell."

"No, I didn't, did I?"

"I am not to see to that?" Kenrick waited, but Rafe didn't respond. "You perhaps wish to do so yourself?" he asked.

"Drop the innocent act, Kenrick. Until I satisfy myself to Miss Cottrell's exact place in that household, I cannot justify the expense, can I? One doesn't buy mounts for the governess, does one?" He turned a glare on his friend, who managed to hold back his chuckles until Rafe turned back to watch his horses. "Kenrick, it is not something about which you should jest."

"I don't see why you are so concerned. If the family accepts her as one of them, then why cannot you?"

"But *do* they? No one indicated she was anything other than governess and general dogsbody."

"I cannot see why you make so much of it. Unless, of course, you have more interest in the beauty than you've admitted."

"Kenrick . . . !"

"Well, have you?"

For half a moment Rafe bristled. Then his shoulders slumped, and he growled, "Yes, damn your eyes! She . . . she intrigued me from the moment she lifted that firm little chin to me! Well, blast and be damned,

I think I've had a facer, Kenrick." The last words were said with despair.

"So. All we must do is discover whether she's a proper lady and you can wed her, or we'll discover she's not and you can bed her. What is the problem?"

"That cynical side you show occasionally does not do you justice. I cannot very well make her my mistress and allow her to remain with the children. But the children have made it clear they would object, and object strongly, to having their Miss Cottrell removed from their schoolroom, have they not?"

"To say nothing of the fact their Miss Cottrell feels a great deal of affection for each and every one of them."

"How did you learn that?" Again, although he hated to admit to it, Rafe felt something he could only call jealousy that his friend had spent more time with the beauty than he had himself.

"It is obvious in the way she hugs them and smiles at them. That sort of thing."

"You are very certain it was not put on for your benefit?"

"Now who reveals a cynical streak?"

Rafe sighed. "That was not well done of me. And, thank the Lord, we've arrived. I hope Roger's cook provides us with at least as good a dinner as he did last night."

"Without the added touch of Roger's homemade wine!"

Rafe laughed. "Oh, certainly. Could we, do you suppose, give his butler a hint?"

"Suggest the man raid the cellars for the good stuff? There's a thought. Perhaps I should go down with him," rumbled the baron.

Rafe let Kenrick off at the front door and drove on around to the stables where he wanted a few words with the head groom. It had occurred to him the marquis's man was just the person to ask about finding grooms for the Easten stables, to say nothing of good local stock.

Should he look into the acquisition of a quiet mare for Miss Cottrell? Then still another bit of cynicism crossed his mind: If, by chance, that young woman did ride the killer-stallion, a quiet mare would not do for her. If she rode the stallion, then there was far too much fire in her veins for the sort of lady's mount he had thought of finding her.

Far too much fire altogether. Surely no true lady would . . . could . . . ride an animal over which a man had no control?

But surely Miss Cottrell was a lady and not—the other thing? Yes, perhaps a nice little lady's mare.

After he had rid the Easten stables of that stallion, of course! Which was still another problem. He had seen the creature. A bullet to the brain of such a beautiful animal seemed a shame. But, of course, he had not yet seen the reputedly vicious stallion indulging in any sort of evil behavior. He might think differently once he had.

Three

"... and then Lord Huntingdon said ..."

"Do you think," said Lydia, forcing a laugh, "that we might finish our dinner with a little less served up of what Lord Huntingdon has had to say?" When she saw how Jasper's face blanked and then turned bright red, she wondered how she could possibly have said such a thing. Not only had it been rude to interrupt the boy, but her words had been excessively uncivil. "Jasper, I only meant ..."

"You only meant I was boring on forever." A muscle jerked, then stilled, in Jasper's cheek. "I apologize."

Lydia sighed. "I think perhaps it was worse than that, Jasper. I mean that I, not you, should apologize. I fear I was jealous."

There was a tumble of words from around the table, the gist of which was a question as to how that could be.

"It is obvious," said Eunice, her dry voice forcing silence on the others. "Lydia has been mentor to you children for years now. You have come to her with each and every problem, and she has done her best for you. Now a total stranger walks in, and Jasper has fallen instantly in love with the man, to say nothing of his every word. Especially his words. I, too, have a gullet full of all his lordship has said to you, Jasper, and although I'm pleased to have heard nothing but good sense, we could now, I think, use just a bit of *nonsense* to spice up our appetites."

Their aunt's wry words roused giggles around the table. Only Jasper had to make an effort to change the tenor of his thoughts. "So," he said at last in an overly bright voice, "what did the rest of you do while I slaved to explain our exceedingly dull accounts to the total stranger?"

It was the sort of comment that in a good mood his father might have made, and Lydia and Eunice exchanged a glance pregnant with unspoken comment. "I spent the afternoon with Cook," said Lydia. "We made lists of all those things a household needs on hand in order to set a decent table. Which reminds me, Jasper, will you present the list to Lord Huntingdon for his approval before it is sent on to our supplier?"

Jasper sent her a teasing look and refused to answer.

"Jasper!"

"But, Liddy, I have been told in no uncertain terms that I am not to discuss his lordship—with whom I have not fallen in love!" He scowled at his aunt, who had made the suggestion. "It would be most improper," he finished with more than a touch of prudery.

Eunice cast a sharp look toward the boy. "That, Jasper Easten, is quite enough of a subject which should never have been allowed to enter your mind, let alone your mouth. I will see you after dinner, if you please. In the library."

Since the library was the scene of their father's worst dealings with his sons and daughters, every child at the table seemed to shrink. Eunice did not explain that she had no intention of getting out the vicious switch her brother had used too often. Not only did she not approve, but she had never had a need of it. By most, her tongue was considered quite vicious enough.

"But . . . ," began Lydia, a worried expression crossing her face.

"Never you mind," said Eunice. "Jasper knows what he said. That is more than enough."

"But," said the boy, suddenly rebellious, "it was what *you* said which—"

"Jasper!"

"Oh, very well. And of course I will present the list to Lord Huntingdon, Liddy. Did you doubt it? Although I don't know why I bother, since he'll very likely say that whatever is needed should be acquired on the instant. That's what he's said about other things."

"In that case I'll go on to the linen closet tomorrow. We might as well see just how much we can get out of him before that fine gentleman surfaces from the facer he received upon discovering how shocking the situation is here. Soon he'll set his mind to more rational thought; and once he does, he will tighten the purse strings, and we will go on much as we have done."

Lydia's tone was more than a trifle sarcastic.

"Lydia Cottrell, when I have finished with Jasper, I believe you and I should have a few words concerning your irrational attitude toward his lordship. Ladies? Have you finished?" Eunice looked around her nephew's dinner table and decided it would do Mary, who was a trifle plump, no harm to leave behind the rest of her pudding. "Come along, now. We will leave Jasper and James to talk of mannish things while we go up to have tea in the drawing room. That is, we'd have tea, as is proper, if we *had* any of that expensive item!"

There were groans from around the table.

Eunice, standing now, grinned. "Don't sound so distressed. I ordered a fire made there." She whispered that last in the overloud whisper of the stage actor wishing to inform the audience of something those on stage were not supposed to know.

The groans turned to giggles, and the younger girls scurried from the room, leaving Margaret, Lydia and Eunice to follow at a more ladylike pace.

"I would say it has been a very good day," said Eunice complacently, as the three trod up the broad stairs arm-in-arm.

"Was it?" asked Lydia. "I thought we were getting along quite well before his lordship turned everything topsy-turvy."

"You truly have taken him in dislike, have you not," said Eunice, surprised.

"I believe I have." She frowned. "And as you suggested, it is quite irrational. I must try to bring myself to a better frame of mind."

Lydia's frown deepened as she tried to understand how someone she had never before met could, so quickly, arouse so much irritation and have done so without the least effort. She thought back over those first moments of their introduction and reached a surprising conclusion.

"Eunice, could it possibly be something so silly as the exceedingly odd way he looked at me when we were introduced? I didn't like it. Not at all."

"How was that?"

But Lydia, not certain, just shrugged.

"Margaret, do you have a notion what she means?" asked Eunice.

"No, Aunt. I was in the schoolroom when they met, of course, so I saw nothing. But Lord Horten, I noticed, looked at her as all men do." Margaret gave her half sister a roguish look.

Lydia blushed. "I didn't notice Lord Horten's eyes upon me, and I'm glad I did not. I wish men would *not* look at me in that particularly upsetting way."

"But, Liddy, it means they like you."

Lydia's flush deepened. "You've no notion of what

you speak, Margaret, and should *not* when you *do*
not . . . which reminds me. Eunice, why were you so
angry with Jasper?"

"You should not speak when you know not of what
you speak," said Eunice, mimicking Lydia's prim tone.

"Which is why I'm asking you to explain it to me."

Margaret again cast her half sister a speculative look,
and then she hurried on up the stairs ahead of her aunt
and elder sister.

Lydia, reviewing the recent conversation, came out
with a totally inadequate, "Oh, dear."

"Yes," said Eunice dryly. "I believe you set yourself
up nicely for Margaret's obvious questions concerning
how men look when they like one and how they look
when they *really* like one." She chuckled at Lydia's horrified expression. "What will you tell her?"

Lydia sighed. "I think I'll merely say that not all re-
lationships between men and women are proper. The
sort of look to which she referred, the kind it is likely
Lord Horten turned my way, implies the man is thinking of a quite *improper* relationship."

"Hmm. A year ago that might have satisfied her. I
don't know that it will now. She may wish to know what
is meant by a relationship, may she not? Proper as well
as improper?"

Lydia groaned.

"I wish you the best of luck," said Eunice with obvious
mendacity.

"One moment, please." Lydia halted Eunice before
the doors to the drawing room. "Do you mean to tell
me why Jasper is in trouble?"

"No."

Lydia cast Eunice a smug look. "I will ask *him,*" she
said. "He'll explain."

Eunice grinned in that singularly irritating way she
had and said, "In this particular case, I predict he will

not." Eunice opened the door and entered the room, leaving Lydia fuming in the hall.

The boys clattered up the stairs before she brought herself to calmness, and she sent James on into the room, catching Jasper's sleeve. "Jasper," she said, earnestly, "what did you mean by what you said? Why was Eunice angry with you?"

Jasper looked at his half sister, his eyes slightly shrouded by drooping eyelids. "Did you ask Aunt Eunice to explain?"

"Yes I did, and when she would not, I said I'd ask you."

"If you do not know, and Aunt Eunice did not think it proper to tell you, then I don't think it my place to do so," he said with an adult dignity which surprised Lydia greatly. Gently, he removed her fingers from his sleeve and turned to enter the drawing room, but found his aunt at the door staring at him. He gulped. "I was just coming to tell you that if you wish to find me, I'll be in the . . . the . . . the . . ."

"The library. Boy, you must learn it is no more than another room in your house." She spoke gruffly. "Come along now." She started down the stairs, and with one more gulp and a look filled with despair cast toward Lydia, the boy straightened his shoulders and went back downstairs, his steps neither so firm nor so quick as his aunt's and every smidgen of that surprising dignity gone as if it had never been.

Lydia smiled to herself. Jasper had obviously not understood Eunice's words with respect to the library, but she did. She entered the drawing room much lighter at heart, knowing that whatever else might go on downstairs, there would be no corporal punishment such as the children's father had seemed to actually enjoy handing out.

"How," she asked, brightly, "about a game of Fish?"

Chairs were set around the table, and the counters were soon dealt out. In the excitement, no one thought to ask what had become of Jasper and Aunt Eunice. It was nearly an hour later that Jasper entered the drawing room and whispered in Lydia's ear that Aunt Eunice wished a word with her before she returned to her dower house.

Lydia handed over her place to Jasper and went down to the front door where, swathed in shawls against the evening cool, Eunice paced. "Ah. Took you long enough."

Since she had *not* taken overly long, coming immediately as she had been informed she should, Lydia merely quirked a brow.

Eunice sighed. "You will not like it, but I have decided to move back into this house while Huntingdon remains in the area."

"You feel Margaret needs a more mature chaperon."

"Margaret! Piffle. You, my dear, are in far more danger than Margaret. She's the merest child in the eyes of those men. You, on the other hand, are not."

"Me?"

"You said yourself that the way Lord Horten looked at you indicated a wish for an improper relationship. It occurred to me that while you insist they consider you no more than the governess, you will find yourself open to insult. I cannot allow that. I owe your mother too large a debt to allow her daughter to be seduced by that bear of a man. Or by the other one, for that matter. I would appreciate it if you'd order a room prepared for me immediately."

"Certainly, Miss Easten."

Eunice chuckled. "Set up your back, did I? You think I mean *you* to do it, but you forget that come morning you'll have a couple of maids to order around. It is, however," she said severely, "up to you to see they do the work properly."

On that dire note she opened the door and closed it with a snap. Lydia was alone at last, at the end of a *very* long day. Except her day was not ended. She must return to the drawing room and see that everyone went properly to bed, must listen to prayers and check that each, James in particular, had washed properly. She sighed.

Lydia very much wished for time in which to think. It was the oddest thing, but now and again and then still again, throughout the long day, while doing this and then the other thing, suddenly a vision would appear in her mind of her first glimpse of Lord Huntingdon as he had looked when he entered the drawing room and had, in the instant she had risen to her feet, stared at her.

His expression had been . . . interesting. It was the only word she could find to describe it. Interesting.

But until the children were in bed, she must contain herself and not attempt to unravel the mystery of just why the expression had seemed . . . interesting.

Roger frowned at his first sip of wine that night at dinner. He stared into his glass. Then he looked up and found both Rafe and Kenrick watching him with something which might have been called a wary look in their expressions. Deadpan, he said, "You see? I told you I could come up with a good wine."

Rafe chuckled. "Or, perhaps you might say your *butler* can come up with a fine wine?"

"I suppose I might." Roger sipped again and sighed. "I cannot understand why my own—"

Kenrick interrupted before they must endure still another dissertation on why Roger's wine *should* taste as good as anything one was once able to import from France. "Roger, I need to find several good ponies for young people. Where might I do so?"

"Ponies?" Roger spoke idly. Then his expression cleared, and when he continued he showed more interest. "I've heard Mr. Simpson wishes to find a good home for two Welsh-bred ponies. Why?"

"I'll need more than two, but that's a beginning. Will you introduce me to the man?"

"Of course, but why . . . oh. The Easten children. Rafe has, as is usual with him, found someone to do his dirty work for him?"

"If you mean I've asked Kenrick to teach the children to ride, then yes I have. Don't tell *him,*" he said from the side of his mouth, "but I thought it might keep him out of mischief." When the others laughed, he smiled and then continued, "However that may be, if we are to speak of riding, do tell me there isn't a whisper going round about the eldest Easten."

"What sort of talk?"

"Something one of the children said. I have the strangest notion the lady may have once ridden, or may actually regularly ride, the stallion with the bad reputation."

"I haven't heard anything to that effect." Roger's hand stopped part way to his mouth, and he laid his fork back on his plate. "The stallion? You mean the animal that is said to be a killer?"

"I was told by the late baronet's sister that the kindest thing to do might be to put a bullet in the animal's head! The younger boy obviously didn't agree." When Roger merely blinked, Rafe continued. "It is one more thing I must decide."

"To shoot the beast?" asked Roger, but was ignored.

"You also have to discover just who *she* is, do you not?" asked Kenrick.

"Who who is?" Roger wished to know.

"Don't remind me," said Rafe. "I detest mysteries. You know I dislike them."

"To whom," asked Roger, distinctly, "do we refer?"

"The eldest Easten," said Rafe impatiently.

"And just why is the eldest Easten a mystery?" persisted Roger.

"Because she doesn't admit to it. She is, according to the whole household, merely Miss Cottrell and no more than their governess."

"Nonsense."

"I'm glad you agree!"

"They all look alike," said Roger.

"She said the late Lady Easten was very kind to her. And that is a rather odd thing to say, now I think of it."

"Very odd. Why should she *not* be kind?" Roger ate for a moment in silence before adding, "Or are you thinking it possible the young woman is a by-blow Sir Jasper's father admitted to his household? I suppose it might be a trifle odd for a wife to treat such a one with kindness."

"I wonder if that wouldn't explain why she goes by a different name and never had a season," said Kenrick.

"Very clearly she *is* one of the family. As you said, Roger, they all have the same look to them." Rafe hated to think Miss Cottrell might be illegitimate.

"What else can it be? I've thought about it, and I am pretty certain the late baronet didn't marry twice. We know the chit hadn't a presentation. She bears a different name and has a menial position. There is a fear on the part of the children she'll be sent away . . ." Kenrick's words trailed off as he noticed how Rafe's expression hardened.

"In a word, a mystery to which you have found a solution, is that it, Kenrick?"

Kenrick shrugged. "You must admit it fills in the holes."

"She doesn't act like one."

"Like a by-blow? And how does such a one usually act?"

Rafe shrugged. "You know as well as I, Ken. That sort act as if they are in a household on sufferance, of course, and as if they have no real place in the family." Rafe refused, himself, to put into words the notion Miss Cottrell was a by-blow.

"If she's been running the house for several years, she would gain a certain amount of assurance, would she not?"

"I believe that even if she did, surely only with the family. *Not* in company," objected Rafe.

"I'll admit she behaved like any young woman I've ever met in tonnish circles," agreed Kenrick.

"Ah!" said Roger. "Did she flirt with you, then?"

Kenrick rumbled a bit, a sound Rafe and Roger both knew well, although it could mean a variety of things. In this case they wondered whether the baron was disturbed or angry and how long it would be before he found his voice and was able to explain.

"She did not," the big man finally said. "In fact, when I tried to set up a mild flirtation, she looked at me as if she thought me quite as mad as any elderly hatter you'd find doing business in a provincial town."

"Do you mean she was unwilling to flirt with you, or she did not recognize your efforts for what they were?" asked Roger, curious.

Frowning, Kenrick remained silent for a long, thoughtful moment. "I had not thought of the latter. Can she possibly be so utterly unaware of her attractions?"

"You do find her attractive, then." Rafe stared at his plate, his profile rather stern.

"Why should I not?" Kenrick cast Rafe a mischievous glance. *"You* did."

Rafe didn't deny it. "Until I discover her place in that household, it behooves the both of us to tread warily. She is, even if only the governess, my responsibility." When Kenrick merely gave him a bland look, he added, "I'll not have her hurt, Kenrick."

"I don't hurt women."

"No, but you've been known to seduce one or two who perhaps should not have been seduced. You'll not try your tricks on this one."

"I *like* women."

"And they like you, but you'll walk a wary route with Miss Cottrell or I'll have your hide!"

"You want her yourself."

"Will you get it through that thick skull, I do not yet know if she is available for sport? I am not convinced she is what you think her. If she were, why would she have put up with the old curmudgeon, who must have been as big a blackguard as one could find anywhere among the *ton*? She did so even when she might easily have found herself a lover and enjoyed life, to say nothing of acquiring some of the elegancies. Instead, she is burdened with responsibilities and, if that gown she wore today is an example, has little enough to show for them!"

"A looker like that—"

"Kenrick!"

"There's a solution," said Roger, breaking into what looked to escalate to a full-fledged argument.

"Solution?" asked Kenrick.

"If you have the answer, tell me. I need to know how to deal with the woman."

"I'll ask Mother."

"Very good idea," rumbled Kenrick. "She'll know."

"It would be a much better idea," said Rafe bitingly, "if your mother were here to be asked."

"Write her," suggested the baron.

"Exactly," said Roger. "I'll write her. Can't promise, however, that I'll get a response any time soon."

Rafe sighed and then looked at Kenrick. "You will behave with discretion?"

Kenrick sighed in turn and put on a lugubrious expression. "I will behave like my sainted uncle."

"Not," said the marquis, startled, "the one who was sent to India!"

"It is true my father's middle brother was no saint. But I referred to my uncle Gerald, my mother's youngest brother, who became a vicar and was given a supposedly temporary living in some hellish hole of a village in Northumberland. Since then he has refused all efforts to remove him to a more salubrious clime and, by so doing, advancing his career." Kenrick's friends stared at him. He shrugged his massive shoulders and explained further. "He says he is needed, if you please."

Kenrick said the last with such an air of wonderment that both Roger and Rafe laughed. The evening improved once that was settled. The men played cards, but trotted off to bed at an early hour feeling quite virtuous.

The next morning Lydia had a great deal of difficulty with her charges. They would not settle to their work. One or another was almost constantly at the window.

"But, Liddy," protested James when she took him by the ear and led him back to his desk.

"But-Liddy me when you have finished your work!"

"They said they'd come again. They said they'd be here this morning. They said—"

"They said," interrupted Lydia, "all too much. You cannot play if you do not work, so it makes no never mind if they come or if they stay."

"Besides," said the children's aunt from the doorway, "it is far too early for bucks of that sort to have gotten themselves out of their beds."

Her words brought an awed silence to the school-room. Slowly, one after the other, the children bent their heads and settled to the work they had been given for that day. Even James, although his round-eyed wonderment indicated this interesting information would, if not immediately, then once he was older, lead to problems. James's mind was a trap for odd information. He would not forget that according to his all-knowing aunt, one sign of such much-to-be-desired sophistication was the lateness of one's rising from one's bed.

Eunice crooked a finger to Lydia, who obliged her by joining the gray-haired woman in the hall. "I forgot to ask just where you meant to put me as I should have done before I left last night. Which room," she added when Lydia didn't seem to understand.

"Oh, dear."

"You forgot."

"Yes, I did, and I apologize. I also thank you for getting the children back to work. I was about to despair of ever seeing them properly studious again!" Lydia frowned ever so slightly before asking, *"Do* tonnish men truly sleep so late?"

"Not so much so in the country, but when dancing and gambling and whatever else is done when in town during the season? I understand their nights don't end until three or four in the morning or, for some, even later, so it is not surprising, is it, that they sleep most of the day?"

"Dancing? Then, the women, too?" Lydia blinked, blinked again. "I do not think I *could* do so. I'd fall asleep in the middle of a cotillion and embarrass my

poor partner to tears when he was forced to pick me
up off the floor."

"You, my dear widgeon, would fall asleep before ever
the dancing began, which might be ten or eleven of
the clock. Or you would, that is, if one didn't quickly
adjust to such hours." Eunice turned toward the stairs.
"Come along now. You must choose me a room and
tell the new maids what to do. I can just imagine the
state things have gotten to since your dear mother
died."

"I've done my best," said Lydia. She realized how tart
she had sounded and bit her lip.

"Of course you have. But, since you've had nothing
with which to do it, it is not surprising your best has
been less than adequate." There was a bite to Eunice's
voice in turn.

Lydia decided the amount of vinegar she had sprin-
kled on her own words was nothing compared to the
children's aunt's! "Since it is warming up so nicely, then
the green corner room might be the most pleasant."

"Also the room farthest from your own, hmm?"

Lydia choked back a giggle. "You wrong me, Eunice.
I've moved into the yellow room which is only across
the hall!"

"Your mother's old room? Why?"

Lydia blinked. "Do you think it wrong of me?"

"I didn't say that. I just wished to know why you
moved."

"If you must know, there is a leak. Along with all else
he would not do, your brother refused to fix the roof.
And," she added before Eunice could say anything,
"that is still another thing, is it not, which I must add
to the list for his lordship?" She grinned a trifle evilly.
"The man will run for his very life!"

"His name is Huntingdon." Eunice gave her a look.

Lydia's lips compressed. "I know."

"Nothing stopping you from using it."

"I don't believe I have been given that privilege." And with that bit of utter nonsense—as if one needed permission to use a man's title!—Lydia opened the door to the green room. She took one look and closed it with something of a snap. "I must find those maids. They'll have much to do to make this ready for you by this evening."

"Things are not the same as when I was a girl."

"Very true," said Lydia. "Among other things, your very generous father was alive then. Or, at least I've heard he was generous."

"So he was. Jasper is very like him, you know."

Lydia blushed. "I apologize. That was outside of enough."

"No, merely truth. You should know I don't get upset at the truth."

"You merely fight back when you think it is not? I'll remember to speak nothing but the truth to you in future!"

"Ah, you mean you'll not respond when I merely ask for your opinion?"

Lydia nodded, her eyes sparkling.

Eunice yawned, patting her mouth with long, work-worn fingers. "How boring," she said languidly.

Eunice's tone poured cold water on Lydia's hope she had finally won a point against her friendly enemy. "I'll see to the maids," she said.

"No, you go back to our children. My words won't have kept them sober for long. No," added Eunice when Lydia gestured at the room, "I'll supervise the maids after all. They'll likely need it!"

Lydia gave her a thankful look which was not noted, Eunice already having entered the room and deciding in what order it was to be cleaned and cared for. Before anything more could be said to Easten Meadows manor's detriment, Lydia fled.

Eunice had maligned the men by suggesting they were still abed. None of them brought city habits to the country, and all had been out of bed for longer than Eunice herself, a fact which would have surprised her a great deal. Eunice was known to be an early bird.

After a more than adequate breakfast, the marquis agreed to ride with them to Mr. Simpson's freehold. They meant to look over the ponies and purchase them then and there, assuming they were suitable.

"I don't know that they will be," admitted Roger as they approached the white-painted gate opening on a short drive leading to a neat manor and well-kept barns. "My guess is you'll find them a trifle long in the tooth."

"Just right, then, for the twins," rumbled the baron. "That is, if they've no odd kick to their gait."

Rafe left Kenrick to look over the animals while he and Roger did the pretty by Mr. Simpson's wife and daughter. The other two men soon joined them, however.

"Pay the man, Rafe," said Kenrick.

Thankfully Rafe looked up from the watercolor he had just been handed. Trying to find words that were neither untruthful nor hurtful was giving him a headache. The chit's muddy little paintings were among the worst he had ever been asked to approve!

"Certainly," he said. "I'll need a receipt, Mr. Simpson, so I may make the charge to the Easten estate."

Mr. Simpson led the three men to his office. "Seem a little young to be guardian to all those children," said Simpson, his eyes narrowed and almost lost in his chubby cheeks, but his tone was carefully nonaccusing.

"I believe their father actually thought he'd left

them in the care of my uncle; but the will was worded badly, so he'd left them to the title. It is not a charge I looked for, but I'll do the best I can to fulfill the duties thereof," said Rafe, speaking with the naive seeming innocence which, at an early age, he had adopted to get himself out of difficulties with those who did not know him well. Very often it still sufficed.

Mr. Simpson eyed Rafe for a long, thoughtful moment and then nodded. "Lord Horten says you'll be looking for smallish horses for the boys and perhaps for the older girls?"

"You know where we might find proper mounts? You realize," warned Horten, "that the children have never ridden? Even the boys will need well-trained mounts."

"Over North Marden way. You, my lord," he turned to Roger, "you'll recall that Irish couple who bought up the old Salway place when the last heir couldn't be bothered to take his nose out of London long enough to see to it? Almost put in a bid myself, but just a trifle more than I thought I could manage."

They heard regret in the man's voice but, showing excellent manners, ignored it. "You mean," said Roger, "the McCormicks. A brother and sister, I believe."

"That's the pair."

"Good breeding lines? Well-trained?"

"Don't know myself, do I? I've heard they do pretty well with a nag."

"Well, Rafe?"

"How far?"

"Good twenty miles, I'd guess," said Roger laconically and added, "one way."

Rafe sighed. "I can't go. Not today. I promised Sir Jasper we'd begin a tour of the estate and make a preliminary list of what needs doing. Kenrick?"

"Promised the schoolroom bunch I'd have ponies for them. Didn't say how many. Two's enough for getting on with. Except"—he rolled his eyes—"I forgot they'll need tack."

"Oh, the price includes the tack, of course," said Mr. Simpson, looking surprised they had thought otherwise.

"You'll not be leaving immediately, I hope," interjected Mrs. Simpson, who stood in the doorway listening. She curtsied when the men turned toward her, her girth making it awkward. "I'm about to lay the men's morning tea, and you are welcome to join us." She glanced at her daughter, whose blushes had begun to fade, then at her husband. "Mr. Simpson, you'll not play the nip-cheese and let your guests go on their way with nothing to warm them?"

"Never say I'd act a skint!" exclaimed the farmer, looking horrified. "Of course they'll stay. Now, Lord Huntingdon, you and I can finish our business while Sally and her mother set out the vittles. The men will come in any minute now."

Rafe tried to think of a way of avoiding any obligation to stay, but he failed, as did Kenrick and Roger. They all, having eaten not all that much earlier, looked at the groaning board in dismay.

Surely the Simpsons didn't eat this way several times a day! Rafe managed to take only a mug of the Simpsons' homemade cider, and Roger a mug of home brew. Kenrick was told in no uncertain terms that a big man must keep up his strength and handed a plate well laded with rashers of bacon, sausage, potatoes and eggs scrambled with more onions than the baron favored.

The marquis chuckled. "Mrs. Simpson, I don't believe my friend needs *quite* so much. He had very nearly that well filled a plate when we breakfasted only an hour or two ago."

"Oh, I should have known." Mrs. Simpson blushed as rosily as her daughter had earlier. "Now, if it isn't just those little differences which make it so difficult to know how to go on. We have only tea and toast at dawn, and then this meal when the morning chores are done. Don't you eat a bite more than you want, Lord Horten. I apologize for thinking odd thoughts about your friends."

Later, when they had ridden some way down the road, Rafe asked, "What sort of odd thoughts could she have been thinking?"

"Wondered that myself," said Kenrick, looking back to see that their pace was comfortable for the ponies which followed on lead reins. "Perhaps she thought you two drank your meals!"

Roger chuckled at the thought. "Perhaps she thought we eat only honey and nectar like Greek gods!"

"Or perhaps," suggested Kenrick, "she suspected we lived on air and sunshine or some such thing. Surely the woman isn't so odd she believes that just because we've fancy titles we aren't human."

"We're quite human enough for her to push her daughter forward!" said Rafe, his lips twisting in faint scorn.

"Ah, but that is simply the disadvantage of being a peer, is it not? Every mother sees an unmarried peer as the answer to her daughter's prayers." Kenrick shrugged. "I'm glad I was with Mr. Simpson and not in the parlor!"

"At the McCormicks', when we look over their stock, I think I'll check the horses and *you* can do the pretty in the parlor!"

"At the McCormicks', unless I've been misinformed," said Roger, "there will be no one in the parlor. It is said Miss Maddy is right out there in the muck with her brother."

"An elderly eccentric?" asked Rafe.

"Elderly?" Kenrick chuckled. "I don't think so. Not

given what Mr. Simpson said. Come to that, I find I'm developing a wee bit of curiosity which needs satisfying soon as may be. Shall we go tomorrow?"

"I will inform the Eastens I'll not be able to come to the Meadows tomorrow," said Rafe, "but I'll not tell the boys why. No need to raise their hopes until we know if there is something suitable. The Irish raise very good horses, but not necessarily natured for the un-schooled young."

Much later that afternoon, Rafe stood near Eunice and Lydia, watching one of the twins have a turn at walking a pony while Margaret sat straight in the side-saddle on the back of other one, trying to get her reins between her fingers as Lord Horten had taught her. He moved nearer the older woman. "I forgot to inform young Jasper that we cannot come tomorrow."

"I'll pass along the word."

"Already tired of your duty to your ward?" Lydia's tone, which she had meant to be teasing, had just a little too much of an edge to it.

"It is duty to my wards which takes me away," said Rafe, wondering how he had managed to get on the wrong side of the beauty when he had had so very little to do with her.

Lydia turned her eyes sideways to look at him and lifted her chin. She turned back to where Margaret, just the tip of her tongue showing, was trying to get her pony to move forward. Lydia decided that poor Margaret would never be a horsewoman, but it was impor-tant she learn the rudiments.

"You don't believe me," said Rafe softly. "I wonder why."

Lydia glanced up to discover that Rafe had moved to her side and was staring, broodingly, down at her. "I am sorry if I implied anything of the sort," she said shortly, turning away from those intense blue eyes.

"No," he said in a measured way, "I don't believe you are the least sorry." When she didn't comment, he added, "Tomorrow I and my friends ride to where we hope to buy the boys mounts suitable to their age and ability."

"You mean their inability." Lydia turned still farther away to hide suddenly heated cheeks. It seemed she could not speak softly to the man even when she wished to do so. "Where," she asked, making an effort, "do you think to find what is needed?"

"Mr. Simpson reminded Maythorn of a fairly new horse farm near North Marden."

"Owned and operated by Sean and Maddy McCormick." Eunice, who had been listening, nodded. "I've heard good things of the operation. I don't know if you'll find anything suitable for the boys, but you might for Lydia."

"For Miss Cottrell?"

Again Lydia felt her cheeks burn. "I am the governess," she said sharply. "Buying a mount for my use would be inappropriate."

"But a governess is expected to take her young ladies riding, is she not?" asked Rafe, once again oozing innocence.

It changed as she watched. She took note of narrowed eyes, a quizzing look she didn't understand. "I . . ." She stopped, then drew in a deep breath. "You mean to get mounts for the boys. When they are in school I'll ride them so as to exercise them."

"I think you should have your own," said Rafe, who had previously thought no such thing. "I will discuss with Miss McCormick the animals she feels suited to a lady."

"Did you say *Miss* McCormick?" Lydia bit her lip, her eyes staring at nothing at all. "Lord Huntingdon," she finally asked, still not meeting his eyes, "is there any possibility I might talk to her myself? I think I would enjoy that," she finished after a moment's pause in which it occurred to her she should hide her true reason for speaking with the female horse dealer. "In fact," she added, a brilliant notion coming to mind, "I think everyone would like to go."

"You mean," asked Eunice slowly, "that we might make a holiday of it and take the children?"

Lydia meant exactly that. With the children milling around, surely she could find a moment in which to have a word with the distaff side of the McCormick ménage. Now she had thought of it, she was almost certain it was the answer to a problem that had been worrying her for some time now. Just then she noticed Sir Jasper approach the paddock from the direction of the house. She turned fully toward him. "You are frowning, Jasper. Has something gone wrong?"

"We have just received a message from old Percell, who heard from someone that Lord Huntingdon has arrived. He would appreciate it, my lord, if you would see him as soon as possible," Jasper added with some diffidence. Almost as an afterthought, he handed over a note.

Rafe read it and sighed. "I haven't a notion what can be so urgent, but I fear, Miss Cottrell, our little jaunt to the McCormicks' must be postponed. I am forced to ride into Storrington and discover exactly what it is which has caused this fine gentleman to write as if the sky were falling!" Rafe glanced at the so-called governess, noting how the corners of her lips drooped and how sad her expression was. "The first good day we'll arrange a holiday. You will all enjoy the treat," he said.

For just an instant a cold, almost cynical, look flitted across Miss Cottrell's features, quickly disappearing to be replaced by her usual blandly polite expression. "Thank you. I'm quite certain we'll enjoy it."

"Now what is going on in what I begin to believe to be an exceedingly convoluted mind, Miss Cottrell?"

"What?" Lydia glanced at him, a startled look.

"I'm almost certain you do not expect to enjoy the treat at all."

"Of course I'll enjoy it!"

Rafe waited half a moment, but she didn't go on. "Very well. It doesn't do to contradict a lady."

"But I am merely a governess," she said with the sort of quick retort she would have made to Eunice in a similar situation. "You may contradict me with impunity, Lord Huntingdon."

Rafe bowed. "Thank you for permission, Miss Cottrell. I'll be certain to remember."

Once again Rafe wondered why Miss Cottrell had taken him in dislike. Perhaps, when he got to know Miss Easten better, he would ask the elderly chaperon if she had any notion. At the moment he didn't feel so comfortable with the sharp-tongued spinster that he could broach something of such a personal nature.

Lydia strolled to where Margaret, very near tears, still sat her mount. Yes, decided Rafe, watching her, an exceedingly convoluted mind—and one he was finding more and more interest in unraveling!

Four

Rafe drove into Storrington, reluctantly leaving Kenrick working with the children and their riding. His only satisfaction was that as he had mounted his curricle, he had noticed Miss Cottrell carrying Baby Alice back to the house, the child's head drooping onto the governess's shoulder and obviously in need of her little cot.

It occurred to him to wonder if Miss Cottrell had not merely *managed* the Easten household, but whether she had done much of the work herself? From the little said, it appeared she had, the children helping where they could. At least that was the conclusion to be drawn from every stray comment dropped accidentally by Jasper, who had finally relaxed enough to prattle on about all sorts of things. He made a note to ask Miss Easten to hire a nursery maid.

The drive would have been pleasant and the town of interest if Rafe had not had so much on his mind. Finding the solicitor's office was not difficult. He simply asked the first man he saw and was directed to the town square where the man's offices were above the draper's not far from the church. Most of one side of the square was taken up by a surprisingly large inn with excellent stabling. Instead of worrying about his matched pair of blacks as he had thought he would do, he left them there, happy in the knowledge they would be properly rubbed down and not given a drink until they had cooled properly.

The narrow stairs to the solicitor's office were covered with a worn drugget. The office itself was so dim and dreary and so crammed with legal boxes and yellowing rolls of paper tied in red tape, Rafe wondered that Mr. Percell could find anything.

"I'm Huntingdon," he said, holding out his hand to the man across the desk. A limp handshake was accompanied by a bemused look, and Rafe added, "Young Sir Jasper's guardian."

The bemused look disappeared in suspicion. "Now what rig be you a'runnin', young man?"

Rafe's brows arched. "I assumed, when you wrote, you knew I had recently inherited my uncle's title." When the man still glowered, Rafe added, "I assure you, I am Raphael Weston Montgomery Seymour, fourth Earl Huntingdon and Baron Seymour."

"Old Easten tol' me particular that Huntingdon would see things done the way he wished them done."

Rafe compressed his lips until he felt himself in control again. "If the situation I found at Easten Meadows was an indication of how the late baronet wished his children to live, then I can only be glad I and *not* my uncle have control of the situation."

" 'Taint right." The solicitor crossed his arms and frowned mightily. His lips pursed in what could only be called a pout.

"Mr. Percell, you, I assume, drew up the will. It was *your* mistake that I must now see to Sir Jasper's estate and am the children's guardian."

"That ain't right neither."

Rafe stifled a wish to throttle the man for his negativism. "What," he asked, evenly, "is wrong in it?"

"Only guardian to Sir Jasper and the estate. No guardian named for the brats. No provision, neither."

"Pernicious if true."

"Oh, it's true enough."

"Mr. Percell, I wish a copy of that will."

"Dinna I send you one?"

"No, you did not."

The solicitor sighed. "So much to do. Can't expect a man to remember everything." Mr. Percell searched under and around the papers littering his desk until he uncovered an inkwell. Next he opened a drawer and chose a pen. After inspecting the nib, he looked around his office with a blank look. "Now where did I put that will . . ."

"I would prefer that you attend to making the copy after I leave and send it out by messenger to Maythorn. I'm battening on the marquis and can be found there most evenings. For now, perhaps you'll explain this impertinent note you sent to Easten Meadows?" Rafe held out the note, but didn't release it when the solicitor reached for it.

"Sent for you, did I? Why did I . . . ?" The man rubbed his chin hard as if the raspy noise might stimulate his thinking. "Why, oh why, oh why . . ."

Absently, randomly it seemed, the solicitor picked up papers from his desk. Eventually, he was about to lay one down where it would soon disappear into the mass when he drew it back and held it close to his eyes. Moving his lips as he read, he perused it.

"Ah, yes," he said. "Now, then, you speak of impertinent notes, do you! 'Pon my soul, never saw such impertinence! Mine to you was written in irritation after reading *that.*" He handed the letter scrawled on a heavy, cream-laid sheet across the desk.

Rafe noted the crest at the top and glanced to the signature at the bottom. "Charingham?"

"You know the earl?"

"We've met. The old man rarely comes to London

these days, so I can't say I know him . . ." Rafe's words trailed off as his eyes traveled down the page. "Of all the . . . !" he said and a bit later, he added, "I can't believe this!" and then, at the end, "This is truly outside of enough!"

"Tol' ye it were impertinent." Percell spoke with satisfaction.

"I am not certain he can, legally, require Sir Jasper's guardian to take on this added burden."

"Yes, he can. He's an earl!"

"His title alone does not give him the right," said Rafe dryly. "Not if the guardian will not agree," he added and very nearly gritted his teeth. "Which I have not done."

He wondered why it had never occurred to him that the children took after their mother rather than their father. Miss Cottrell, it seemed, was connected to the Earl of Charingham. *His* daughter, perhaps? Had the earl arranged for his mistress to become Lady Easten? There had been, Rafe remembered from his study of the estate business, a rather large dowry come into the estate upon that marriage.

Percell interrupted his thoughts. "You see he don't want Miss Cottrell to know of the annuity 'cepting she needs it. But this'll make it easier for you to throw that female out, won' it? *To get rid of her*, you know?" he added when Rafe turned a glowering look his way. "Can't have a by-blow in charge of all them children, can ye?" suggested the solicitor piously.

"She's been in charge with the late baronet's full approval."

"Tol' me she got above herself. Tol' me one day she'd go too far and he'd be done of her. That he did, dinna he, then!" Percell finished when his words seemed to make his visitor more angry than ever.

"The children love her very much."

Percell blinked. "So? What's that to do with the price of eggs in Lonnen?"

Rafe sighed. "If you do not understand, I won't attempt an explanation. Whatever Miss Cottrell's origins, and I'm not satisfied I understand them despite what might be read between the lines in this letter, she has done a good job of work with the children, and unless something occurs to change my mind, I've no intention of turning her off."

"What ye mean, her origins? Clear as a bell!"

"Not entirely," said Rafe who had had a moment to think. "Even after all these decades, there are tales about the Charingham Romance. The earl is said to have fallen deeply in love with a certain woman he first met when she was about to wed another. He is said to have waited over a decade to marry her and that he never looked at any other woman from the moment they were first introduced at his future wife's first wedding. He is said to have sworn he'd marry her and no other. Luckily, the groom that day was a rather elderly man who popped off in a not totally unreasonable length of time."

The solicitor blinked. "So?"

"So," Rafe elaborated, "given that history, I've great difficulty believing he had a long-term affair with the late Lady Easten, Miss Cottrell a result of their improper union."

Percell shook his head vigorously. "Musta done."

"There are other possibilities," said Rafe, waving aside the man's next impertinent question. If asked *what* possibility, he had not yet thought of one and could not have answered. He reread the earl's letter. "A goodly sum. It'll make her a very nice annuity, will it not?" he said at one point. "But not to tell her, to give her no options, I don't like that."

"Already an uppity woman. No sense in putting notions into her head."

"You don't like her, do you?"

Two spots of color appeared on the solicitor's cheeks. "Why should I dislike her?"

"I can think of one reason. You offered to marry her and she refused."

"None of your business!" growled the man. Hectic color came and went.

"How true." Rafe was sure he had guessed the situation. "Just as she is no business of yours. My solicitor will be in touch with you. I believe he means to visit, actually. You may safely put all Sir Jasper's business and Miss Cottrell's business, as well, into his hands."

Rafe made a mental note he was to instantly inform his solicitor of the need for an immediate journey to Storrington.

"Mr. Caruthers, my solicitor, is a very busy man," he said when he realized it would take time to organize, "but, in the next week or two, you may expect him. He'd appreciate it if you have everything in order," added Rafe, although a glance at the messy office left him without much hope the man would oblige. "If you've everything ready for him, it will take as little time as absolutely necessary to transfer the Easten affairs to his hands."

"Thought something like this would happen," said Percell and heaved a great sigh. "Don' know how it is; don' seem to have the business me da and me used to have. Everyone thinks someone else knows better."

Rafe looked around the office. "May I give you a hint?"

Percell looked interested for the first time that day.

"This office is a mess," said Rafe sternly. "Your desk looks as if you'd lose your clients' work and never find it again. Your own attitude leaves one with less than a measure of confidence that you'll manage anything with any sort of competence. It is your own fault your business is taken from you, you see."

"Nonsense. Always a trifle disorganized. Never had no complaints afore Da died!"

"And now you have had complaints. And no business?"

Mr. Percell, who had been glaring at Rafe, dropped his gaze to his desk. "Nonsense," he said, but he said it softly and with a lack of emphasis which indicated he feared there might, after all, be something in what Rafe said.

Roger supplied a carriage for the girls' ride to the McCormicks' farm. It was a lovely, warm day, so Lydia didn't object when the boys were each offered a seat in a curricle, Rafe and Kenrick each driving his own. The carriage was a trifle crowded with the twins and Mary riding with their backs to the horses and Eunice, Margaret, and Lydia facing forward. Lydia fretted about Baby Alice; but the new maid seemed competent, and Alice had seemed to like her. Besides, there was nothing she could do unless she demanded she be taken back at once.

"A problem, Lydia?" asked Eunice.

Lydia explained.

"You spoil them." When Lydia merely shrugged, she added, "Such nonsense you should feel so responsible!"

"You forget that my mother died knowing I'd see to them. I have every reason in the world to feel responsible!"

"I cannot believe she meant you to devote your whole life to them."

Lydia noted how pale the seven-year-old twins grew.

She smiled at them. "I haven't a notion what she expected in the long term. But I know I love each and every one and have no desire to leave them. As they know." She made a face at the twins. They relaxed and giggled.

"Still," said Eunice, "you should not deny yourself rational entertainment. It is a blessing you no longer have an excuse to stay home from church. The new maid will deal with Alice, and you will take your proper place in the Easten pew."

This time the grimace Lydia made was unconscious. "I would not mind attending church if that were the end of it. What I cannot like are the whispers and the sly looks and the young men's insinuating manners and even the reverend looking down his nose at me and giving me one finger to shake at the end of the service."

Eunice had not noticed that the countryside treated Lydia differently after her mother's death. In a startled voice she said, "But you were his daughter!" She thought about that. "Stepdaughter, of course, but still . . ."

"But nothing. The worst is widely assumed. At least it must have been or why would I have suddenly become a byword?"

"What do you mean by the worst?" asked Margaret. "That he beat you like he did the rest of us?"

"I suppose they did think that," said her aunt Eunice quickly. The conversation had gotten out of hand. "I'll see what I can discover . . ."

"I am perfectly content to stay at the manor with Alice, Eunice. Don't worry your head about me. Especially under current conditions."

"Lord Huntingdon and Horten. I understand. We'll discuss it later."

Margaret sighed. "When will I be old enough that you needn't discuss things later?"

Lydia laughed. "I hope that day doesn't come too soon, Margaret. Right now your situation seems to be improving, and I would like you and the others to have something of childhood before you are forced into the problems of adulthood."

"Problems?"

"Adults may seem to you to have grown beyond problems, Margaret," said Eunice bitingly, "but I assure you that now that you needn't worry that each and every word or action might result in punishment, you will discover life is quite good. Enjoy it, as Lydia suggests you should do, because, no matter what your future as a woman, it will not be so free and easy as your years in the nursery."

Lydia quickly added, "And in the schoolroom, now you are free of those concerns your aunt spoke of."

Margaret looked puzzled. "But adults go to parties and dance and . . . and I don't know . . ."

"That is exactly it," said Eunice sternly. "You *don't* know. Think of all the work your Lydia does. She must see to your education. She must see to the management of the house. She must decide, with Cook, what we'll eat each day. She must nurse you children when you are ill. She must . . . do all sorts of things."

"And *she* doesn't go to parties and dance," said Mary.

"But Margaret will," said Lydia quickly. "And so will you, Mary, and the twins and, someday, little Alice. Your guardian will see to it that you all have proper seasons."

"You didn't," said Mary. "Why didn't you?"

"My situation is a trifle different, Mary. My mother was sick about the time I should have been presented, and I'd not have wanted to leave her in any case. Then, too, I've no dowry. You girls will not have large dots, but you'll have something. A man rarely marries a woman with no dowry. It wouldn't be good sense, would it?"

Lydia was beginning to feel just a trifle upset by the

subject of her own future, a concern she had thought she had put behind her years earlier. She was exceedingly glad that just then the carriage slowed and turned in between stone posts. A wooden gate, made of heavy planks with beaten ironwork, stood open to the world. The gravel drive was raked, and the tree-dotted lawn well-clipped. The flock of sheep to one side obviously kept the lawn under control, but the raking could only have been done by a man hired to see to it. The farmhouse, too, had a prosperous look, but their carriage followed the curricles around the house to a scrupulously clean stable area.

As Rafe helped first Eunice and then Margaret from the carriage, a tall, almost angular woman a few years older than Lydia stepped into the wide doorway of the barn. Seeing the cavalcade which had drawn up, she strode forward, a rather mannish stride swinging the skirts of her starkly designed habit rather more than was proper.

"Sean," she called, twisting her head from side to side and revealing long, wild red hair which had merely been pulled back and tied with a leather thong. "And where the divil have you got to, then?" she shouted, moderating her tone before adding, "Hello, now. And what may we be doing for you this fine day?"

"And what do you be supposing we can do for them this foine day," said her brother with a somewhat heavier Irish accent.

Sean opened a half door in the stables, a long ell extending forward from the barn and, after a pause to survey his visitors, strode forward. He was just in time to see Lydia exit from the carriage, her hand in Huntingdon's. She found her feet and looked up. Seeing the blazing look in the Irishman's eyes, she had to force herself not to turn and crawl right back into the carriage. But her hand must have tightened convulsively around Huntingdon's, because he winced slightly and gave her a questioning look.

"Miss Cottrell?" he asked.

"What? Oh. Nothing." Lydia forced herself to relax. "No, nothing at all, of course."

What, after all, could the man do here among all her brothers and sisters, to say nothing of Eunice and the gentlemen? Once again Lydia wished she had not inherited her mother's face. She was tired of the effect it had on most every man who saw her. Especially since it wasn't the *man* with whom she wished to speak. It was his sister. And she must watch for her opportunity since it might be fleeting.

Horten had already come forward with the boys, and it was he who explained their needs. "The boys have been deprived of ever learning to ride. For them we need a pair of small and well-trained mares. We need two more ponies and then, if you've a really gentle mare, something for Miss Margaret?" Horten glanced at his friend at that last, and Rafe nodded his agreement.

"Ah. Three horses. Two ponies. And all for novices." Sean looked at his sister, who grimaced.

"The ponies, yes," she said. "Well-trained horses, yes. Horses for novices." She shrugged. "Well, you'd best decide for yourselves, then. We don't approve of *plodding placid* horses, you'll understand." She stared at the disappointed faces on the children and smiled. "Then again, perhaps we can find you something."

She and Sean moved a trifle away from the group from Easten Meadows. Lydia was amused to note that Horten stared at Miss Maddy as he had been in the habit of looking at her. Men were strange, she decided. That a man could, in the blink of an eye, transfer his attentions from one woman to another was something she doubted she would ever understand. But, that someone, anyone, would turn his attention from her was just fine.

Unless, the thought intruded when Horten approached the Irish couple, *he prevents me from talking to Miss Maddy!*

Huntingdon gave the boys permission to go to the nearby paddock rail for a better look at the young horses grazing on new grass. The girls closed around Lydia and Miss Eunice and looked around with a great deal of curiosity. They had too rarely visited other estates so were bemused by all they saw. It was so different from their own ill-cared-for home.

One of the twins, Fenella, Lydia thought, jerked at her sleeve. "Liddy!"

"Yes, dear?"

"Why doesn't our home look like this? It's so beautiful here!"

"What do you mean, love?"

"So . . . pretty?"

"So clean," added the other twin.

"You mean the nicely whitewashed stone and the painted woodwork?" asked Lydia, referring to the well-kept barn and stables. "And that there are no weeds and no litter?"

"Yes," they said together. "And the windows shine like . . . like . . . ."

"Like jewels," said Mary on a long, satisfied sigh. "Like beautiful, sparkling jewels."

"Will our home ever look like this?" asked Margaret softly.

"It used to," said Eunice gruffly. "When my father lived. I think Lord Huntingdon will see that it looks that way again, but it'll take time. You can't put back in an instant what took years to spoil!"

"Why . . . ?"

"Not now, Mary," interrupted Lydia, but with a smile.

"I think they are going to bring out some horses for the men to look at. Don't you wish to see them?"

In the next hour over a dozen young horses were paraded before Horten and Huntingdon, the boys hanging on their every word and, occasionally, daringly, asking for an explanation of some comment or criticism.

Huntingdon realized that James, especially, was interested in learning how one told a good horse from a poor one—not that they had seen any really bad stock that morning. He began taking pains, making his comments in such a way the boy could follow his reasoning. Maddy was nobody's fool, or so Lydia soon decided. She, too, took care to phrase her words in such a way James would understand. At one point she noticed Lydia's appreciation, and her quick smile flashed, showing white teeth in her rather tanned face. When the men and boys, including Sean, headed for the pasture behind the barn, Maddy approached the girls.

"Now, then," she said on a smile. "Would it be lemonade, perhaps, that would be pleasing ye?"

The twins nodded, Mary hung back, and Margaret, in her newly adult fashion, said, "That would be very pleasant, thank you."

"Then, off with you. See you that plump woman, her hands wrapped in her apron, then? She'll serve you. Might even find a ginger biscuit or a brandy ball to go along with it, then," she added in a slightly louder voice as everyone but Margaret ran toward the house.

Margaret, after a glance at Lydia for permission, walked in a far more ladylike way in the younger ones' wake. "I'll see they behave, Liddy," she called back over her shoulder.

"Alarming, isn't it, how they suddenly become such terribly refined young ladies?" asked Maddy once Margaret was beyond hearing. Again her teeth flashed in that audacious grin. "And now, then, a drop of wine, perhaps, for the two of ye? We have it in the office here." She gestured toward the end of the stable nearest the house.

There were wide windows, and Lydia could see through to a comfortable arrangement of leather-covered chairs and a sofa. She feared that if she were trapped in there with Eunice, she would never find a moment in which she might confide her problems and her fears to this wonderfully free seeming woman who was so friendly and yet, with it, maintained a slight reserve.

"I'd like wine, thank you," said Eunice. "The miles were a trifle rough on these old bones of mine."

"Wine it is, then."

"Would you object if I took a closer look at the bay in the second loose box?"

"Ye liked the looks of my Selena, did ye? A good eye you have. Feel free, then. She won't object if you want to go in with her."

Miss Eunice had already reached the office and awaited Miss Maddy before entering. Lydia, moving toward the mare, hoped Maddy would return to speak with her. She doubted she had much time before the men returned, since they merely intended catching the ponies that the McCormicks had taken in trade when their owners had outgrown them and needed horses.

Her wish was filled when she had about given up on it. The light dimmed as Maddy leaned against the half door, her arms crossed atop it. "The best mare we've got," she said. "And not for sale, if you be thinking she'd do."

"I'd think not. We've a stallion I'd like to see put to her," said Lydia, blushing at the topic, but it was the only opening she had been able to think up.

"The killer stallion?"

"You've heard."

"I've never believed in killer horses myself. Only badly treated horses who will take no more."

"You do understand!" Lydia moved to join the older woman. "I thought you might. It is only men he cannot bear. With women he is a lamb. And they are saying they may shoot him! I couldn't bear it. Such a waste. Such a terrible terrible waste.

"You ride him, then?" Maddy backed so Lydia could come out into the sunlit lot.

Lydia looked both ways. Except for a groom some distance away who concentrated on cleaning a harness, no one was in sight. "I ride him. No one knows. I'm one of those people who need very little sleep, and very early, when no one is up, I take him out once or twice a week. He has wonderful conformation, and his action! You'd not believe how easy a ride he can be."

"And?"

Lydia drew in a deep breath. "Maybe if you were to make an offer for him?" She bit her lip. "I've no business saying this, but you could very likely get him cheap. Sir Jasper's father tried to sell him; but the stallion is known for having a vicious temper, and no one would buy. But he *doesn't*. Truly. It is—"

"Only with men. Yes, I've heard of such. The trouble is, I often wear trousers. Ah, then, I've shocked you. But you see, this is as much my business as it is my brother's, and I do my share of the work." She looked thoughtful. "I suppose I could keep an old skirt hung by the boyo's stall. I could slip it on when I had to do with him . . ."

"You'll make an offer?"

"Miss Easten . . ." Maddy's brows rose when Lydia shook her head.

"Miss Cottrell. I am the children's half sister."

"Ah. Miss Cottrell, I can't make a decision like that

without talking to Sean. He'll agree, I think. He thinks as I do about mistreated horses." Then Maddy asked if Lydia truly believed the stud should be mated with Selena or if that had only been a ruse for bringing the stallion into the conversation.

"I know very little about such things as bloodlines and all that, but I know two likely looking animals, and these are both beauties. I think you'll agree when you see him."

"Some bloodlines don't mix well," said Maddy. "I hope your Sir Jasper knows where to lay his hands on his stallion's pedigree."

"The old groom would know the dam and sire, I'd think, if nothing else."

"Old Herbie?"

"You know him?"

The woman's smile flashed again. "Tried to hire him when we heard the late baronet was ridding himself of staff. The man wouldn't come. Said he was needed."

Lydia frowned. "That's incredible. He was turned into a gardener, of all things. He hates it. But he stayed, knowing he might have gone elsewhere?"

"No hope of getting him now you'll have horses again," said Maddy, and glanced around. "Ah. The ponies."

"I'll just join Eunice while you and the men discuss the horses," said Lydia after one look at Maddy's brother, who was, once again, looking at her in that way she hated.

"Don't you let Sean scare you, Miss Cottrell," said Maddy with a knowing look. "He may flirt a trifle, but he won't embarrass you beyond that."

"I don't care to be embarrassed at all!" Lydia turned and was soon seated on the couch beside Eunice. It occurred to her she might, instead, have gone to find the children and been well out of the way of embarrassment, but it was too late now that she had a glass of wine in her hand.

"And did you discuss that bloody-minded stallion with Miss Maddy?" asked Eunice.

"How did you guess?"

"You either didn't know or forget that I, too, am a very early riser. Once or twice I've seen you on that killer's back!"

"And you never said anything?"

Eunice smiled. "You seemed to be enjoying yourself, and since I don't think you stupid, I assumed you knew what you were doing."

"It is only men he hates . . ."

"Ah. So as long as this Sean person will don skirts, he'll be able to handle him?"

Lydia laughed at the notion. "I can see it now. All the stable hands dressed in skirts and our stallion behaving like the angel he is!"

"How very nice to hear you laugh," said Rafe from the door.

How long, wondered Lydia, casting him a horrified look, had he been there?

"We've finished our arrangements. Mr. McCormick will deliver the animals tomorrow."

"What did you buy?" asked Eunice, a question which interested Lydia but one she would not have dared ask.

"We have the ponies and two mares. The other will have to be found somewhere else. The stock here is much too lively for Margaret."

"Good." Eunice glared. "I feared you'd insist she ride some fool mount she'd no business attempting."

Startled, Rafe asked, "Why would I do anything so stupid as buy her a horse she couldn't ride?"

"Why," asked Eunice, airily, "do men do any of the stupid things they do?"

Lydia glanced quickly at the wine carafe. Just how

much, she wondered, had Eunice drunk while she talked to Maddy?

"Not all men do stupid things," said Rafe, obviously on the defensive.

"My experience," said Eunice, heaving herself to her feet and moving toward the wine in that careful fashion of the inebriate, "has been quite otherwise." She nodded. Once. By then she had reached the carafe and poured herself one last glassful. She downed it and turned, steadying herself on the edge of the buffet. She blinked once or twice and hiccoughed. "Oh, dear," she said. Red in the face, she covered her mouth. "Lydia, dear, do you think," she said carefully, "you could give me your arm to the coach?"

"Take mine," offered Rafe, his face sober, but his eyes twinkling. He turned his head and winked at Lydia. "Careful now. There is a sill just here . . ." He gently led Eunice to the carriage and helped her in. When everyone else was collected, ready to leave, he asked Sir Jasper if he would go with his sisters, that he thought Miss Cottrell might enjoy a ride behind his team.

Jasper, not noticing Lydia's quick negative shake of her head, obediently crawled into the carriage behind the last of his sisters. Rafe nodded to the coachman, and the carriage rolled gently down the lane.

Lydia frowned at Rafe. "You might have asked!"

"And if I had?"

"I'd have said no, of course. It isn't proper."

"It will not offend against propriety for you to ride with me in an open carriage, Miss Cottrell." He waited for her response, but she merely stood there, dithering. "What *will* offend is if we trail too far behind the rest. Will you come now?" he asked.

Lydia watched as James and Kenrick tooled down the drive. She had no choice so she approached his curricle. She gasped when strong hands clasped her waist and she was lifted easily to the rather high seat. Her lip between her teeth, she settled herself.

Maddy approached. "A moment, then," she said. "I'll go find you a parasol against the sun. I don't worry about such things, as ye can see for yourself, but *you* should. I think I've one tucked away . . ."

She was off, that ground-eating stride carrying her quickly toward the house. Lydia sighed. She would have denied the need for one, but knew her bonnet's brim was not wide enough to shade her face. It would be far better if she had one.

"Now, then," said Sean from just below her, "are ye fearful to ride in Huntingdon's curricle? I'd be happy to harness up a carriage and take ye meself if ye'd be more comfortable?" His eyes gleamed up at her, and Lydia looked away.

"I will be fine, thank you. It isn't the carriage . . ." Then she realized what that sounded like. "I mean, I should be with the children. I should—"

"Are you, then, their mither? No, no, too young, ye are! And far too beautiful!"

"And made uncomfortable," said Rafe from just behind the Irishman, "by your blarney."

"Nay, then!" Sean adopted an expression of extreme surprise. "You'll be saying she is not beautiful?"

Rafe grinned. "You know very well I cannot say that. Merely that she doesn't seem to appreciate our appreciation of it. See how she blushes?"

Lydia hid her face in her hands. "Please . . ."

"We are teasing you, Miss Cottrell," Rafe said, his tone sober. "You must not allow us to overset you so."

"I have never learned to accept compliments gracefully," she whispered. "I am sorry I—"

"Ah, then," said Maddy's voice as she approached in that same long-legged stride. "I feared it. They've been putting you to the blush. Men! They don't know from anything, do they, then?" She opened the parasol and handed it up to Lydia. "I'll be seeing you tomorrow, then?" she whispered. Her back to the men, she winked.

"Tomorrow," Lydia whispered back. The reminder she had managed to do what she could to save the much maligned stallion from destruction helped her to relax. "I'm ready, my lord."

"Good. We'll see you about noon, McCormick, and have a luncheon for you before you ride back," said Rafe . . . and then realized he was offering hospitality in someone else's house. He glanced at Lydia.

"An excellent notion," she said, and wondered just what one should feed a man who would be dirty from the ride and very likely smelling of the stables. Besides, Eunice would very likely have a few words on the subject of allowing him in the house . . . assuming, of course, Eunice was not laid on her bed with a hangover!

Perhaps, Lydia decided, assuming the weather remained good, they could have a sort of picnic on the terrace just beyond the library. She must remember to check on the condition of that area and have it swept and scrubbed down early enough so it would be thoroughly dry by the time they must lay a nuncheon.

"You are very quiet. Was it wrong of me to invite him? I'd have done so in my own home, you see, and I forgot how ill-prepared you are, as yet, for company."

"I believe it might be possible to arrange an alfresco meal on the terrace." She glanced at him, then away. "I've been going over what must be done to arrange it."

"Then, I'll let you think. But, before we reach home, I'd like a word with you about that animal still in the stables." He glanced down at her. "Something must be done about him, and I rather hoped you might have a suggestion?"

Lydia blushed, glanced at him and looked back down

at her toes which peeked under the hem of her one and only walking dress.

"Have you no suggestions?" he asked, after a long moment.

"Let me think about it," she said, and desperately tried to make up her mind to confide in the man who unsettled her in ways she had never before been unsettled. But how could she? How would she dare allow anyone to know she had actually ridden an animal that was thought to be a killer? She couldn't. If he believed her, he would think her a hoyden, and he might send her away from the children, thinking her unsuitable to have charge of them.

"I had thought, perhaps," he said, "from something James said, that you had a fondness for the creature?"

"I think it would be a terrible waste to kill him." She could safely admit that much.

"I cannot allow the grooms to be endangered."

"I understand the difficulty, but—"

"But you hope we'll find another solution. It occurred to me, as we were leaving, I might ask Mr. McCormick's advice when he comes tomorrow."

"Or his sister might . . ."

She began firmly enough, but trailed off, once again deciding not to tell Lord Huntingdon of her conversation with Miss Maddy. It was not her place, after all, to put her nose into business matters concerning her brother's property.

Rafe glanced sideways, but all he could glimpse was that firm little chin, her bonnet hiding the rest of her face. "Or McCormick's sister," he agreed, wondering *why* Miss Cottrell made that particular suggestion.

Five

The Eastens' brand-new butler cleared his throat. Lydia looked up from the schoolroom floor where she was engaged in helping the twins put together a dissected map of Europe, teaching them, as they worked, about the recent wars Napoleon had instigated all over the Continent.

"You wanted something, Brean?" she asked.

"A female just arrived, Miss Cottrell. I put her in the small salon."

"The back parlor," corrected Lydia automatically, although she had almost given up trying to convert the stubborn man to the traditional family names for the various rooms. The parlor was small. It was to the back of the house and not a room used for company, although very popular with the children. As she rose to her feet, she glanced around the schoolroom. "James, you will *not* leave, even once you've finish that bit of Latin. You've maths to do as well, have you not?"

The boy sighed and nodded. His hopes of escape while his eldest sister was absent from the room had been neatly foiled.

"Margaret, you have your essay to do and the twins their map. Mary? Will you play with Baby Alice if she becomes fretful? Your sampler should wait until I return since you have still to master the silk stitch." The butler cleared his throat. "Yes, Brean, I'm coming."

He cleared his throat again, his gaze resting on her hair.

"You think I am too mussed to see guests," guessed Lydia. She sighed almost as deeply as James had done. "Who has come?" she asked as she led the way down the hall toward the stairs.

"She called herself Miss Madeline McCormick," he said repressively.

Lydia's step quickened. "Oh, good. Miss Maddy will not mind if I'm a trifle less than perfect!"

She took the stairs in something very close to an unladylike gallop, leaving the butler to follow at the stately pace he deemed proper to his dignity.

"Miss Maddy! Has no one offered you refreshment?"

"What?" Miss McCormick looked up from the ancient ladies' magazine she had been perusing, a rather cynical expression implying it was all nonsense. "Ah! Hello. My brother'll be bringing the stock you bought. He doesn't know I've come atall, you see, so if we could just see the creature, then?"

"You wish to be as expeditious as is possible. Of course. This way."

Lydia moved briskly toward the back door and then on to the stables. "He has his own loose box which opens into an attached paddock. Old Herbie rather let him go his own way, and the new groom, after nearly being savaged his first morning, does likewise."

Lydia began to hum as she approached the back of the barn. There was a whinny in response, and the stallion's dark head pushed through the half door and nodded so Lydia could reach his forehead.

Maddy approached slowly, noted the stallion's nervous reaction, and paused. "A beauty, indeed," she said softly. "Sooo, boyo," she added in a soft singing voice and came on. "What's his name?"

"I don't know that I ever knew his official name. The late baronet called him Devil's Spawn. I, however, call him Angel's Wings."

Maddy chuckled, and the stallion's head jerked back. After an instant he extended his muzzle to sniff her offered palm. He gently bit into the chunk of carrot which had appeared from somewhere, his strong yellow teeth crunching it noisily. "I would like to see his reaction to a man. Is there anyone near?"

Lydia shook her head. "The grooms will not help us. I don't think I dare ask Sir Jasper to risk his neck. And James is too small. There are only the new footman and butler, and you have seen the butler?"

Maddy's chuckle was even warmer. "That one would not oblige. It would not suit his notions of his great position, I think!"

"Exactly."

"Would I do?" asked Rafe from about halfway down the galley.

Lydia swung around and found him lounging against the rough boards that formed the end of an open stall, his arms crossed. One foot was raised, the toe set casually in the dirt on the far side of the other foot.

"What are you doing here?" she asked sharply and then, when Angel moved nervously, moderated her tone. "I'm sorry. That was uncalled for. You have every right to be here."

"Yes, I do. But do *you*, Miss Cottrell? By what right, I wonder, do you show that dangerous beast to a dealer in horses?"

Her chin rose sharply. "The fact I know he is *not*. Not to me."

"I tried to ride him one day last week. Thought the brute might be grateful for the exercise," said Rafe on a musing note. He rubbed his chin between fingers and thumb.

Lydia hid her quick response to a guess as to how that ride had ended, but wasn't quite quick enough.

"You think it humorous that I parted company with him not five minutes after mounting him?"

"No. Not really." She bit her lip and then, eyes twinkling, admitted, "But I'd have liked to have been there!"

"Only my old friend Kenrick was there. He hasn't let me forget it, either. On the other hand," said Rafe softly, "he hasn't offered to try the animal himself."

Lydia realized he was several yards closer and wondered when he had moved, since he looked just as relaxed as before, his pose very nearly the same.

"Don't come nearer, not atall," said Maddy. "Poor boyo, here, smells you. He's sweating like a coal heaver!"

"But he wasn't when you and Miss Cottrell approached?"

"Not atall, atall. Soooo, boyo," she soothed.

"Miss Cottrell," said Rafe softly, "I believe you've a lady's saddle in the tack room."

"Is that a crime?"

"Perhaps a trifle odd in a mere governess, but then you are a very odd governess, are you not?"

Lydia felt the heat flowing up from her well-covered breasts into her totally uncovered ears. "I haven't a notion what you think you mean by that, my lord, but if you think a governess should not ride . . ."

"I don't believe I said that," replied Rafe, his tone still thoughtful. "In fact, I had it in mind that perhaps it might be a good notion if I were to put that saddle on the Spawn here, so you could put him through his paces for Miss McCormick's edification."

"I will saddle him myself," said Lydia.

"Then, you do ride him?" He was satisfied that he had been correct when she nodded hesitantly. "Regularly?"

Lydia sighed. "Since I require little sleep, my lord, I've found that an early morning ride does both Angel," she emphasized the name, "and me a great deal of good."

"A very early ride."

She stared. "Very well. A *very* early ride."

"You see," he said softly, "I've been here early. Twice. I arrived at seven the first time. The Spawn had obviously been ridden and rubbed down. I arrived at six another morning. It was the same. Just *how* early do you ride, Miss Cottrell?"

"Does it make any difference? Miss Maddy will buy Angel, and I'll have no opportunity in future to outrage your sensibilities."

"I cannot believe it proper that you roam the countryside in the late-night hours. Not *everyone* is asleep at that time."

"Nonsense. No one has ever seen me."

"A poacher perhaps?" His brows rose. "Worse, a swag man or another of the more nefarious sorts?"

"None of which would say a word, would they, for fear someone would ask why *they'd* been out and about!"

"She has you there," inserted Maddy with a low chuckle. "Now then, if ye'll be telling me where to find the tack room, I'll just fetch the saddle meself?"

Rafe took the hint and returned the way he had come. He brought back a very nice saddle, a good quality pad, and had a heavy bridle hanging over one arm.

Lydia stared, shocked. "Not that bridle! That bit's a horror."

"Miss Cottrell, when a horse is as unmanageable as that one is, you need every aid to control you can get."

"He is *not* unmanageable . . . except for a man. It is my belief he has been badly treated by men. He is a very intelligent beast, but he is a beast. You, whom I have seen treat your teams very well indeed, are to be trusted, but he cannot know that. On the other hand, I wear a skirt. He recognizes that, and also, I think, the higher feminine voice. It is possible, if one were to put him in skirts, he'd allow Jasper on his back. But I'm not about to test that hypothesis."

"Assuming, of course, you could get Sir Jasper into the necessary skirts!" said Rafe half-amused and half-shocked by the notion.

Lydia smiled. "Yes, there is that, of course."

"Which bridle?" asked Maddy. Lydia described the one she used, and the woman strode up the center aisle.

"When did you ask her to come? When we visited their farm?"

"Yes."

"Why?"

"Everyone has urged that Angel be destroyed. I could not bear to see such a magnificent animal shot."

"And you feared I'd order him destroyed?"

"Were you not thinking of it?"

Rafe grinned roguishly. "For five minutes after he threw me, yes! But I agree that he's too much a good thing to be put down if there is any alternative. And you, Mystery Lady, may have discovered one."

Ignoring his intriguing name for her, since she rather feared to discover just what he meant by it, Lydia took the saddle and moved toward the loose box, humming as she had done at her earlier approach. The stallion looked out, saw Rafe and set up a violent tattoo of hooves against wood. Lydia sighed. "Lord Huntingdon, I would appreciate it if you would go away. If you insist you must watch, there is a shed with a window that looks over the back paddock. You may secrete yourself there. Angel's Wing is not going to settle with you around."

"If you were a man, I'd stay just to see the fun. Since you are not, I am forced to go."

"Thank you."

"I was not being polite."

"I know, but I thank you just the same!"

His eyes narrowed in sardonic appreciation. He nodded to Maddy, who returned with the desired bridle, and with his exit, Lydia soon had the stallion calm again.

"You heard him carrying on?" asked Lydia as she tightened the girth, waited for Angel to relax, and pulled it another notch. She looked around and saw Maddy studying the stallion.

"Poor ol' boyo," said Maddy softly. "I agree with your assessment, but I've a problem if I'm to buy him for breeding purposes. Which is not yet decided, is it?"

"What's the problem?"

"Much to my disgust, my brother has forbidden me to participate in the mating of our breeding stock." The two women shrugged at the incomprehensibility of men. "So who, one asks," added Maddy after a moment, "is to handle Angel, here, if I do not?"

"Tell your brother his alternative is to put himself into skirts!"

"Aye," said Miss Maddy sardonically, "but ye do not ken that he will likely try it!"

"If it is only the skirts, then it might work. If it is also the voice, then I don't know that it will."

Angel's Wing was ready and dancing, impatient to go. Lydia led him into the paddock and, using the fence, mounted him. She was forced to soothe him again when he realized he was not going to be allowed a good long run, but he settled to her voice and touch, and obediently showed himself off for Maddy.

When Lydia trotted back to the barn door, Maddy approached, again handed the animal a chunk of carrot, and then set herself to going over every inch. She examined the stallion with a thoroughness that would have put to shame some knowing bucks buying new stock at Tattersalls, or so Rafe later told his friends as he described the scene after dinner over their port.

"So that's where you got to today," rumbled Kenrick.

Rafe nodded. "Later I had another argument with the tenant who farms most of Sir Jasper's land. If I can get him to go along with the necessary changes, the other two, who have smaller farms, will fall into line."

"Stubborn, is he, about adopting modern methods?" asked Roger. "I might have my land agent pay him a visit."

"Your land agent, being local, might have more influence, you think? Then, by all means, ask him to make that visit!"

Rafe fell silent after that, his thoughts returning to how regal Miss Cottrell had looked seated on the high back of the huge stallion. Much too big and strong for her, of course. She had no business riding such a large animal, even one that hadn't such a nasty reputation. He wondered what she would think of the feisty little mare he had told Miss McCormick to deliver as part payment for the stallion . . . which, after she herself rode him, she had bought without consulting her brother.

He had looked at the mare twice when they had bought the other stock, thinking he might like her in his own stables, possibly as breeding stock. He had reluctantly left her behind since she wasn't up to his weight and he had really had no need of her. But watching Lydia—Miss Cottrell!—on Devil's Spawn's back, he had wondered how she would look on the mare and

given in to temptation to find out. Now he wondered
at himself for doing so.

However that might be, off and on all evening, he
found himself anticipating Miss Cottrell's reaction and
very much wished to watch her enjoyment when she
first rode the mare. Just how early, he wondered, *did*
the woman ride?

*Which is, is it not, just another way of asking how little
sleep the woman needs?* he asked as he himself drifted into
sleep that night.

Rafe woke before dawn, his mind occupied with com-
posing a letter to Lord Charingham. Rafe not only
wished to berate the man for assuming he, a total
stranger, would take on the trusteeship for such an odd
annuity, but he wanted, very much, a clarification of
the woman's situation in life. Of her birth, to be exact.

That was a mystery the old man would completely satisfy or Rafe would refuse the trustee position! He would
tell the earl the annuity had resulted in rumors that Miss
Cottrell was his lordship's by-blow. Of course—he allowed the thought headroom reluctantly—there was the
possibility that that was exactly what she *was*. If it turned
out to be the case, the additional problem arose of a
bastard remaining as governess to the children for whom
he was guardian.

Besides, the girl was a beauty, and if word were to get
around she was illegitimate, all the bucks in the area
would be hounding her, pushing her into an illicit
life . . . perhaps forcing her . . .

That thought had Huntingdon gritting his teeth, and
he pushed it from his mind. He would finish the letter
by informing Charingham that he himself, aware of the
story of Charingham's love affair with his own wife,

didn't believe the girl was any such thing. Still, given the problems, the truth must be made known.

Rafe wondered just how harsh he dared be. Charingham's letter to Sir Jasper's solicitor truly had been impertinent, just as Percell had claimed. Still, it hadn't quite gone beyond the proprieties. The letter Rafe was thinking of writing in return *did*. Which was rather insulting to an old and valued neighbor, which Charingham had become once Rafe became Huntingdon.

On the other hand, if it turned out that Miss Cottrell was illegitimate . . . No. Rafe rearranged his pillows into a more comfortable pile and sighed. He could not seduce her and take her away to the cozy house he kept in Chelsea, not when the children loved and needed her. But that was another thing, was it not? Dared he leave her in charge of children if she were not quite the thing herself?

He put a fist into the center of his pillow. *Lord, will my thoughts never cease circling?* he wondered.

Rafe chuckled as he heard, in his mind, the tirade Miss Eunice would deliver if he attempted to relieve Miss Cottrell of her position. *She* would not stop with the merely polite! Which decided him. He would be just as blunt as need be in his letter. Besides, for his own peace of mind, he must discover the truth and soon.

Peace of mind? What did he mean by that?

Rafe pushed the confusing thought aside and kicked down the covers. Sometime later he was wrapped in his banyan and standing, staring, out his window. Was Miss Cottrell out riding one of the boy's horses? Or was she still snug in her bed, her hair tousled and her eyelids, if she were to be gently awakened, heavy with sleep. . . .

Still later his valet crept in quietly, astounded to discover the earl already out of bed and at work at his desk.

Lydia *was* riding. She returned to the stables just as
the sun broached the eastern horizon, feeling unhappy,
and telling herself she was a fool to feel that way. She
missed her gallops on Angel's back. Jasper's mare was
not only lacking in spirit, but she would be needed later
for the lad's lesson and must *not* be overworked just
because Lydia needed to rid herself of the restlessness
which seemed much worse these days.

Yes, she missed Angel, but far better the stallion have
a new home than that he be destroyed! She *must* remember that, calling up the thought whenever she self-
ishly regretted telling Miss Maddy about him. Lydia
continued lecturing herself as she unsaddled the mare,
but was startled when a disheveled stable lad, yawning
widely, appeared in the stall and, still yawning, assured
her in a grumbling tone that he would rub the mare
down properly and that it was his job and not hers and
she had better take herself up to the big house where
she belonged.

And then, awake, he opened his eyes wide, wondering
how Miss Cottrell would take what was, after all, an insult even if it *was* the truth. He didn't understand why
she laughed, but he grinned, relieved he had not said
something so stupid as to find himself summarily let go
and without a character.

Lydia felt chagrined she had arrived home so late the
servants had begun to stir. When she went through the
kitchen, the little workhouse girl who slept before the
fire was also up and beginning her work. Only once
before had Lydia disturbed the child as she passed silently through the large, low-beamed room. And on
that occasion the little girl had been awake because of
a toothache she had been reluctant to tell Cook about
for fear she would be sent to the tooth drawer—which,
of course, she was, but once it was over, she admitted

she was pleased to be done with the pain which had been with her, off and on, for some months.

Lydia, still unused to having competent help in the house, ladled water which was still warm from the night's coals into an ewer. Once again she was startled when the new footman, still in his shirtsleeves, took it from her and led the way up to her room. "Thank you," said Lydia.

The footman, peering down his nose in emulation of the butler, nodded. The pose was quite humorous when combined with his young and freckled face.

Lydia, manfully restraining her giggles, merely nodded in response. But, once alone, she instantly forgot the young man and his idolization of the snooty butler. Instead she went back to worrying over Lord Huntingdon's words when he had called her Mystery Lady. What could he have meant by it? Why did he think her an oddity, something other than the governess she insisted she was to one and all.

Is he—she bit her lip until it hurt—*thinking of asking me to depart? Of telling me I'm not needed?*

A tutor was to arrive shortly. Had his lordship also hired a proper governess? Agitated by the thought, Lydia buttoned up her day dress all wrong and had to begin again. When she finished, she discovered she had not improved matters, but merely ended with the *other* side of her collar sticking up oddly. She sighed, telling herself she was to cease worrying about what she could not change and put it behind herself.

If worse came to worse, she decided, giggling a slightly hysterical giggle, she would throw herself at Sean McCormick's head. She hadn't a doubt he would find a way of obliging her! And keeping her.

For a while, anyway, until he tired of her.

And what nonsense. She would never do it, so why even think it? Instead, she told herself sternly, she must plan the schoolroom party's lessons. So, finally having gotten proper buttons into proper buttonholes, her collar lying primly against her shoulders, she took herself off to the schoolroom . . . where, much to her surprise, she found James.

"James?"

He turned from his desk, his lower lip pushed alarmingly far forward. "I don't want a tutor. I want you."

"What are you really worrying about, James?" she asked softly.

"What . . . if I'm ever so far behind? What if . . . I can't do the work?"

"Hmm." She crossed the room and laid her hand on his shoulder. "Have you ever had difficulty doing the work I set you?"

"No, but you're—" he cast her a glance from under his lashes, "I mean, well, a governess, that's not the same as a tutor, is it?"

"What you mean is that I'm a mere female and that you've known for some time I can no longer keep up with you—or at least, that I've difficulties doing so?"

He dipped his head, staring at his desk. Finally, he nodded.

"Then, it is a very good thing you will have someone who can stay ahead of you. I was rather proud of the fact that when he first went to school, Jasper was actually somewhat ahead of the boys his age. I know you are now a trifle older than he was then, but not so very much. And you've weeks before you'll leave for school. James, I don't believe you need fear that you'll be behind the others who have been in school for a year or two."

"But . . . you can't know."

"I can't. What I can do is tell your tutor you are concerned about it and ask him to discover if, and in what subjects, you may need extra help. He has been hired to see that you and your brother are up to snuff, you know. For his own future prospects he will see that you are."

James sighed. He sighed again. "I suppose he'll expect us to work all hours of the day," he finally admitted when urged to do so.

"Your riding lessons will not be forfeit, James, *assuming,*" she added sternly, "you do your assigned work and do it properly." She tried to catch his eye, but he wouldn't look at her. "James?"

"But . . ." James drew in a deep breath and turned, staring up at his oldest sister, his eyes opened painfully wide. "Perhaps I'll not be allowed the . . . the freedom I've had in the past. He won't understand, Liddy! I know he won't."

"You mean your love of a good ramble. James, will you be allowed to go off on your own that way once you've gone off to school?"

"I don't suppose so," he grumbled. "That's the only thing I don't like about going. What is so wrong with liking to find birds' nests and watch them feed their young and how they go about it and what they feed them and all the other things I like to do. Like, did you know there's a new badger's hole near the mill stream? He's beautiful, Liddy," he finished softly.

"It isn't wrong that you enjoy such things, but I fear any serious study must be postponed until you are older, James, and have more control over your own time. For now, you will have to think of it as a special treat saved for the hols, will you not?"

"I suppose," he said glumly, looking back at the Latin book he had just opened. "The next three paragraphs?"

"The next *four,*" she said, pretending outrage. "They are rather short, are they not?" She turned away as the girls traipsed into the room, setting each to work on whatever it was they were supposed to be doing. Once she was certain everyone was busy, she beckoned to Margaret, and they went down to the back parlor.

"We've a special treat," she said, moving to the old piano. "It has been *tuned.*"

"Play for me?" begged Margaret. "So I'll know how the piece is supposed to sound?"

Lydia nodded and seated herself. She played through the piece twice before looking up at Margaret, who stood beside her. "You see?"

Soft clapping from the doorway had her swinging around on the stool.

"My lord!"

"I don't know how you could bear the instrument as it was. It can't have been tuned for years."

"Not since it was purchased when Mother first married the children's father and we came here. It was his wedding gift to her . . . I think," she added hesitantly, since the recently deceased baronet had not been known for giving gifts even before he grew quite so curmudgeonly.

Surely her gentle mother hadn't had the courage to demand a pianoforte as part of the marriage agreement, had she? But Lydia could not help but remember all the hours her mother had spent teaching her in the years before her health began to deteriorate. By then, Lydia had become more than reasonably competent, and even her stepfather had occasionally asked that she play of an evening.

Rafe realized that for the first time someone in the household had admitted that Miss Lydia Cottrell belonged there, and, miracle of miracles, it had been Miss Lydia herself. But he still didn't know whether the chit was legitimate or not! Well, Charingham would satisfy that particular mystery—or he would take a couple of days and go visit the man. Face-to-face he would not be put off!

"Miss Easten? Are you meaning to play now?" he asked Margaret.

"To practice. It was quite wonderful to hear the notes as they should be played. Now I can do the same."

"Assuming," he teased, "that you touch the proper keys!"

The girl smiled, knowing he was teasing, and Lydia, who had instantly bristled, ready to defend her sister, relaxed as she, too, belatedly recognized the impish quality to his lordship's smile. "Yes," said Margaret, "assuming I don't make mistakes. Which I will, of course. It might be better, my lord, if you were to take yourself elsewhere so that your ears won't suffer."

"I may just do that. Miss Cottrell? Might I have a word with you?"

Lydia felt herself tremble. Sternly, she told herself not to be a fool, but even if she was forced to leave Easten Meadows, there would be a place for her in the world . . . somewhere. She rose to her feet and followed his lordship to the front door.

And stared.

Almost in a dream, she drifted down the shallow steps to the badly graveled drive. Slowly, she approached the dainty mare standing there, her reins hanging to the ground. Carefully, she extended a hand to the animal. Gently, she scratched the mare's forehead, touched her velvet nose lightly, backed away reluctantly.

"My lord. How lovely she is . . ."

"I'm glad you approve, Miss Cottrell," he said, his voice so dry she was forced to look at him. "You will, of course, be expected to take her out daily in order to exercise her. I am very sorry to have to add another, er, burden to your many duties," he continued, his face and voice bland, "but I'm certain you'll manage to find time to add this one to your exceedingly busy schedule."

Lydia, absorbing his words, swung back to the mare. "You mean . . . !"

He chuckled. "I mean, Miss Cottrell, that I have purchased you a replacement for Devil's Spawn."

"Angel's Wing," she corrected reflexively. "But, for me? Why?"

"Why not?" he responded insouciantly, unwilling to probe into the exact *why* of his decision.

"She's lovely."

"Go put on your habit and we'll try her paces. I'd like to assure myself she is—" looking at the storm clouds forming on Miss Cottrell's face, he altered his ending, "—well-trained."

"And not that she is too much for me?" asked Lydia with more than a touch of belligerence.

"That is what I was about to say, but I recalled, just in time, that you were used to riding Dev— er, *Angel's Wing,*" he said, with the mildest of apologetic tones.

"I am quite certain that if the McCormicks had a hand in her training, she is well-trained," said Lydia.

"But we cannot know. Go change, Miss Cottrell. Let me ease my mind before I leave her for you and your early rides of which I do *not,* you see, approve. I still think it dangerous," he added when she would have responded. "If, for instance, your mount put a hoof in a rabbit hole and came down. If you were hurt? What would you do? Far from home? No one knows who might find you, helpless and alone."

"Nonsense . . ."

"You seem a trifle less certain, my dear. Would it be a terrible loss if you were forced to give up your lonely rides and go later? With a groom in attendance?"

Lydia didn't want to admit that she might rearrange her schedule so that she might wait for a groom to be up and around. She could still ride before the children were likely to be up, and she no longer had the excuse that since she rode Angel she must do so secretly.

"I will think about it," she said abruptly.

"And now? Now you will put on your habit?"

Somehow, although it was phrased quite gently, Lydia did not feel he was asking so much as ordering. "If I must, I will do so." She swung on her heel and returned to the house. Once she was beyond his sight, however, she picked up her skirts and rushed up the stairs, going beyond the bedroom floor to the nursery and school-room above.

As she had hoped, she discovered Eunice helping Mary with her embroidery, and the twins moaning and groaning softly over the essays she had set them. "I have been ordered into my habit so that I may try the paces of a mare his interfering lordship has bought for my use," she said all in a rush. "I don't know exactly how long I'll be," she added, looking at Eunice, a tiny frown marring her brow.

"If Lord Huntingdon wishes to see how you handle your gift, then of course you must go. Take a groom with you, of course," finished Eunice a trifle more pointedly than she had begun.

"A groom . . . but why—"

Eunice stared at Lydia, a hard look in her eyes.

"Oh." Lydia realized Eunice meant her to be chaperoned.

Fifteen minutes later she once again exited the house and found not only Lord Huntingdon but a groom, the men's horses and the new mare. And why the fact Lord Huntingdon obviously didn't wish to ride alone with her but had, himself, with no prompting, brought along the groom—why that should bother her, Lydia didn't know and *didn't want to know.*

Six

Despite the odd and inexplicable sense of disappointment, Lydia was too impressed by the mare to remain in a blue mood. They had only to reach the road for Lord Huntingdon to let his long-legged gelding out into an easy canter. The mare followed, and her spirits soared. The mare could never match Angel's Wing for strength or stamina, but she was surely as soft a ride and, Lydia suspected, would show a nice turn of speed if allowed to do so.

"Where would you like to go?" asked Huntingdon after some moments during which he had fallen a pace or two behind.

"If you are quite satisfied I'll not tumble off at the first jump, I would very much like to test the mare's way with wall, fence, and hedge."

"In other words, a cross-country run. Lead on," he said.

And she did. When she pulled up some three or four fields later, her cheeks were flushed, and one long tress had fallen to lie against her shoulder. Patting the mare's neck, she grinned at Huntingdon when he pulled up beside her. "She's wonderful. What is her name?"

"That's up to you. She's to be your horse."

"She must have had a name, surely."

"Her papers read that she is Princess Mara by King Tara out of Princess Regan."

Lydia blinked, and then, reprehensibly, she giggled. "If I'd known she was of such royal background, I'd not have dared to ride her! Sitting on the back of a princess? It must be lese majesty, do you not agree?"

Rafe grinned. "Give her another name, then, so you'll not feel you must curtsy whenever you approach her."

"Princess Mara. I could call her Marvelous, but . . . no. Although she is, of course, but I do not like that so . . ." Lydia's eyes narrowed, and she stared at nothing at all. "Marigold! There is a nicely plebeian flower, and she is certainly golden when the sun catches her hide. Yes. Marigold it will be."

"And you needn't feel the least bit of awe at the majestic lineage she boasts."

"Exactly."

Humor faded, and Rafe stared at her, his eyes serious. "Miss Cottrell, I have brought you out here for another reason, as well." He glanced to where the groom waited some distance away, where he could watch but be well beyond hearing. "I feel I must inform you of something . . ." He trailed off, wondering how to continue.

Lydia felt herself tense, a fact that communicated itself to the mare, which objected. Automatically, she brought the animal back under control. "My lord?"

"You will recall the message from your brother's solicitor which took me into town one day not long ago?"

"Yes."

"It concerned you."

Lydia once again went stiff, this time with rage, and again Marigold sensed it. Even as Lydia controlled herself and then the mare's fidgets, she found herself ranting. "If that presumptuous bag of wind dared to renew—"

Rafe grinned, his eyes dancing.

Lydia bit off the rest. "He didn't, then. I apologize for interrupting."

"I guessed he'd asked for your hand and been rejected. He informed me it was none of my business, but warned me of the uppity miss who would get above herself! No, it has nothing to do with him, but"—once again Rafe sobered—"involved *another* impertinence. One directed at me. I was informed that I was to administer an annuity which was yours but about which you were to know nothing unless, for some reason, you were in need of it. I have written the, um, gentleman that I find the whole notion iniquitous and will do no such thing.

"I did not," he continued after only the briefest of pauses, "inform him I meant to tell you of the annuity. You see, I feel it unfair that you are not allowed awareness of your options. Nor is it fair that you have taken on the duties you bear with such grace only because you don't know that you have an alternative. The annuity, you see, would be quite large enough to keep you in comfort in any of our country's nicer provincial cities. Bath, for instance, or Tunbridge Wells." He grimaced. "Not, I fear, in London, if that is your desire, but you could go nearly anywhere else and enjoy the advantages to be found in a town where there is a theater, music, conversation. Or you could travel. Despite the difficulties. Naples is open to one, and there are the Americas which are interesting and—"

In the face of her growing agitation, he paused.

"What have I said to upset you?" he finished.

"Are you saying I must leave the Meadows? Leave the children?"

"Not that you *must* leave. Definitely not! The children love you and you are very good with them, but you are a young woman who should wish for a life of her own rather than the constant pressures of rearing a family which is not her own."

"But it is."

"Excuse me?"

"It *is* my family." In her agitation she forgot his lordship was meant to believe her merely the governess. "My brothers and sisters. Half, anyway. Unless you tell me I *must* go, I would much rather stay. You say they love me, but they cannot love me half so well as I love them. I am *needed*, my lord," she said earnestly.

So, thought Rafe. *She admits, finally, that she is family. And where does that leave us?*

"My lord?"

"I believe you should think about your situation before you make a decision which may affect the whole of your life."

"I made my decision at my mother's bedside the morning she died, my lord. She asked that I have a care for the children. She asked knowing I would say yes, and she died in peace knowing they would have all the love and care I could give them."

"From what I have seen of their father's methods, I am much surprised he allowed you to stay on."

"My stepfather." Her eyes widened and then she chuckled. "But no, my lord. You did not know him at all. I don't believe he'd have allowed me to leave had I'd wished to do so!"

Lord Huntingdon tipped his head, his expression one of query.

"You haven't thought, my lord." Her eyes danced with humor. "I eat moderately; I work hard; I took the place of not only a governess but housekeeper and nursed my mother. The day she died he gave notice to the household maids, and I took on their duties to the degree I could." She frowned. "I believe," she added, "that he'd have rid himself of Cook as well; but he was

aware I don't know which side of a kettle one sets in
the fire, so he didn't dare. He liked his food, you see."

"I see." What Rafe saw was that this young woman
had been used as a drudge by a man who had known
very well she had no alternative but to do her best. Now
she had that alternative. "What you do not seem to
understand is that you are no longer forced to do all
that."

"No, of course I am not. You've allowed us to hire
proper household help. I have so much time on my
hands I don't know what to do with myself."

"You still don't understand. Have you no desire for
the entertainments any woman even half as lovely as
you accepts as her right? Proper clothes and dancing,
card parties and the theater? All those things which go
to make up a season?"

Lydia glanced quickly at his lordship and then looked
down to where her fingers fiddled with her reins. Her
voice faintly choked, she said, "I might have done some
years ago, my lord, but now my hopes and dreams are
centered in Margaret and my other sisters, who will have
some sort of season when they reach an age where Sir
Jasper must introduce them to the world. I feel a trifle
sorry for Jasper, my lord. He has five sisters for whom
he must find suitable dowries. I fear it will burden the
estate excessively."

"Thank you for reminding me. I must discuss with
him a plan whereby monies may be set aside each year
for that purpose so it will *not* be such a shock to his
finances when the time comes. Still, that is some years
in the future." He eyed her, a faint frown line appearing
between his brows. "Have you no hopes of meeting
someone whom you might wed, someone with whom
you might have a home and children of your own?"

She gave him a shocked look. Again she looked away,
this time across the meadow toward the thinly wooded

hillside, then on toward the far roofs of Easten Meadows. "At my age, my lord? I have been on the shelf for any number of years. I no longer think of such things." She did, of course, but it was not something she would admit to anyone. "I will miss very little," she continued doggedly, "if I may watch my family grow and stretch their wings. Someday they will wed and have children, and I flatter myself I will be welcome in their nurseries." She saw that he frowned, and a fine line drew down between her own brows. "I've no reason to mope," she said, putting a firmness she didn't feel into her voice. "Nor, my lord, do I fear a lonely old age."

"You would play the spinster aunt to nieces and nephew?" he asked, the faintest of acid bites to his tone.

"Yes."

His mouth tightened. "And you do not wish me to look into the legal standing of the annuity? You are, I believe, of age. I might see that you receive a quarterly allowance?"

"When you first spoke of it, I think you mentioned that I must be in need before I was allowed to know of it. I am not in need, my lord."

"Are you not? You receive an allowance from Sir Jasper? Or perhaps one should call it wages, given the work you do?" The bite was even sharper.

"When I need something, a length of material to make up into a dress, for instance, I will not fear to ask Sir Jasper to pay the bill. Other than such things as shoes and an occasional bonnet—why, I am fed and housed . . . what else do I need?"

"Ridiculous."

"I am not ridiculous!"

"Not you, but that you need nothing. Have you no notion of how lovely you would look in silk, your hair properly dressed? Do you not care that you would outshine nearly every woman to grace the *ton* last season if you were properly gowned? Have you no ambition to join them in their play?"

"No."

He waited half a moment, realized she would say no more and chuckled. "You are a delight. You are able to surprise me again and again. Just a simple no. No explanation. No reason why you should not behave and feel as any other woman I have known would behave and feel. Just *no.*"

"Beauty can be a curse, my lord, as well as an advantage," she said, looking between the mare's ears.

A curse? What could she mean?

Lydia, realizing she had very likely given away more than she should, drew in a deep breath. "Sir, we have been gone far longer than I meant to be. Miss Eunice will be worried. We should, I think, return now."

Still pondering what she could possibly have meant, he didn't respond.

"My lord?"

"Hmm? Oh." After a glance at the sun's position, he settled his reins, agreeing it was time they returned. Once they arrived at the Meadows he dismounted and moved to lift her down.

As soon as her feet were on the ground, Lydia tried to step back but found herself held, his hands firm at her waist. He looked down at her. "Miss Cottrell, you no longer need play a menial role here. Miss Eunice Easten has done very well at restaffing the house. I mean to give orders that you are to be treated with respect."

Lydia glanced up, startled. Then, a mischievous look to her eyes, she shook her head. "Unnecessary, my lord! I have never been treated any other way."

She tugged at his hands which had tightened slightly. When he released her, she practically ran toward the house. When she reached the door she looked back.

He was staring at her in a very odd way, she thought. Once again she found herself wondering what was going through his head.

She would have been quite startled to discover that it had to do with her supposed bastardy and his surprise that given she had worked her fingers to the bone for years, she felt she had been well-treated. It was *not*, after all, treating one well when one was made a servant in one's own home!

Lydia would have been surprised by that thought, too. She had never thought of herself as a servant. True, what she had done had been, in part, expedient. But mostly it was because of love for her siblings and her mother. She was not put upon—at least not in her own mind. She had merely tended to those she loved as would anyone who truly loved another.

"Yes, James?" asked Lydia the next day. She looked up from where she helped Mary with her sampler.

"Lord Horten sent me up to find Jasper and I can't. It's time for his lesson. He isn't with Lord Huntingdon," he continued before Lydia could ask, "because his lordship left with that new agent to tour the farms. He said Jasper could go along on their next round once Mr. Black is familiar with what there is and what must be done."

"Which is pretty much everything! I am so glad Lord Huntingdon authorized new roofs for the tenants' houses. Have you looked in Jasper's bedroom?"

James cast her a look of scorn. "Of course. I've looked everywhere. Even in *Father's* rooms."

Jasper had, so far, refused to move into his father's old room, saying there would be time enough for that when he reached his majority and was truly in charge.

Lydia frowned. "Surely he would not forget such a treat as his riding lesson."

James shook his head, once, short and sharp, in the way he had when he disagreed.

"James?"

The boy shrugged, obviously embarrassed he had allowed his eldest sister a glimpse of his thoughts. "Oh, I dunno . . ." He dug a toe into the worn drugget carpeting the hall. "I'll go look again. Maybe I just missed him somewhere."

"James!"

The boy sighed but, obedient to her tone, turned back. "Yes, Lydia?" he asked.

"Don't try that baby-innocent trick on me, young man! Now, what do you know that I *don't* know?"

"Not a thing," said James promptly. "May I go?"

Lydia's eyes narrowed. "What have you *guessed*?"

He scowled. "I don't wish to say. I don't see how I can possibly be correct, so I must be wrong." He brightened at the thought. "Is that not logical?"

"James."

James looked at Mary and then at the twins. His scowl returned, and once again he toed a worn place in the drugget.

Lydia rose to her feet, looked at the girls, saw they were occupied, and, putting a hand to James's shoulder, turned him and pushed him gently down the hall. "Now, James . . ."

The boy drew in a big breath and whooshed it out. "I don't think he likes our lessons. He doesn't say anything, but I don't think he even likes horses." James grimaced. "He isn't any good at it, Lydia."

"He doesn't enjoy the lessons?"

"I'm pretty certain he does not. He doesn't say so, but you can see it. He gets all tensed up, and the mare *knows*, you know what I mean?"

"Oh, dear . . ."

"I thought it the other day . . . but I couldn't," he went on in a rush, "believe it. But, well, he didn't come for his lesson today . . ."

Lydia sighed. "Tell the twins they must have their riding lesson now. Lord Horten is kind enough to teach you all, then we must not waste his time, must we?"

"But what about Jasper?"

"I'll try to find him and I'll talk to him."

"I just don't understand how he cannot like it!"

"Some people do not like horses, James. They are very big animals, and many people are a trifle afraid they'll not be able to control something so much larger than they are themselves."

"What nonsense. You *don't* control them. It is a partnership. You take care of them and they let you ride. Besides, they like a good run, and most of them like to jump, too. It's all a game, don't you know?"

"You continue to think of it that way, James. Just so long as you remember you are responsible for the care of your animal and remember there are limits to what they can do. If you are sensible in what you ask of them, well, I think it a rather good way to think. But not everyone is able to do so. You take the twins down and tell Mary she may set aside her stitching for today. Tell her I wish her to practice for half an hour, and then I'll come to her to hear her piece."

James grinned. "I was never so glad of anything that Lord Huntingdon has done as that he had the tuner in to fix the pianoforte. Even the horses!" he exclaimed. "I don't know how you could stand to help the girls play."

Lydia smiled in response. "It is much kinder on the ears now, is it not? And your sisters are doing ever so much better since they may hear the way a piece is supposed to sound."

"Actually, I *was* gladder he bought us horses, but you know what I meant," he said and ran back up the hall to tell the twins of the treat in store for them. James would never have believed it, but to practice the piano rather than do her stitching, which she hated, was very nearly an equal treat for Mary.

Lydia walked briskly down the stairs. She would do something James would never think of doing. She would ask their brand-new butler if he had seen Sir Jasper that morning, and if so, she would also ask if Brean knew where her brother was to be found.

Brean did know. Sir Jasper had gone into the library something over an hour earlier and, so far as Brean was aware, had not come out.

"The library!"

Lydia almost left the boy alone. Of all the places he might have gone in the house or on the estate, the library was the one place she would not have thought to look. The children still avoided the room, the scene of too much violence at the hands of their father. That Jasper chose to go there indicated to Lydia he truly did not wish to be found.

And yet . . . why did he not wish to be found?

It was, she decided, her responsibility to discover what bothered her brother and to consider if there was anything at all she might do about it. Still, she opened the door with far more reluctance than she usually felt when confronting one of the children. She hated to pry into their problems before they were ready to come to her and discuss them; but occasionally it was necessary, and this, she feared, was one of those times.

"Jasper?"

"Hmm?" He glanced around, his shoulders tense. "Oh. Hmm, Lydia . . ."

"You appear to be trying to think up a good excuse

for being here, Jasper, which is very foolish of you. There is no reason why you should not be here."

He turned back to the window, his hands clasped behind him. She watched as his fingers closed around each other, opened, closed again.

"There is some problem you are reluctant to discuss with me," she said. "Is it also something you cannot discuss with Lord Huntingdon?"

"He wouldn't understand."

"I, too? I would not understand?"

"No."

"Why don't you try me?"

"You'll laugh at me."

Lydia was silent for half a moment. "Jasper, have I ever laughed at you children or at any of your problems?"

"No . . ."

"Then, why would I now change?"

After a moment he turned. "I don't want to learn to ride." He almost spat the words at her before twisting back to the window.

"Would you rather learn to drive?"

He swung around and stared at her. "Drive . . . Liddy, did you not hear me? I don't wish to learn to ride."

"Lots of people dislike riding. They'd rather drive."

He blinked. Very slowly he relaxed. "Are you serious?"

"Well, perhaps it isn't *lots* of people, but you are not alone in disliking to ride. The thing is, sometimes it is easier to get somewhere if you ride rather than drive. You can go across country in a way you cannot with a rig."

"*You* love to ride," he said accusingly.

"Yes. I think James will like it enormously, too, but if Margaret learns to sit a horse properly and manages to get from here to there at a walk, I will be pleased. Mary will do well, and I believe the twins will become excellent riders. I hope that you will manage to do at least as well as Margaret, Jasper, but only because, as I said, it is sometimes *necessary* to ride somewhere. One needn't insist that you enjoy it as well. So, would you rather learn to drive?"

Jasper drew in a long breath. "I hate horses."

"No. You hate *riding* horses. You haven't a notion whether you'll hate driving."

After a moment," he said, "I think I would prefer it. Liddy, I really thought you'd think me a . . . a . . ."

"Prime noodle?"

He chuckled. "Something like that."

"It isn't something one boasts of, a dislike of riding, but there is no reason why one should force oneself to do more than learn the basics. Would you prefer to learn on one of the twin's ponies? I believe you are still small enough . . . no. All right."

"James *would* laugh at *that.*"

"Jasper, do not try to be like your brother."

"I never could," he said.

Lydia heard a certain amount of sadness in that. "Jasper, you are yourself and you have value in our eyes for the things which are your strengths. That they are not so obvious as your brother's more . . ."

"Manly?"

"*Never.* More *common* tricks, I was about to say. If your strengths are less obvious, that does not make them any less important. In fact, they are the truly important things. Your loyalty to those who need you. Your sense of responsibility. Your ability to offer friendship and generosity without burdening others with it. Oh, many things. You are young yet, Jasper, and you do not value such traits as you will when you are older, but they are, if anything, more important than your brother's headstrong nature which will not admit to wholesome fear."

"Far more important, actually," said Lord Huntingdon from the open window on which he leaned his arms. "May one ask why you have fallen into the dismals or is this a very private conversation? Perhaps I should tiptoe away and pretend I have not heard a single word?"

Jasper turned a raging red color, and turning to Lydia, his eyes begged her not to say anything.

"We were merely discussing the fact that people are different. Sometimes very different. Oh, and before that, I discovered Jasper would like to learn to drive. He will, of course, continue his riding lessons, but he is concerned that he will never be a horseman and thinks it would be best if he didn't attempt the impossible, but only learned the basics, and that driving might be more the thing?"

At first Huntingdon wanted to laugh. Then, as he considered how carefully Miss Cottrell's airy delivery of information he needed had avoided exacerbating Jasper's low self-esteem, all desire to laugh faded. "I think that's an excellent notion. Not everyone is an equestrian. I remember that my own father much preferred to drive rather than ride."

That his father had weighed very nearly as much as the Prince Regent did was something Rafe hoped the boy didn't learn until he was much older and much more secure!

"I will see about a horse to hitch to the dogcart which is a very good vehicle for someone just learning to drive." He nodded and disappeared.

"He is wonderful," said Sir Jasper, relief and hero worship fighting for dominance in his expression.

"He is certainly a far better guardian for you children than I feared you'd have." Lydia was a trifle surprised herself at how easily Lord Huntingdon had picked up on her hints. "But now, Jasper, do you think you might manage to take that riding lesson you've been avoiding all morning?"

He grinned. "Now I know I'll never have to learn to jump those hedges and walls James already wants to go over, I think maybe I can manage to learn to sit a horse well enough that I won't totally embarrass you."

"I'd much prefer it, Jasper, if you learned to sit it well enough you'd not embarrass yourself!"

"We mustn't," he said with a completely solemn face, "ask miracles, Liddy. It isn't right. I mean," he went on, "one miracle a day is quite enough, is it not?"

Before Lydia quite sorted out his meaning—that was, that Lord Huntingdon had not dripped scorn all over him but had, instead, agreed to the driving lessons—Jasper seated himself on the windowsill, swung his legs over to the outside, and jumped down. She smiled as she watched him race off toward the paddock to join the twins, who were riding their ponies.

Lydia returned to the nursery far more slowly than she had come down in her search for Jasper. Lord Huntingdon was proving himself admirable in far too many ways for her comfort. She had, she believed, gotten her initial jealousy under firm control, but it still irked her that he could, without the least thought or contrivance, arrive at instant solutions to problems.

When she had suggested to Jasper that he might prefer to learn to drive, it had not occurred to her that a carriage horse had yet to be purchased and that quite possibly his lordship had had no intention of spending estate money for still another horse. And yet, faster than one could snap one's fingers, he said he would find one. Still, perhaps it was an expense the estate should not be asked to bear?

What, she wondered, would she have done if he had not been agreeable? Tried one of the mares, probably, to see for herself if the animal would work between the shafts.

Nor had Lydia expected Lord Huntingdon to appear in that rather magical way. She had expected to find him alone somewhere and make the request where she might argue with him about the benefits to Jasper and where she could warn him of Jasper's need for respect, his fear of ridicule.

But Lord Huntingdon had seemed to understand instantly. She had not needed to argue her points . . .

. . . and she didn't quite know how to deal with the notion there was a man in the world with whom it wasn't necessary to organize a full debate in order to gain one's point. Were such common? Had her own experience with the children's father and, briefly, his solicitor been so skewed she didn't know how a normal man acted?

Perhaps Eunice might know.

Lydia picked up her pace but, upon reaching the schoolroom, discovered it was empty. Silently, she berated herself. Mary was practicing, and she must go listen to her. The twins were riding. Margaret had been allowed a morning with Cook, where she was, Lydia hoped, learning the secrets of making good pastry. And James, of course, always disappeared the instant he was not supervised.

So . . . where was Eunice?

Eunice was in the salon. She had ordered a tea tray and settled into her favorite chair with one of Cook's more lurid Gothic novels. She was not particularly pleased to be interrupted by Lydia's whirlwind entrance to the room, but set aside the book and folded her hands.

"Now, Lydia," she said, her glower well in place, "tell me what has upset you to the point you have forgotten to brush your hair which is, for reasons beyond my comprehension, quite unruly."

"Is Lord Huntingdon a normal representative of the male of the species?" the younger woman asked all in a rush.

Eunice blinked. Then she blushed. "Lydia!"

"He isn't like your brother, and he certainly isn't like that awful little man from Storrington who asked permission to approach me about marriage, and he isn't like vicar, and he—"

"Stop."

It was Lydia's turn to blink. "Yes, Eunice?"

"Tell me what happened to bring on this tantrum. At once."

Lydia sighed, huffing out her breath in a rush.

"Start at the beginning, now."

"It *started* when James came to find Jasper for his riding lesson."

"His riding lesson?"

"Hmm. James said he didn't think Jasper liked learning to ride."

"I assume this has something to do with Lord Huntingdon? Eventually?"

"You did say I was to begin in the beginning."

"I was wrong."

Miss Eunice scowled; but her lips twitched slightly, and Lydia knew she wasn't really angry. Lydia herself smiled and discovered she felt better. "So," she said, "I went to find Jasper and discovered him in the library which just goes to show how much he didn't wish to be found . . . you know?"

Eunice, pursing her lips, nodded.

"So I tried to discover the truth, and James was quite correct. Jasper does not like horses."

"So you told Huntingdon, and Huntingdon said he didn't need to learn to ride? I don't believe it!"

"You need not. What I did was suggest to Jasper that he might prefer learning to drive, but that since at times it was important one be able to get somewhere only a horse might take one, he must learn the rudiments."

"Sometimes, Lydia, your sensible nature surprises even me, who know you so well."

"Thank you. I think." Lydia shook off the compliment if that was what it was, and continued. "Anyway, Jasper thought that might be a good idea . . . and so did Lord Huntingdon, who listened to part of our conversation at the window! I didn't have to argue with him." She frowned. "More, I didn't have to explain more than the least little bit. Eunice, I simply do not understand it. So—"

"Is Lord Huntingdon a normal male! I see." Eunice, who had been sitting poker straight throughout Lydia's agitated summary, relaxed very slightly and reached for her teacup. The tea was cold, and she poured the dregs into the covered container provided for them and poured herself another cup of tea from the cozy-covered pot. "I think perhaps Lord Huntingdon is a trifle more intelligent than most. There are others, of course, who are as sensitive to another's needs when they are brought to understand them. Not all men are as dense as my brother nor so out of this world as our vicar."

Lydia smiled again, more broadly, and felt still better. "You do not mention Mr. Percell," she said. The ungenerous would have said there was something almost coquettish in her teasing comment.

"And I never will," snapped Eunice. Then, more calmly, she added, "Percell's father was a good man. It is too bad the son is—" she grimaced, obviously searching for an ending to her sentence, "—as he is."

"With any luck we'll have nothing more to do with

him. Jasper told me Lord Huntingdon is having Percell turn Easten Meadows' affairs over to his own solicitor."

"I rather hoped he'd do something of the sort."

"But you didn't suggest it?"

Eunice looked down her long, narrow nose. "Lydia, it is not my place to tell another how to discharge his duties!"

"Which is why you never interfered in your brother's way of doing things. I see."

"You understand me, but you do not approve. That, Lydia, is *your* way of doing things. I leave you to your methods, do I not, as I do others?"

"I don't believe anyone could accuse you of inconsistency, Eunice," said Lydia dryly. "I must go listen to Mary now. Assuming she hasn't given up waiting for me. It will soon be time for her riding lesson, and she will not have finished with the piano."

Eunice watched Lydia leave the room, the slim, graceful carriage a compliment to the mother who had raised her to believe in herself and her abilities. For a moment or two Eunice considered promoting a match between Lydia and Lord Huntingdon. It had crossed her mind more than once that the pair might do very well together.

But, as she had done in the past, she dismissed the notion. Her policy of noninterference in the lives of all others, except, very occasionally, that of her nieces and nephews, made it ineligible to interfere in what would or would not happen between Lydia and Lord Huntingdon. Eunice poured herself more tea, picked up the book, and settled deeply into her chair.

Except that what would *not* happen would include improper behavior on the part of either of the two. To that degree Eunice would bring herself to interfere.

But, as usual, she would for the nonce do just exactly as she pleased. *She* knew—although she would never have admitted it to a soul—that while far more benevolent, she was, in her own way, very nearly as selfish as her brother.

Seven

Rafe sat slouched, staring into the small fire cheerfully crackling away in the library hearth. A pewter mug, half full of ale, rested on one chair arm, his hand fisted around the handle. He hadn't sipped from it for some time when the marquis passed by. Three letters drifted down into his lap. He glanced at them and back at the fire.

"Where is Kenrick?" asked Roger from behind his desk. He broke the wax seal on the first of his own pile of correspondence.

"I don't know." When that abrupt phrase sounded churlish even to his own ears, he added, "He said something about hunting."

"Kenrick? *Hunting?*" Roger chuckled. "The only thing our lazy friend ever hunts is the female of the species. *Our* species."

"Now you mention it, I think he said something about Miss Maddy."

"Yes, that makes sense, although, from what I've heard, he'll not get far with her."

"Kenrick won't repine. You well know he lives by the adage of nothing ventured, nothing gained. He won't mope if he fails." Rafe picked up his mail one piece at a time. The first he laid aside. It was from Mr. Caruthers, his solicitor, and was likely to require a thoughtful response which would require quiet, a bit of time and a desk on which to write. The second he threw directly into the fire. Roger chuckled, and Rafe glanced at him.

"From La Bellissima?" asked Roger.

"I wonder," said Rafe sarcastically, "how you guessed."

"It was rather highly scented. The whole mail bag was contaminated. She not taking her congé well?"

"I've been told it is the first time anyone has left her rather than she leaving them. Given what I learned of her, I don't know why it *hasn't* happened before. Often. She's beautiful, that I admit. But she's greedy to the point there is no satisfying her, and demanding of one's attention until one wants to throttle her. Too, she has a temper far beyond anything you would ever guess." Rafe shrugged. He opened the last missive and scanned it even as he absently continued his conversation with Roger. Suddenly he sat up, his mug tipping, almost spilling. Only his quick reaction caught it, saving it from disaster. His eyes never leaving the letter, he set the mug on the floor. "Roger . . ."

"Hmm?" Roger had opened one of his own letters and was deeply into its contents.

"Roger, pay attention."

The marquis looked up, noted the odd look on Rafe's face, and set his letter aside. He came over and took the other chair. "I am," he said gently, "all attention."

"This is from my aunt."

"Aunt?"

"My London aunt. Lady Freward."

"And why do you look at her words as if they were direct from heaven? I don't believe I've ever read such awe in your expression!"

"Did you never hear that the late Lady Easten was Charingham's daughter? That she was a widow when she married the children's father?"

"A widow." Roger tipped his head. "Is that so surprising?"

Rafe cast him a look.

"Well," said the marquis a trifle defensively, "many women are."

"You don't appear to understand. If she was a widow, then she was previously married."

"I believe that follows," said Roger, carefully, if not quite successfully, containing a desire to smile.

"And, that," continued Rafe, who wasn't fooled by his friend's tight expression, "means Miss Cottrell is not . . . was . . . was not . . ."

"Miss Cottrell, despite your fears," Roger supplied when it appeared Rafe would never finish his sentence, "would appear to be perfectly, er, *acceptable* as a governess to your young wards."

"Thank you."

"The word you were trying to avoid is 'illegitimate,' Rafe, and your aunt's news would appear to make that impossible."

"What do you mean by that?" asked Rafe, rising to his feet. "*Appear* to make it impossible?"

Roger bit his lip, studying his friend's belligerent expression. "Rafe, that missive from Lord Charingham. You surely haven't forgotten you don't yet know the reason why your Miss Cottrell's grandfather wants nothing to do with her!"

Rafe's shoulders slumped, and he slouched back into his chair. "Damn," he muttered.

"You wrote Charingham?"

"Her grandfather? Yes. I've received no response, so either he has decided to make someone else responsible for the annuity or he can't decide what to tell me. I must respond to my aunt's question, however. She will be glad to know what has become of Miss Cottrell."

"That's her question?"

"Hmm. Evidently she knew Miss Cottrell's mother quite well. Which is reasonable, of course. The Huntingdon estate is very near Charingham's, you see. According to my aunt, her presentation followed the season in which Miss Cottrell's mother was presented."

"So the mother did have a season . . ."

"Perhaps I will ask my aunt if she didn't *take*. It might explain her father's reaction. If he were half so enamored of his wife as I've heard, then he might have hoped to be rid of his daughter who must have taken up much of her mother's time."

"A jealous *father?*" asked Roger, chuckling.

"Not impossible," retorted Rafe, but even he heard the defensive note to his tone.

"What is not impossible?" rumbled Kenrick, entering just then. Roger's butler followed carrying a tray on which rested not only decanters and glasses, but a plate of small but hearty sandwiches made of thinly sliced ham and a good strong, well-aged, local cheese.

"Find Miss McCormick at home, Kenrick?" asked Roger, pouring wine from the largest decanter, then lifting it toward Rafe.

Rafe shook his head and picked up his mug.

Kenrick gave the decanter a suspicious look and stared at Roger. Roger sighed. "The smallest decanter is a Portuguese Mountain sherry. The middle one is brandy bought in France during the 1803 Peace, which was *not*. Peace, that is."

"I'll have a drop of the sherry," decided the baron. "And no, I did not find Miss Maddy to home. She crossed to Ireland with her brother to attend a sale and will not return for some days." He approved the sherry. "Very good, Roger. I'd like the name of your supplier. Their head groom says they are looking for a few likely mares to breed to that devil stallion."

"Who is caring for him while Miss Maddy is absent?" asked Rafe.

Kenrick's rumbling chuckle worked like a volcano, rising from the depths to break out all over. Roger and Rafe were forced to smile, a not uncommon reaction to Kenrick's infectious laugh.

"Well?" prodded Roger.

When he had controlled his chuckles, Kenrick told them. "They've put the youngest groom into skirts and it answers very well. What will happen when the lad's voice begins to break I haven't a notion, but for the time being the two creatures are very tolerant of each other!"

Roger grimaced. "I can just imagine the poor boy's response to being told he must wear skirts!"

"The head groom is something of a mimic. If his portrayal was anything accurate, then it was a sight not to be missed. It took three of them to hold the boy down and put him into a dress. I am sorry I did. Miss it, that is."

Rafe smiled as he rose to his feet. "I think I'd better go to my room and try to answer this letter from my solicitor. Then, if there is time before dinner, the one from my aunt as well."

"Did your aunt know anything?" the baron asked, curious.

"She says that Lady Easten was Charingham's daughter, a widow before she married Easten, and wants to know what happened to Miss Cottrell." Rafe shrugged. "Perhaps if I ask direct questions, she'll give direct answers. I was too cautious in my last epistle."

"When you wrote before you didn't know Lady Easten had had a prior marriage. You were concerned lest Miss Cottrell—"

Roger interrupted with a wave of his hand. "We've been through all that. A former marriage implies Miss

Cottrell was born within wedlock but does not explain why her grandfather is behaving in such a gudgeonish way. You would think he'd want his only grandchild close to him, would you not? Instead the noodle appears to want nothing to do with her."

"I must write him a second letter as well, must I not?" asked Rafe. "Behave, my children, while I am absent," he said with a facetious air. "I don't wish to return and discover you've gotten into mischief!"

"I believe I'd wait a few more days for Charingham to respond to your first letter, Rafe," said Kenrick before Rafe had left the room. "It may seem as if we've been here a long time and have known the Eastens and Miss Cottrell for ages, but it hasn't truly been all that long. Certainly not since you learned of that ridiculous annuity Charingham provided for when or if Miss Cottrell is in need of it."

Rafe paused and counted on his fingers. He blinked. "You are correct. It hasn't been so very long. I wonder why it seems as if it has been wee—?"

His voice was cut off as the door shut behind him, and the marquis, one brow arched, stared questioningly at the baron.

"He told me he feared he'd been handed a facer," explained Kenrick. "Perhaps I should not have told you that if he hasn't mentioned it himself."

"I'll not say anything. Is there anything we might do?"

"Did you write and ask your mother what she knows of the situation?"

"Yes, but you well know it may be some time before I've an answer. Mama is traveling in the Lake District, and heaven only knows when my messenger will catch up with her."

"Messenger?"

"I didn't send him specially, if that is what you won-

der. I am to forward her mail at intervals, and I send a
personal message whenever I do."

"You just happened to forward it, this time, a trifle
more quickly than you might have done?"

"Hmm. Well . . . yes." Roger grinned, and once
again Kenrick's basso laughter filled the room. This
time Roger laughed, too.

The next day, instead of riding over to the Meadows,
which was his usual mode of going, Rafe drove the gig
Roger kept for the use of those among his staff who
needed transport. It was pulled by an older horse the
head groom swore would not give a boy trouble. He
was approaching the Eastens' and about to turn up the
lane past the dower house when he saw, coming down
it, the Eastens' dogcart, one of the mares hitched to it.
Miss Cottrell was, very obviously, in difficulties as the
horse, trained for riding, objected strongly to the con-
traption trailing it.

In fact, it appeared the mare was doing her best to
run away from it.

Rafe pulled across the end of the lane and then,
jumping down, ran toward the panicked runaway. His
heart pounding with fear for Miss Cottrell, he placed
himself just where the lane curved, ready to jump for
the mare's head.

Faintly, through his concentration on the horse's progress, he heard Miss Cottrell shouting at him to get out
of the way. He ignored her, crouching slightly, and leap-
ing at just the right instant. His weight alone began to
slow the light-limbed animal. His soothing voice helped.
And Miss Cottrell's steady pull on the reins completed
the task. Shaking in every muscle, sweating horribly, the
mare halted, her head drooping.

Silently, Rafe began unharnessing her. He finished

and, without even looking at Miss Cottrell, walked the mare back up the lane, leaving the young woman sitting in the cart. The harness had been dropped just anyhow and the reins sagged uselessly between the shafts and into the ruts making up the lane.

Lydia half turned and stared after him. She felt very near to tears. Her arms ached terribly, and, she knew, before too much longer the pain would be next to intolerable. He must have known it, too. And yet, he hadn't even asked how she was. He hadn't so much as looked at her. He had simply walked off leading the mare.

Walked? *Stalked.*

The man was a boor and ungentlemanly and unworthy of a single thought. So the fact she could think of nothing and no one else as she climbed down from the cart irritated her. Her legs felt more than a trifle shaky; but she began the rather long walk up the drive anyway, and that, too, made her angry.

One of Eunice's servants, who had seen the runaway, came rushing out of the dower house carrying a glass of wine. She scolded and chaffed and was obviously very concerned for Lydia, which soothed the young woman somewhat. And she was grateful for the wine. Once it was finished, the maid reassured and sent back into the house, Lydia remembered the gig and horse with which Lord Huntingdon had arrived. Sighing, she turned her footsteps back toward the head of the lane.

The marquis's elderly gelding had moved no farther than required to reach a succulent patch of clover at the edge of the road. And, well-trained beast that he was, he insisted on only one more mouthful before heeding Lydia's pull on the reins. He backed easily, just enough so he could turn up the lane, and didn't object to walking past the stranded cart with care, the off-side wheel of the gig rolling into the grass in Lydia's concern she not scrape the two vehicles together. She was nearly back to the house when one of the new grooms came rushing around the house and, seeing her, stopped short.

"Miss!"

"Yes? You are Ben, are you not? What can I do for you?"

"Miss! I been tol' to fetch the gig. That gig?"

"Hmm. Yes, once it is parked out of the way, you must take this animal back and bring up the dogcart. I am very sorry to put you to such extra work, but you see, I thought perhaps the mare was gentle enough to be used as a carriage horse. I was wrong."

"Yes, miss. His lordship—"

"His lordship, I presume, had words to say about the general stupidity of women and of this one in particular. Well, you may—" She tipped her head. "Why do you shake your head?"

"His lordship never would! Just as well he didn't say such things, too. Ol' Herbie, he'd have his guts for garters if he was so disrespectful to you, miss. Ol' Herbie, he wouldn't even let the fact it were a lordship stop him!"

"I am glad to know of Herbie's loyalty, but in this case"—she sighed softly, hiding it as she climbed down from the gig—"I fear it is misplaced! It was a stupid thing to do. I should not have attempted it."

"I am glad to hear you admit it," said an icy voice from the doorway to the house.

She turned quickly and was appalled to find Lord Huntingdon standing there, glaring, his arms crossed and a frown such as she had never before seen on his brow.

"Miss Cottrell," he continued, "I would appreciate a few words with you. In the library." Rafe turned on his heel and disappeared.

Lydia glanced at the boy whose face was bright red, but whether with anger or in an attempt to stifle laughter, she didn't know. She nodded toward the gig and turned on her own heel. Well, perhaps his fine lordship had words to say to her, but she had a few to say to him, too! Determined to say them, she stomped on into the house and down the hall.

"Thank God I was there to stop that beast," he said as she came through the door. "You might have been hurt. You might have been *killed . . .*"

"But I wasn't." Lydia frowned slightly. Where was the angry man ready to berate her? Why was he looking at her in that intense, worried way? "I am fine. *Truly,*" she added when his frown didn't fade a jot.

He studied her for a little longer and then walked to the window. Staring out it, he asked, "Miss Cottrell, what must I do to give you a modicum of faith in me?"

Lydia felt heat rushing up from under her bodice and into her face. "I don't know what you mean."

"I think you do." He turned. "On more than one occasion you have acted in such a way as to make it quite obvious you do not expect me to fulfill my duty or that you fear I'll fail in keeping a promise or whatever else it is you have decided I'll *not* do which I should do. Did you truly think I'd forget that Sir Jasper wishes to learn to drive?" He held up a hand. "No, you needn't answer. Obviously you thought just that. Otherwise you would not have had that riding horse harnessed to the cart. That you did, I can almost understand. That you then proceeded to attempt to drive the cart yourself, I *cannot.* You have grooms who have a responsibility to take such risks. You should *not* have put your own self into jeopardy." His frown returned. "That you did so, I find incomprehensible. When you are such a necessity to the children's well-being, how could you have done it?"

"I . . ." Lydia closed her mouth. In the face of his conclusion there was nothing she could say. "I have admitted it was a stupid thing to do, although my reason was not what you suggested. You heard me admit it. What more do you wish me to say?"

"Tell me *why* you thought it necessary."

Lydia looked at the rug, at the portrait over the mantel, at the window. "Jasper . . ."

"Jasper has waited a fair number of years," he said on a dry note. "He could have waited another few days if that had been necessary."

"I feared you would feel it more than the estate could afford. There is so much to do, so much *expense*, and you've already bought too many mounts; so I thought if one of the mares . . ."

He had eyed her in a judicious manner as she had spoken, and now interrupted. "Although that may have been part of your reason, I think it is something else. I think you feel I have usurped your place in this family, and that you must prove, again and again, that you are necessary to it. Or something of that sort?"

Lydia's blush had faded. Now it returned. "You would say I am jealous." She sighed. "I will admit that at times I have felt that ignominious emotion and have berated myself for it. I know you've a responsibility here. I have watched you go far beyond what many would think necessary. And a great distance beyond what the children's father expected or even desired, miser that he had become." It was her turn to walk to the window and stare out. "I do not like myself very well when I stop to think of my reactions to you. I do not know myself." She felt his hands on her shoulders and wondered when he had come so close to her. She also found she liked the gentle warmth, the support it implied . . . and still more, just the feel of him so near.

"I do not wish to steal the children's love from you.

I could not even if I would. You are far too important to them."

"I know that. But I also know you will go away, and they will miss you!"

"I won't go forever, and you may tell them so. Besides, I have been thinking that it might be a good thing, once I have the work here in hand, if they were all to come to Huntingdon Chase. You and Miss Eunice as well, of course. I doubt very much that this house will be at all comfortable once the roofers begin work. I've noticed we must also have the carpenters in for several problems, and they must be followed by painters. You will be much more comfortable elsewhere."

"I . . . don't know what to say . . ."

"I hadn't meant to mention it just yet. I have only just written to my aunt and meant to wait until I knew she'd come to the Chase to play hostess. She knew your mother, by the way. They grew up near each other."

Her reluctance to leave the Meadows faded. Someone who had known her mother when young? Knew things to tell the daughter! There was so much Lydia wanted to know, so many questions and no one to ask. And, besides, she missed her mother and would feel closer to her if allowed to talk about her, learn about her. . . .

"I shall, of course," he added when she didn't speak, "discuss this with Miss Eunice Easten. She must be the final arbiter, I think."

"Yes, perhaps it would be best to discuss it with Eunice. I do not feel I can make a proper decision."

And not only, she berated herself, *because I'd have an opportunity to learn more about Mother. I am also, I fear, becoming far too interested in you, my fine lord!* She squirmed, and his hands dropped from her shoulders; and although it was what she had wanted, she felt a surge of disappointment . . . *why* she didn't know.

"I must go. Margaret will be coming in from her les-

son." She paused, her hand on the doorknob. "By the
way, James is rather fearful he is not up to snuff and
cannot achieve a proper degree of erudition before
Michaelmas term. You might reassure him if you can."

"Thank you, Miss Cottrell."

She turned. "Why do you thank me? What have I
done?"

"I believe you have just offered me that modicum of
trust for which I asked."

When she looked confused, he smiled.

"You offered," he explained, "and with *no prompting
whatsoever,* information about one of the children and
asked that I do something about the problem. So far
as I can recall, it is a first."

Lydia felt chagrined. Had she truly been so . . . surly?
"I will try to do better, my lord." She curtsied and swept
from the room.

Because they had seemed to end their confrontation
in the library on a more positive note, Lord Huntingdon was at first surprised and then depressed that Miss
Cottrell appeared, over the next few days, to be avoiding
him. When, three days later, he walked into the salon
in the late afternoon and discovered Miss Eunice Easten, Miss Cottrell and the baron sitting over nearly
empty tea cups, seemingly enjoying an interesting cose,
depression turned to irritation.

"My lord! Welcome," said Miss Eunice. She leaned
forward and lifted the lid to the teapot. "Oh, dear. I
must call for more hot water, my lord. We seem to
have—"

"No, that is quite all right. I just had a nursery tea
with the younger girls." He had gone to the nursery in
the hopes of catching Miss Cottrell there. She was not,
but the twins, who now accepted him without reserva-

tion, pounced on him and insisted he share their toasted muffins and marmalade. Despite his disappointment his quarry was absent, he enjoyed the half hour with the girls.

When James came in and discovered they had eaten up everything already, his complaints resulted in much teasing, but when the boy would have gone down to the kitchen for his tea, he received lessons in punctuality and consideration for the servants instead. In fact, Rafe put his foot down quite firmly. James was not, he was told, to put the servants to extra work. They had their duties, and they were not to be put off stride by a scrubby schoolboy who could not watch the position of the sun and get himself home accordingly! Instead, James must wait for his evening meal, and to distract him from his hunger pangs, he would bring his Latin text and show his guardian how far he had gotten in his studies.

James, grumbling and dragging his feet, had complied. And had been astounded to discover he was well ahead of where he need be in that particular field of study. He did not, however, like to learn that he should have the rudiments of Greek under his belt, although his facility with the globes was approved, and when tested in his maths, they were pronounced adequate.

"When Mr. Minchwell arrives he will work with you on the Greek in particular. You are quite intelligent enough that you will easily pick up what is necessary over the summer. After all, you will be expected to have no more than an introduction to the language. That does not mean you'll not need to apply yourself. I will tell Mr. Minchwell he is to keep you up in other subjects, but is to concentrate on the one you have yet to be introduced to. Will that do, do you think?"

"I like to study nature," mumbled James, staring at

the floor where the toe of his shoe rubbed at a bad place in the schoolroom drugget.

"I did not hear that, boy," said Rafe.

Taking a big breath, James repeated himself. "I like to spend time outdoors. I like to observe how birds behave and how animals do things."

"Hmm. Yes, most boys take an interest in such things if they have an opportunity to do so. I believe you will be required to write essays as part of your work. I will tell Minchwell he may allow you some time for your observations if you will then proceed to write down what you have discovered in proper form."

"How much time?" asked James, wary.

"He likes to stay out for hours and hours and hours," said one twin.

"He sometimes doesn't come home until after dark," said the other.

"Be still," whispered James, scowling at them.

"It's true," said the first.

"You know it is," said the other.

"Hours and hours and, most certainly, 'until after dark,' will not do," said Rafe firmly. "I believe Minchwell may wish to go with you a time or two and will set boundaries for you, James, which you will observe. Your life at school will be far more circumscribed than it has been here. It will be just as well for you to learn, now, that you must keep to a schedule."

"But . . ."

"Yes?" asked Rafe gently.

James hung his head. "Nothing."

"You already knew that, did you not?"

"Jasper explained."

"That is one good thing about older brothers. They are there to explain what one needs to know about things which they had to learn the hard way!"

James grinned a quick grin at that. "He didn't mind

going to school. Even after the caning. The headmaster isn't so bad as our father, you see." He grimaced. "I mean how he *was.*"

That scene with James passed through Rafe's head as Lydia rose to her feet and began excusing herself. "I've something to discuss with you, Miss Cottrell. Miss Easten, thank you for the offer of tea, but it will be unnecessary. Miss Cottrell? Perhaps we'll not interfere in the conversation here if you will join me by the window?"

He offered his arm, and Lydia hesitantly placed her fingertips on his wrist. He seated her in the window seat and stared down at her bowed head. "I finally managed to talk to James," he said.

She looked up. "And?"

"He is well up on his Latin . . ." He continued, explaining what he had told James. "Mr. Minchwell should arrive any day now. He will see to the boy's Greek. You needn't blush, Miss Cottrell. You are not, you know, expected to know *Latin.* Why would you be expected to know Greek?" It suddenly occurred to him that her knowledge was surprising. "How, by the way, does it come about that you know Latin?"

"Before Mother remarried . . . before . . ." She brushed hastily at a tear tracing a path down her cheek.

"Never mind," said Rafe quickly. He glanced to where Kenrick was entertaining Miss Eunice. "Please. Don't cry," he said softly.

"It is stupid . . . so long ago . . ."

"Were you one of those Wordsworth called a Model Child? As in his poem? *'This model of a child is never known to mix in quarrels . . .'*"

"My early training was of that sort." Lydia turned slightly, so she was looking out the window rather than at him. "My mother didn't completely approve and did her best to give me a certain amount of time each day to be, well, I suppose one might call it being free. But she never understood that I enjoyed my studies and especially the languages. I have, I fear, forgotten much of my French and German, and we had only opened the book for Greek; but I learned maths and the globes and more than one might think a woman needed to know of the new sciences . . ."

"Do I hear a defensive note? I wonder if perhaps the combination of study and free time is not a good one." He eyed her bent head and continued more softly. "I know it is if a child, so taught, grows into the sort of person you have become."

Lydia, raising her eyes quickly, stared up at him. "Surely you cannot approve that I'm a . . . a bluestocking!"

"Are you? You are not at all like the women I've met in London who revel in that label. They are, far too often, affected in their manners or overly belligerent. Too many of them believe they know a great deal when they've only a smattering of this and that, although there are exceptions, of course. No, I do not think you a bluestocking, Miss Cottrell. What I think is that you are an educated woman of great principle and still greater integrity."

"Nonsense. I am nothing so special."

He smiled, a gleam in his eye. "Are you not? And what, or should I say *whom*, do you use as a comparison that you think yourself average and in no way special?"

"Miss Eunice!"

He chuckled. "Perhaps you are correct. Miss Eunice is certainly an exception to many rules. Nevertheless, I will hold to the belief you, too, are special. Now, have you plans for tomorrow?"

A tiny smile tipped her lips at his laugh. It was reinforced by his compliment, at which she felt a secret pleasure. The smile faded, however, at his question. "Plans?"

"I was thinking that perhaps we should take advantage of this excellent weather and give the children an outing. If we were to drive into Brighton, I could take the boys to a tailor there, and you could choose material for clothes for the girls. We could all go somewhere the children would like and, at the proper time, have a meal at the Old Ship or at the Castle Inn. Do you approve that plan?"

"The boys certainly need new jackets."

"From what I have seen," he corrected her with only a faint hint of scorn, "very nearly everything else as well."

"And, although the girls are less rough on their clothing and can hand things down one to the next, there is poor Margaret, who is, like Jasper, becoming a trifle large to be comfortable . . ."

"You frown. Why?"

"I had hoped, when I next went shopping, they'd no longer need deep mourning. They had not come out of it, you see, for our mother, when their father died. I had thought to wait until I could buy them half mourning."

"They are children. I see no reason why, if you are restrained in your choice, they cannot go back into colors."

"It has been only—"

"I know to the day how long it has been! You will oblige me by not being hypocritical about this. Not a one of those children mourns their father. If they did, I'd think them total nodcocks! Buy the girls less drab clothing, my dear."

Lydia glanced at him, and away, blushing slightly.

"All of them. And, Miss Cottrell," he finished softly, "something of a happier nature for yourself as well?"

A stubborn look crossed her face, and that firm little chin rose a notch. "No."

"No?"

"I admit that I have not mourned the loss of my step-father, but I am still in mourning for my mother and will be for some few more months."

"I had thought little Alice more than a year old."

"She is just over ten months. On her birthday I will, I think, lighten my mourning. Some. I will adopt half mourning, assuming it feels right, when she is a year and a half."

"You mean to adopt formal mourning for a full two years."

"You disapprove."

It occurred to Rafe that she would be less likely to go into society, less likely to meet a man who would become his rival, if she remained in mourning. "I don't believe," he said carefully, "that I've any right to either approve or disapprove."

"I agree," she said evenly.

"But the children . . . ?"

Lydia hesitated. As their guardian, he had the right to decide such things. Still . . . "I will consult Eunice."

"Very well. I will inform her of the treat in store for her. She will, I'm certain, enjoy going into Brighton."

"With seven children? I doubt it!"

"Six children," said Rafe gently. "Baby Alice will remain here with the maid hired to care for her."

Lydia bit her lip. She had not yet adapted to the notion she was not, every moment of the day and night, responsible for all of the children. Especially, it bothered her where the youngest was concerned, the one she felt most truly her own.

Rafe touched her cheek with one finger very lightly. It was no more than a feathery whisper of a touch; but it burned her clear down to her toes, and once again, she rose to her feet, meaning to escape. The door opened and, the nursery maid in attendance, the children came in. Baby Alice, held by the maid, squirmed to be let down, and a trifle wobbly but far more proficient than the day Rafe first arrived, the child walked to where Kenrick sat and patted his knee.

Rafe was astonished when, without looking, without breaking off a word of what he was saying to Miss Eunice, the large man leaned forward, lifted the child to his lap, and settled her there. The little girl, her finger in her mouth, leaned her head against his chest and looked exceedingly content. Rafe heard an odd sound and looked toward Lydia, who was still staring at the small tableau. He heard the sound again.

"My dear," he said softly, "I'd not do that if I were you. You will very likely do damage to your teeth, will you not?" He gave her an understanding look when, startled, she glanced up at him, and then he turned to stroll across the room. "Miss Margaret, may I request that you play a piece for us?"

For the first time, Lydia noticed there was a new piece of furniture at the far end of the room. A very new, very modern, and, with the inlay work and ivory keys, very expensive piano. When had it arrived? And why?

Slowly, feeling as if her world were changing around her in ways she didn't, couldn't, understand, Lydia sank back to the window seat where she was joined by the twins. They watched Margaret, blushing furiously, settle at the piano and choose from the music waiting there. And then Lydia listened, critically, as the girl played. Stilted, perhaps, but technically, well performed. If there was less emotion than Mary gave to her playing, there was far more accuracy. But still, something must be done to encourage Margaret to put just a little feeling into her music.

Not, of course, too much. That, too, would not do. A chit of an age to be presented should not, after all, understand the emotions the composers so often relied on when looking for ideas on which to base their work. Certainly so young a musician would not.

Mary played next, and then, much to her surprise, Lord Huntingdon asked that she play for them. Lydia had itched to get her hands on the piano from the moment she had realized it was there. But now, asked to play, she wondered if her fingers would cooperate.

She needn't have worried. It was such a fine instrument she soon forgot she had an audience. The various composers, whose work she played from memory, would have approved the verve and elan with which their music rose into the air to fall on eager ears.

There might, however, be high sticklers who, had they been among the audience, would have looked askance that the youngish spinster was capable of producing such sounds. It was, actually, no more suitable for Lydia, unmarried and an innocent, to have so much understanding of some of the emotions on which a composer might base his work than it was for Margaret or Mary to do so.

Eight

Lydia was still playing when, quietly, Lords Hunting-don and Horten excused themselves so they might re-turn to Maythorn's estate in time for dinner. She was too deeply lost in the music to either know or care they had gone and was startled into hitting an extremely odd chord indeed when, sometime later, James laid his hand on her arm.

"James! Oh, dear . . . where was I?" She played a phrase or two. "Did you wish something?"

"Dinner has been put back *twice,*" he said on a plain-tive note. "Cook says it will be ruined if it is put back again." He was more than usually anxious since he had missed the nursery tea earlier and was, boy-fashion, fam-ished.

"Twice . . . ?" Lydia lifted her fingers from the keys and looked toward the windows where, she discovered, the long shadows of the trees bordering the lawn nearly reached the house, dimming the light in the room. "Twice? What is the time?"

Eunice, handing Alice to the maid, strolled across to join them. "Late, but never mind. No one wished to stop you, but, since Cook must be pacified, we are forced to do so. I knew you could play, my dear, but up to this point you've not had an instrument to do you justice. That was truly special."

Lydia remembered the two men had been among her audience and glanced around. She breathed more easily when she realized Lord Huntingdon was gone. The feeling of relief was instantly followed by one of deep disappointment that Huntingdon hadn't found her playing of a standard to keep him listening to her.

"Lord Horten," added Eunice, "insisted he and Huntingdon must leave." She chuckled. "It was obvious his lordship had no desire to do so, but when reminded the marquis warned them they'd have company this evening and that they were not to be late, Huntingdon managed to take his leave with a semblance of proper manners."

Once again Lydia's inner being lightened. And then she wondered at herself—because, almost immediately, she was depressed by the knowledge the marquis had invited in company. Who would join the three young men? Who would partner his lordship at dinner?

Just then she noticed James's worried face and remembered that Cook feared for her reputation. Putting thoughts of Lord Huntingdon firmly out of her mind, she eyed her younger brother sternly. "Hands, James."

He glanced down at them before holding them out. For once they did not look so terribly grubby, so despite Eunice's grunt of disapproval, Lydia decided that this evening he would be allowed to go directly to the table.

It wasn't until much later, not until the children were all in bed and she had felt able to close her door and enjoy the privacy of her own room, that Lydia wondered at the odd shifts in her emotions where Lord Huntingdon was concerned. It occurred to her that perhaps they were the sort of thing one experienced when one spoke of suffering the pangs of unrequited love.

Then, chiding herself for foolishness, she told herself she was not to be an idiot. She was far too old to fall in love like some starry-eyed chit enjoying her first taste of company.

Still admonishing herself, she prepared for bed. Falling in love at her age was such a ridiculous notion that really one must laugh at it . . .

. . . and then she wondered why she could find not the least little bit of humor in the thought. That thought depressed her so much, she once again, quite firmly this time, put all thought of Lord Huntingdon from her mind.

Once her pillows were well-pummeled and shaped to her liking, she set herself to deciding just exactly what was needed when they went shopping for the girls. Three gowns for Margaret. Two for every day and one for good. And perhaps a good dress for Mary. The twins tended to damage their clothing far more than their older sisters ever had and needed nearly everything, which was an expense she worried about for all of five minutes, but then it occurred to her that Baby Alice was very well outfitted so that was a saving. One grew so quickly at her age which meant she had acquired new mourning clothes when her father died, so that was all right.

Poor child. She had been forced to wear mourning for all of her young life. The reminder of her mother's death saddened Lydia, drawing her thoughts into the not so distant past. She wondered if her mother would have liked Lord Huntingdon. She wished she knew more of just who and what the man was, had been . . . would be? And then she reminded herself such thoughts were outside of enough and that she had already determined she would not waste time thinking about him.

So she fell asleep and dreamed about him instead.

Which, she decided, when she woke to the clear but subdued predawn light, was far worse. So, what to do

to keep her mind occupied and off topics that would
do it no good? Formerly, she would dress in her habit
and take herself off to the stables, saddling Angel for
a hard ride over the countryside; but Angel was no
longer there, and several grooms *were*—and would still
be sleeping. It was much too early to wake the hard-
working young men, one of whom had been ordered
to ride with her whenever she rode the new mare. Much
to her disgust.

At that point Lydia remembered the new piano. She
would don her habit; but then she would practice until
she thought the grooms were stirring, and *then* she
would take Marigold out for a run before the children
roused and needed her.

It wasn't that she wished to postpone her ride. But,
out of consideration for the youth detailed to go with
her, she felt forced to await a more reasonable hour of
the day. The order had made her particularly displeased
with Lord Huntingdon, who, although he obviously had
control over the doings of her siblings, did *not* over her.
She was not an Easten. Besides, she was far too old to
need a guardian!

It was, therefore, with a sense of ill usage she went
down to the salon and seated herself at the new piano.
Then she felt something far different when she recalled
that the piano would not be there if it were not for his
interfering lordship. And *then*, irritated by her roiling,
unstable up-and-down emotions, she played the angri-
est and most violent music she knew in an effort to
work off the tension such emotions roused.

What was more, the music helped. She went to the
stables much more in charity with her world.

Hours later, after Lord Huntingdon accompanied
them to a tailor, Jasper and James rejoined the distaff

side of the family in the inn yard where they had left the carriage. James was bubbling over with all he had seen and done that day.

"He did what?" asked Lydia, staring at James in growing horror.

"A complete wardrobe, Liddy," reiterated the glowing boy. "New shirts and everything. Even a watch," James ended on an awed whisper.

"I have my own watch as well," said Jasper somewhat more complacently, "and two new coats and trousers and shirts and small-clothes and I don't know what all. Now," continued the older boy, "he's gone to look at carriages. Liddy, he said we were to ask that you ladies order a luncheon be served in the private parlor he ordered before we set off for the tailor's. I asked about that last, and he says he doesn't think it proper for us to sit in the common room. And we will have sweets as well as roast and vegetables—"

James grimaced at the mention of vegetables.

"—and something for everyone to drink and . . . I don't remember what else. But Aunt Eunice will know, will you not?" Jasper hugged his aunt, who fended him off and pushed him away. He grinned at her as she resettled her hat and scowled. "Well, you *will*. And he means to look at carriage horses this afternoon while we are at the waterfront. He says there are donkeys, Liddy, and bathing machines, and we may each have a dip if we wish and I don't know what else."

Somewhere deep inside her, Lydia felt a hard, cold ball of fear. What did Lord Huntingdon think he was doing? Surely, with all the expense of restoring Easten Meadows, he shouldn't be spending money so wildly on frivolities such as watches and carriages. And to order shirts and small-clothes made up for the boys was outrageous. She had already bought material from which Eunice, Margaret and she herself would sew such

things. She must have a talk with him and soon before
he ran poor Jasper so far into debt he would never recover!

Perhaps, she tried to excuse him, it was that he did
not understand that Jasper was not so wealthy as were
the people he must know in London. She supposed
that there it was common to be extravagant. And perhaps the womenfolk living there hadn't the time to do
proper white work for their families and that was why
he had ordered shirts. Or perhaps. . . .

Oh, she didn't know, but a carriage and horses and
such a very large bill at the tailor's and she herself suc-
cumbing and ordering a fourth outfit, a new habit, for
Margaret to encourage her in her riding. Even if it *was*
a sturdy material, which could be turned and restruc-
tured later for Mary, she should not have succumbed,
perhaps.

And now they were to order a feast in a private parlor,
and why didn't Eunice object? Why was she calmly guid-
ing the twins into the inn, asking for the owner and . . .
and serenely ordering him to provide an impossibly
large meal for them all.

Oh, dear, had the whole of the family run mad? Was
she alone in her concern for Jasper's pockets? Surely it
was just thoughtlessness on the part of his lordship. He
simply hadn't counted up what all this was costing, perhaps. He wasn't thinking of a future in which Jasper
must provide his sisters with dowries and for which the
poor boy must save every penny. And there would be
the roofer and the other workmen at the manor and
the roofs for the tenants and hedgers and new farm
equipment . . . and was there no end to it?

Where were the funds to come from? Surely his lordship didn't mean to mortgage Jasper's property. But
how else could he deal with so much expense?

The money she and Jasper found in a bound and

locked chest in his father's room had surprised them
and pleased them, since it meant they could pay local
bills immediately, which was just as well since after doing so, they were told they had headed off an irate delegation of local suppliers who had meant to come out
to the estate en mass and demand that their bills be
paid. Instantly. Which would have been excessively embarrassing for everyone if they had not found the
money. The chest had been a wonderful windfall, but
there had not been so much coinage in it that his lordship could cope with all he was doing.

Surely there was not enough. The tightly coiled, cold
fear began to unwind and change to hot anger. Which
upset Lydia a great deal when she found it interfered
with her appetite and she could do no more than pick
at all the lovely food the inn provided. She couldn't
even enjoy the fancy walnut cake which came in along
with treacle tarts and a trifle for their desert.

"What's the matter with you?" asked Eunice when
she managed to corner Lydia with no small ears nearby.
"Are you feeling ill?"

"Ill?" Lydia laughed harshly. "Ill with worry. Ill with
fear. Ill with the thought our fine lordship will run Jasper so deeply into debt he'll never recover!"

Eunice frowned. "Because he provides a few elegancies along with necessities?"

"That piano must have cost a fortune. And watches
for the boys . . . particularly a boy like James who is just
as likely to take it apart to see how it runs as he is to
take proper care of it! And a new carriage and horses
and, Eunice, James tells me he has ordered shirts and
small-clothes which you know we always sew for them.
It is a ridiculous extravagance. If he spends all Jasper's
money in such a lavish way, then how will Jasper provide
the girls with dowries which he must begin doing in
only a very few short years. Two years for Margaret or

perhaps, stretching it a bit, three. And then Mary and
then the twins and finally little Alice. Well, she of course
is only a baby, so it will be a while before *she* requires
such a thing, but Eunice—" Lydia finished over and
around the fingers which had been pressed to her lips.

"You are hysterical," scolded the older woman.
"Calm yourself."

"You don't understand . . ."

"No, I believe it is you who doesn't understand. *Nothing* has been provided for a very long time. Much is
needed. There are bound to be heavy expenses in the
beginning."

"Fancy meals at the inn? Watches and pianos and
that mare he bought for my use when I'd no need of
one? And clothing which might be provided much
more cheaply from our needles than from a—"

Once again Eunice stopped her tirade in the most
direct way possible. This time Lydia nipped the fingers
covering her lips. In response, Eunice glared, but she
did remove her hand.

"The only thing about which you have been correct,"
she said, "is that we must cancel the order for shirts
and small-clothes. We are, as you pointed out, quite capable of providing those, and we shall do our duty in
that respect. I will discover from Jasper where the shirts
were ordered and cancel it myself. You bought a very
nice selection of linen and cotton materials for that purpose."

"I believed myself quite extravagant in what I ordered," said Lydia bitterly. "I see I've no notion of what
extravagant means!"

Eunice chuckled, called Jasper to her side and, after
determining where the shop was to be found, went off
to cancel the one order, telling the boys they were to
take good care of Lydia and their other sisters and that

she would find them along the promenade. And they were *not*, she insisted, to enter the water without her.

"Perhaps she is worried she'll drown if she is not with us," suggested James.

"More likely she fears we'll drown if she is not there to watch us," retorted Lydia.

And then could have bitten off her tongue for her bitter thought. She must not, she told herself firmly, take her anger out on the wrong person. The person deserving her sharp tongue was not available, so with difficulty, Lydia put aside all thoughts of the terrible spendthrift ways of his fine lordship and did her best to help the children enjoy their treat of a few hours among the amusements of the fashionable seaside town.

Lord Huntingdon, feeling quite pleased with himself for a day's work well done, awaited the Easten family's exit from the water. He paced slowly up and down the landward side of the bathing machine, wondering what Miss Cottrell had bought for herself.

He pictured her in a sprigged muslin gown like the one floating past him just then, the young lady flirting up at him from under her parasol and quite chagrined he didn't even seem to see her. And then he wondered if she wouldn't look better in the clean, neat lines of the walking dress approaching from the promenade, the grosgrain ribbon emphasizing the woman's striking figure and repeated along the ribs of her parasol . . . but no, perhaps it was too stark.

Another lady, a friend of the first, had on a slightly more ornate walking dress covered by a short pelisse held together by simple frog closures. Miss Cottrell would look charming in a similar gown, but in a rose color rather than the almost muddy green from which this gown had been constructed.

Perhaps she had ordered a new habit. He had noticed

that her old brown habit was extremely well worn, shiny in spots from wear and revealing one neatly mended shoulder seam where, very likely, she had parted company with her horse and the seam opened. Yes, very likely she had ordered a new habit. He tried to envision her in a dark blue habit with military collar and braid here and there but decided that would not do. Again something less stark in structure. Perhaps with a white shirt and lace at the throat and wrists the way it was in the portrait of his mother that hung in the study opposite another of his father standing by his favorite hack, his hand half-covered with lace as well and tapping his riding boot with his crop, the longer coats of that earlier era standing out stiffly around his hips.

Yes, lace would look very well on Lydia, he decided, and wondered what modiste the women patronized. He was almost certain Lydia would not order lace. Dare he modify her order, ask that the lace, which would be so very flattering, be added?

Reluctantly, Rafe set aside the notion. It would not do. Word would get around that he was ordering clothing for the young lady, and her reputation would be in shreds. Perhaps he might have Miss Eunice do it for him. He imagined Miss Eunice's response and shook his head. That thought, too, must be put firmly aside.

In fact, all such notions must be put from his mind. James had just poked his head out of the back of the bathing machine and ducked back in. The boy hadn't seen him, but his appearance meant the others could not be far behind. When they appeared he would suggest they stroll up around Prinny's Pavilion before returning to the inn. There he would order a light repast and something to drink, and then they must be on their way home. It would, very likely, be dark before they reached Easten Meadows, as it was. He sighed. He did not particularly enjoy traveling in the dark, and could not for the life of him remember if there was to be a moon later.

He would be late returning to Roger's, too, but that didn't bother him. He had found the company the evening before excessively boring and was glad he would miss dinner and, with luck, much of the evening. Perhaps his rudeness would convince the marquis's dark-haired cousin there was no hope for her, and she would turn her eyes in some other direction. Back, he hoped, to the young man who was traveling with the Littledon cousins and obviously had hopes where the young lady was concerned.

Another thing Rafe could do without were the young man's black looks whenever the girl set herself to flirting with him!

It had been particularly painful last evening to force himself to listen politely to the chit's unmusical playing when, only a few hours earlier, he had reveled in Miss Cottrell's exceedingly delightful performance. The sounds coming from the child's fingers were more than usually painful in contrast to the lyric expression that had issued from the piano at the Meadows.

Ah! There they were!

"Did you enjoy the sea dip," he asked Lydia.

Before she could respond, Miss Eunice grinned at him. "I have always been enthralled by swimming. The greatest of good fun! I enjoyed myself immensely." She scowled what was obviously a pretend scowl at James. "And would have been still more entertained if that brat—" she pointed at her nephew, "—had not insisted on splashing us all at each and every opportunity!"

"I quit when you told me to," said James, thrusting out his lower lip.

Miss Eunice grinned. "So you did. Because you knew that if you did not—" she glared ferociously "—I'd grab a very good hold of one ear and dunk you, did you not?"

James grinned, finally realizing his aunt was teasing him. It was not something she did often, so it was no wonder he hadn't immediately recognized it for what it was. The bantering went back and forth between aunt and children with giggles and chuckles and even the occasional full-throated laugh, and it was lost on the others that Lydia was exceedingly quiet.

She was pleased to discover she could eat a few of the tiny sandwiches provided by the inn and a small bowl of berries and cream. Then, finished, she took the twins to the convenience at the back of the inn, returning to discover that Eunice was about to go off on the same errand with Margaret and Mary.

While waiting for their return, she sorted through the packages which had been delivered to the inn, discovered the one she wanted, and allowed the remainder to be carried out to the carriage. She followed with the twins, tucking them inside and climbing in after them while Lord Huntingdon was answering a question James asked about the high perch phaeton parked near the far wall of the inn yard.

Huntingdon returned to discover her inside the carriage. He opened the door. "I had rather hoped you'd return to the Meadows in my curricle, Miss Cottrell."

"I think I'll be needed here, my lord. You'll have to excuse me."

He was startled by how hostile she sounded, but nodded, and backed away to allow Mary to climb up, then handed up Margaret, who shyly gave him her hand when he held out his own. Last he handed up Miss Eunice. "The boys can ride with me, which will leave you a trifle more room. We'll follow you and be available if anything unwarranted should happen. Not that it will, of course. Not where one of Lord Maythorn's carriages is concerned." He grinned up at the Maythorn driver and winked. The driver nodded, but obviously hadn't much of a sense of humor and, just as obviously, slightly resented Huntingdon's jesting. Huntingdon sighed softly. He didn't seem to be doing very well all the way around.

The next few days Lydia managed to avoid Lord Huntingdon. She didn't know what she would say to him but was quite certain she would *not* say it, whatever it might be, in any form acceptable to polite society!

At first Lord Huntingdon felt irritation that he kept missing any opportunity to speak with Miss Cottrell. Eventually it dawned on him that she was deliberately avoiding him. He was deeply hurt by her behavior even as he wondered what he could have done, this time, to insult her to the point she would have nothing to do with him.

The letter arrived from his aunt, and although he had concluded it was true, he was still relieved to be informed in so many words that Miss Cottrell had, indeed, been born within wedlock but that the marriage had not been approved by her grandfather. In fact, Lord Charingham was so thoroughly angered by it, he had disinherited his daughter and refused to have anything to do with her from that day forward.

"So. Now you know," rumbled Kenrick as he cut his breakfast beefsteak into small pieces.

"I think I've known all along. If I'd not been responsible for those children and if the silly chit hadn't behaved in such an odd fashion, it would never have crossed my mind she was anything other than legitimate." Rafe grinned. "I feel a bit of a fool for allowing the children to bamboozle me in that way. I should have laid out my problem before Miss Eunice at the beginning and demanded the truth."

"Which would have been all very well, given the situation. But what if you had discovered she was born on the wrong side of the blanket?" asked Roger.

Rafe compressed his lips, but Kenrick chuckled his deep-chested, rumbling laugh. "Easy," said the big man. "He'd have seduced her and set her up somewhere in a neat little house."

"It isn't funny," said Rafe defensively. "Not at all funny."

"No, don't suppose it is—" Kenrick smiled placatingly and then spoiled it, "—to you."

"Kenrick . . . !"

"Peace, peace. What else has your aunt to say?"

"She will be at the Chase by the end of the week and will see that everything is ready for the arrival of my wards."

"And of Miss Cottrell?"

"Well, of course."

"You consider her a ward, as well, do you?" asked Roger, smiling slyly.

Rafe felt heat in his throat and was glad of his high neck cloth. "She is not only of age, but not an Easten. I do not think of her as my ward, but I do consider her necessary to the well-being of the children," he finished somewhat primly.

"Oh, of course. We understand exactly what you mean." Kenrick chuckled.

"I had thought, Kenrick," said Rafe coldly, "that I would invite you to join us. Now I'm not at all certain I will do so."

"Couldn't come in any case," muttered the larger man, his ears reddening.

"Ah!" exclaimed Roger. "We can conjecture Miss Maddy has returned from Ireland, can we not?"

Kenrick, rarely put out for long by anyone's teasing, merely grinned before stuffing another piece of meat in his mouth.

"Roger? Will *you* join my party now your own has moved on?"

"You needn't call it a party in that odious way, Rafe. My cousins stop here every year, both on their way south in the spring and then again when they return home from London. I can hardly meet them at the door and tell them it is inconvenient when I've room enough for an army in this old barracks!"

Rafe sighed. "I know. I was merely irritated more than usual by your young cousin's antics. She did no more than any young woman does who is on the prowl for a title, so I don't know why I found her in particular such a nuisance."

"Never before have you had your mind occupied by your own flirtation," suggested Roger, lifting his glass to inspect a bowl of buttered mushrooms. He shuddered. "What is this?" When told, he shuddered again.

"Ah! Excellent," said Kenrick. "I asked if they might be added to the menu. I'll have some, Jeffrey," he finished, speaking directly to the footman.

"I will *not*," said Rafe, waving the man on when he would have stopped as he rounded the table to Kenrick's seat. "I do not know how you eat the things for breakfast. Roger, you have not said if you will come with me."

"I would like to, but . . ."

"You needn't stay here for me," said Kenrick, correctly interpreting the glance cast his way. "I have been thinking of moving my traps over to an inn nearer the McCormicks' in any case."

"You have found it possible to approach Miss Maddy, then?" asked Roger, curious.

"Up to a point. Only up to a point," said Kenrick,

grinning. "So far, that point has been quite good enough to keep me nearby."

"You aren't thinking of courting her seriously, are you?" asked Roger, alarm added to his curiosity.

"I . . . don't know. She is a fascinating lady."

"She is not, exactly, a lady, old man," said Roger gently.

"She isn't? Well, she isn't the other thing either!"

"Have you met her?" Rafe interrupted the obviously tart response Roger was about to make.

"No." Roger compressed his lips before bursting out with, "And I've no desire to meet her!"

"I *have* and I agree with Kenrick. She is definitely not the 'other thing' as you so deftly put it, Kenrick. What she is is Irish gentry. So I, too, do not understand why you are pursuing her."

For a moment Kenrick chewed thoughtfully. "I don't know that I know either. I know she fascinates me. I know she doesn't bore me. And that she doesn't treat me to the vapors if I say something not quite in line. Nor does she expect me to hold back my steps to a mincing little gait. And she knows a great deal about horses."

"Which are your passion." Roger sighed. "Beware, friend. I would dislike it more than anything if you were caught by an adventuress."

"I doubt very much," sighed Kenrick, sounding somewhat aggrieved, "if I'll be caught, because she isn't doing any chasing."

"Which may be the most subtle form of chasing there is."

Rafe noticed that Kenrick's temper, usually slow to rise, was definitely simmering. "Roger," he said, "Kenrick is a big boy. He'll not do anything foolish."

Roger's brow arched. "Are you quite certain about that? What if he actually marries the wench?"

"If he does, it will be because that is what he wishes to do. And not because she has somehow tricked him into it. I have faith in Kenrick."

"I, on the other hand, am exceedingly suspicious of the female of the species. Including the one in whom *you've* an interest."

"You haven't met her either."

Roger lounged back in his chair and frowned slightly. "I do sound something of a cockscomb, do I not? Making pronouncements about women I haven't even met?"

"I always said he was the brightest of us," rumbled Kenrick, pretending to look pleased with himself.

"So you did. Roger, will you or will you not join my house party?"

Rafe didn't see Kenrick solemnly nod his head or notice that Roger grimaced in response.

"If," said Roger, finally, "you very much wish my support, then I suppose I must agree to accompany you back to Huntingdon Chase. Besides—" he brightened, "—if your aunt is to be there, I know I'll enjoy myself. I don't believe I know a sprightlier little lady. Now, if she were only twenty years younger, I might think seriously of marriage." He adopted a sad look. "Unfortunately, they don't make any like her anymore."

"I will inform Miss Eunice we will be leaving early next week. At least, I believe the new clothes should be ready by then, and if they are, I'll ask her to see that everyone is prepared for travel."

"You have everything moving along at the Meadows?" asked Roger.

"Yes. Thanks to your agent. He convinced the farmers to try the new methods I wished introduced. And the man I've hired seems competent to oversee the repairs. I will have to return with some regularity until I am certain of that, but everyone will be far more comfortable away from the noise, dirt and smells of what must be done to put that manor back into shape."

"You've made miracles already."

"Yes, well, if the old miser hadn't had all that coin he probably liked counting, along with the surprisingly large amount invested in the funds, I couldn't have done it half so quickly. As it is, all will soon be settled, and Jasper will have quite a nice income . . . assuming I can keep him from falling into bad company." Rafe grimaced at the thought of bear-leading the boy through the shoals of a London Season. "He won't have sufficient for gambling in the hells or going wild at the tracks."

"You'll manage it. I believe the boy has pretty good sense already," said Kenrick, finishing the last of his mushrooms.

"Say rather that Miss Cottrell instilled proper values which makes my job much easier. Kenrick, I have noticed you are no longer doing your job."

"Old Herbie was itching to take over." Kenrick grinned. "So I let him." He shrugged. "Besides, you only asked me to teach the children as a means of keeping me away from your beauty. I've my own interest now, so you needn't concern yourself."

"Which comment reminds me," said Roger dryly, "that we *do* have something about which we must worry."

Kenrick growled, frowned, and then exited the dining room, closing the door with a snap.

"Oh, oh," said Roger softly.

"You should know by now that to push him usually makes him go exactly the way you wish he would not!"

"Yes, I suppose I should know that." Roger sighed. "Rafe, do you think I should stay here after all and keep an eye on him?"

"Do you think it will help?"

"No."

Rafe grinned at the simple response. "Then, you might as well come and enjoy my aunt's company, might you not?"

Again Roger sighed. "I'll come." He eyed his old friend. "But mostly because I wish to get to know this young lady with whom you've become enamored."

"Ah. The misogynist must see what sort of female can come between himself and his friend? What happened to you that you so thoroughly dislike women?"

Roger grinned. "I don't believe I dislike women so much as I distrust them. We'll see."

"So we will." Rafe wondered if he dared ask the obvious next question and discover why Roger *distrusted* women. He decided he did not. "And now I'd better be off and tell Miss Eunice my news."

Nine

"Go *where?* Eunice, you know I cannot do such a thing."

"Of course you can, Lydia. In fact, you must."

"He can hire a governess, a real governess, and I will come to the dower house. I'll stay with you."

"That might be possible if I were to be there myself, but I will not."

"Will not?" Lydia's air of confusion faded. "You? You, too, are invited to Huntingdon Chase?" And then she blushed furiously at the dry look she received. "I do not mean," she went on hurriedly, "that there is any reason why you should not. It is just that I'm surprised he would ask . . ." She trailed off, knowing she was making bad worse.

"You needn't feel *quite* so stupid as you think you should," said Eunice at her driest. "I suspect I was invited merely to assure you are properly chaperoned. His aunt will be there, of course, but a London matron! Well. We all know about them, do we not?" For a moment Miss Eunice pursed her lips in a shrewd look. "Very likely she's a flighty piece who will not concern herself with a spinster she believes was invited merely because Lord Huntingdon's wards require the young woman's presence. It was quite proper of his lordship to invite me, and I cannot help but think better of him that he did so."

That she might have been asked to join the exodus to the Chase simply because the children required her presence had not crossed Lydia's mind. His lordship had, more than once, revealed he was no better than other men who stared more blatantly, not to say *rudely.*

True, his lordship's manner was less easily read, and he was never rude, of course; but she had come to realize he was *flirting* with her. More elegantly. More subtly. But obviously with the same thoughts in his head as those others. It had been the fear that away from the Meadows she might be fool enough to succumb to his lures that led to her intemperate words and the impropriety of actually inviting herself into Eunice's home.

"It is true," Lydia said, "that the children will be happier if I am there." She frowned. "I wonder. Do you suppose the nursery and schoolroom floor includes a suite in which you and I may live?"

Eunice very nearly choked on the laugh she was forced to swallow. "I am certain we will be properly housed, my dear," she responded after an internal battle against an impolitic remark. It would be unwise to say anything to further to upset the chit. *Not* when she was on the verge of agreeing.

Luckily Lydia missed both the sly note and the suppressed humor. "I suppose, if proper provision is made for us so that we are not underfoot as it were . . . well, then, if you approve, then I suppose . . ."

Lydia realized she was dithering and firmed her mouth above that already firm little chin. She did not want to go. She wouldn't!

"Eunice," she said, speaking with only a trace of belligerence, "I truly do not wish to leave the Meadows, and what is more I believe I *should* not. I will stay in order to oversee the work his fine lordship has ordered."

Miss Easten scowled. "Nonsense. The new agent will do that. Lydia, I detest people who interfere in the lives of others, but I am about to do so. When his lordship asks for your decision, you will—" she glared one of her most powerful glares, "—*politely* respond that of course you will go."

"I . . . don't know if I can."

"Be polite?" If anything, the glare, which had been as good as it ever got, improved on itself. "Furthermore, you will cease and desist from this ridiculous attitude you have developed toward his lordship."

"You do not understand. I truly fear for Jasper's future. You were not about when we counted the coin in that chest."

Eunice paused. It was true she had no notion of how much was available to the guardian in his need to right the wrongs of years. At the time Lydia and Jasper had been so awed by the magnificence of their discovery, she had rather assumed it a fortune. On the other hand, their attitude had been based on the need for immediate payment of the bills at local merchants, *not* at re-roofing the manor or buying carriages.

"No," she said at last, "I was not. But you fret about things you know little about. It would be better if you simply asked for an accounting."

"I've no grounds, Eunice." It was Lydia's turn for a quick, sly look. "As Jasper's aunt, *you* might do so."

"But *I* haven't a distrust of Lord Huntingdon, have I?"

Lydia ran the notion of discussing Jasper's finances with his lordship through her mind, playing out the scene in which she confronted him and demanded to know the details of her brother's inheritance, demanding also that Lord Huntingdon justify his expenditures against the estate. But no. She could not see herself

facing him with such questions. She shook her head.
Definitely not.

"I cannot. You know I cannot."

"Of course you could if you truly wished to do so,
but you don't. You don't wish it for the simple reason
you might discover he knows exactly what he is doing,
and if you found that were true, you'd no longer have
an excuse to avoid him."

Lydia looked at Eunice, horror in her eyes.
"Surely . . ."

"Surely I do not believe that is your reason for sus-
pecting him of gross dereliction of his duty?" Eunice
adopted a patently false look of deep thought. "Do I
not?" she asked. She shrugged. "To the contrary, I fear
I do. You are afraid of him."

"Afraid? Of him? Why would I be afraid?"

Eunice gave Lydia a look which had the younger
woman blushing. *"Exactly,"* said Eunice smugly before
she stalked off to enjoy herself immensely in a rousing
good argument with the new butler involving the
proper way to polish the best silver. Not that there was
much to polish, of course. That was another thing her
brother had sold off.

Lydia watched her go. "Exactly *what* did she mean by
that?" she whispered, very much afraid she knew.

But it would not do. Definitely not. She had not,
would not, could not, *must* not fall in love with his lordship! Especially she must not if he were the sort who
would thoughtlessly put poor young Jasper deeply in
debt just so that everything looked properly up to the
knocker at the Meadows.

Lydia frowned. Assuming, of course, he was the reckless spendthrift she thought him. Eunice did not seem
to think so.

Lydia's mind was in a muddle, which had not been
an unusual condition for days. But, instead of trying to

smooth it all out and make sense of it, Lydia went off
to the laundry to order everyone's clothing washed,
dried and pressed, ready for packing no later than Tues-
day.

Once she had assured herself the laundry maid understood, she went off to find Cook, who, since the ad-
vent of Lord Huntingdon, also acted as housekeeper.
With her Lydia had a long discussion concerning how
to deal with the house in the family's absence while it
suffered the indignities of repairs, painting, waxing and
polishing and all the rest his fine lordship had ordered
done in their absence.

That task completed, Lydia decided to reward herself.
After changing into her habit, she collected Mary, who
had quickly become quite a distinguished little equestrian, and went off to treat the girl to a gentle ride along
the lanes—a decision she soon regretted.

Mary, it became clear, was thoroughly incensed that
her eldest sister was on the outs with Lord Huntingdon,
whom Mary considered quite the best thing to have
happened to the Meadows in her memory. Not only did
Mary ask for an explanation of Lydia's behavior, which
Lydia would not give, but she insisted Lydia *not* behave
so much like a gudgeon.

Lydia would not promise to reform, but did, adopting
a meekness she did not feel, promise to try. But then,
despite an outwardly calm manner, she found herself
angry with the child for daring to berate her right after
Eunice had scolded her for exactly the same fault.
"Mary," she decided, "the groom will escort you home.
I have determined I want a harder ride than you can
yet handle."

And, basely deserting the young man who was supposed to stay with her whenever she rode, she took off
across the fields at a speed his hack could not have
managed in any case. Of course, in this case he would

have been unable to follow even if his horse were up to it. Not when he had been left the responsibility of the untried Mary.

And so Lydia was forced to explain to Lord Huntingdon when, worn out and careful of her equally tired mount, she returned home. She approached the stable from the side, but upon hearing an altercation going on around the corner and wishful to avoid still another scene, she dismounted. Leading her horse, she approached quietly and was astounded to overhear the voices of not only an exceedingly unhappy Mary, but an insistent Jasper and a disapproving Eunice.

"You cannot send him away," insisted Mary.

"If Lydia went off and left them, I do not see what poor Jamie was to do," said Jasper. "I tell you, you do not know Liddy when she gets the bit between her teeth."

"Miss Cottrell is aware she is not to go riding without an escort," said Lord Huntingdon in icy tones. "It was the groom's duty to stay with her."

"You would say he was to leave Mary behind on the road, alone, in order to obey that order?" asked Miss Eunice, her tone pure acid.

"It wasn't Jamie's fault," said Mary tearfully. "It *wasn't*. You cannot send him away."

"Not often but occasionally Lydia allows her temper free rein," explained Miss Eunice, more calmly. "She'll expect no one but herself to take the brunt of your anger. Certainly she would be surprised and unhappy if you were to blame the young man who was forced to choose between a fully adult and experienced rider and a child who has only begun to learn."

"He knew—" began Lord Huntingdon.

"He knew," interrupted Lydia, coming around the corner, "he'd been ordered back to the stable with Mary. If there is trouble here, it is not"—she looked at

the children—"did you say Jamie? Not Jamie's fault,"
she finished when Mary nodded.

"He had his orders."

"Pretend, Lord Huntingdon"—her voice dripped
ice—"if you are *able* that *you* are a young groom. You
are in attendance on two females, one of whom is young
and inexperienced and the other known to ride the
wildest horses available over all terrain and at all times
of the day. The experienced lady takes off on her own.
You have been ordered to ride with that lady whenever
and wherever she rides, but you are, now, left with the
child who has only begun her training. What would *your*
decision be?"

Rafe grinned. "Put that way, Miss Cottrell, I assume
I'd have done what Jamie did. Very well. I will not send
him away. On the other hand, you and I must talk, and
we will do it now. If you will excuse us, Miss Easten?"

Lydia found her arm grasped above the elbow and
had barely an instant in which to gather up her skirts
before she was led off in the direction of the side garden
at a pace she found difficult to maintain.

"You will, Lord Huntingdon," she began in a low and
intense tone, *"release my arm this instant."*

"I'll do no such thing. You, my fine lady, have been
avoiding me. If I were to release you, I'd take the gam-
ble you would run off and avoid *this* discussion as well."
He glanced down at her, his eyes narrowed. "I am determined you will not."

They reached an old stone bench which had been
set there in days when a large tree had shaded the area.
The tree was long gone, felled by a thunderbolt. One
corner of the bench had cracked off in its fall; but the
bench was stable, and it was isolated in the middle of
a largish lawn. They would know if anyone were to interfere, either by accident or by deliberately seeking
them out and, on the other hand, would not contravene

society's dictates concerning the impropriety of being alone together since anyone could watch what they did.

"Sit," ordered his lordship.

"Arf arf!" she said and held up her hands in the fashion of a begging dog.

Rafe rolled his eyes. "Please, Miss Cottrell, have the kindness to take a seat."

Lydia listened carefully but heard not the least sign of sarcasm. Of course, she heard nothing that might be taken for humor, either, so she feared that perhaps she had gone too far in her objection to being ordered around. She sighed and, sweeping her skirts to the side, seated herself.

"Thank you." He eyed her. "I would very much like to know how I have offended you."

"Ordering me to sit—"

"Miss Cottrell," he interrupted, "I am not referring to this moment. Some time ago I did something you resented very much or you would not have proceeded to do your excellent best to elude me. Unfortunately, no matter how I search my mind, I can think of nothing which would result in your taking me in such dislike you cannot bear to say so much as good day to me."

"You have done nothing to me."

He thought about that. "Then, the insult is that I have paid you too little attention? I am sorry, but I have been very busy organizing—"

"Nonsense," Lydia interrupted in turn. "You have insulted me in no way whatsoever. And I haven't a notion what you mean that I cannot bear to speak with you. We are speaking now, I believe?"

"You are not stupid, Miss Cottrell. You know very well what I mean."

She determinedly shook her head, refusing to acknowledge she had any notion at all what he was going on about.

"You cannot deny you've avoided me." He stared pensively down at her. "For days now."

Lydia bit her lip. "If I have insulted *you,* my lord, it was unintentional." *In actual fact,* she thought wryly, *it was in order to prevent myself from insulting you!*

"You have not insulted me. How could you when you will have nothing to do with me?"

"You are not my guardian, my lord. There is no reason why you should have to do with me."

"No reason . . ." Lord Huntingdon drew in a deep breath and let it out slowly. "No reason, Miss Cottrell? You cannot be so naive."

Lydia rose to her feet, her face red. "I must change out of my dirt, my lord," she said, again coating each word with ice. "This conversation has turned in a direction of which I cannot possibly approve." She turned on her heel and stalked off.

Lord Huntingdon watched her go. This time when he drew in a deep breath, it was a sharp one of anger. *With himself.* Somehow he had managed to sit with her, bantering away on everything but that which had brought them there: she must *not* ride off by herself, and he had managed to forget he had brought her out here for no other reason than to get her promise she would never again do so!

"What have I done?" Rafe asked Kenrick as the carriage took the three men to Baron Rovert's home late that afternoon. "She will not even speak to me."

The invitation to dinner had arrived unexpectedly early that morning. None of the three had wished to attend a country dinner where they would be required to do the polite to every young woman with any pretension to gentility and, on the other hand, to every old lady in the region who would state quite firmly they had known 'that boy' in his cradle even if they had never laid eyes on him before. Unfortunately there had been a note at the bottom of the invitation, handwritten by their host, which had particularly requested that they oblige him by accepting.

"Since when?" asked Roger, as always interested in the ups and downs in his friends' affairs. Even when he didn't approve.

Rafe's eyes narrowed. "I believe it must have been that day in Brighton. As I recall there was no problem when we set out. I believe it was only when I met them after finalizing the purchase of a strengthy pair for the carriage I'd ordered earlier that she turned into an icicle. I recall that she dripped cold water down my neck when I merely asked that she return to the Meadows in my curricle!"

"You saw to the boys and she to the girls?"

"Yes."

"Did you ask about their purchases? Show an interest in what they'd ordered?"

Rafe bit his lip, a frown creating a ridge between his brows. "I don't believe I did. But surely that isn't the sort of thing about which one holds a grudge for days and days. No, that isn't at all like Miss Cottrell. I don't believe it can possibly be anything so simple."

"You can't know that." Roger spoke so quietly it drew Rafe's attention as a more general comment would not. "Rafe, you *don't* know her. You can't possibly know her. Think, man. When you were merely an officer in the King's army, you might have looked seriously on a young woman in her situation, but not now. Now, unlike those days, you've a position to maintain. You have title, land, and wealth. You are expected to wed someone quite different from the penniless little spinster over at the Meadows, even if she is legitimate. Which you do *not* know. It would be just like your aunt to have a soft spot for her friend's daughter only because she *is* the daughter of a friend."

"But what she said . . . Miss Cottrell's mother's marriage, Charingham's disapproval . . . ah! You have forgotten my aunt's *second* letter. Miss Cottrell *is* legitimate."

"Your aunt said, in so many words, that the chit was the legitimate product of that marriage?" When Rafe nodded, Roger went on more gently. "She is still nothing more than an undowered spinster."

Roger's words deflated Rafe. He felt as flat as a silken bag awaiting gas for an aeronaut's ascent to the skies. Or perhaps one which was returned to earth and from which the gas had escaped, which was rather a different sort of thing. He turned to look out his window, staring into the rapidly deepening dusk. It grew dark, but he continued to stare, just as if there were something to see.

There was quite a surprise for him at the Roverts'. A colleague from Rafe's military days was among the guests. And it was the military man Lord Rovert wished to discuss. Rafe pulled himself out of his blue state for long enough to give his old friend a rousing commendation.

"Ah, then. I need not forbid the banns," said his lordship, a sad look about his eyes. "Can't say I'm happy about it. Military man, you know. Never know where he'll be sent next, do you? Could be the antipodes and then where'll my poor girl be? And what happens to her if something happens to him, hmm? But can't make her see sense, and if you say he's a good man, my lord, well, there you are, are you not?"

Manfully, Lord Huntingdon managed not to laugh. All desire to laugh faded when it occurred to him that in the not too distant future he would very likely be suffering the same qualms when deciding whether to approve, or not, some suitor for Margaret's hand.

He drew in a deep breath. "My lord," he told Lord Rovert, "we can only do our best when it comes to allowing the young women in our care to wed. We find out what we can about the man, and we try very hard to determine exactly why he wishes to wed our chit. You may commiserate with me in future when it is my turn to approve my wards' choices."

"Ah, yes. Forgot. Don't envy you that job. Not when you've so many girls to see to!" He shifted ground and asked, "How are you managing? Is it possible things may be improved at the Meadows?"

The ensuing discussion of land use and modern farming methods took them far afield, conversationally speaking, to the point a harassed footman finally tracked them down in his lordship's library and suggested, politely if with a little strain, that they might like to join the other guests in the salon so that Peeps, the Rovert butler, might perhaps announce dinner.

Dinner was informal. There were only a dozen or so guests, and the table was small. Everyone talked to everyone else. For nearly two hours Rafe managed to forget his problems while reminiscing with his old friend about army days, although they were careful to choose stories proper for feminine ears . . .

. . . at least, they were until the ladies left and the covers were removed!

The stories became a trifle warmer, recalling, as they did, one or two Spanish ladies and an evening of carousing after one particularly sanguinary battle, none of which would edify the ladies. Then they answered questions about the tactics used in other battles, an equally unsuitable subject for feminine ears. Nevertheless, Rafe was glad when the time arrived they might

climb back into the carriage and return to Maythorn
Hall.

While Rafe dined at the Roverts', Lydia spent several
hours at the new piano. She played simple pieces while
trying very hard to order her thoughts. What, she wondered, was she to do?

Eunice insisted she must attend the children at the
Chase. That would put her still more in Lord Huntingdon's way because, there, he would live under the same
roof. At least now he left each day and returned to
Maythorn Hall for the night. She had the evenings in
which to stiffen her backbone and reaffirm her decision
she must have to do with him as rarely as possible.

Because if she did not avoid him, she might weaken
and have far too much to do with him, and that would
not do. Before his arrival, when they didn't know if she
would be allowed to stay, they had joked that she could
make her living on the streets. It had been no more
than a joke.

Then.

Now, if she were to follow where her heart led, she
would very likely find herself ruined, and when his lordship tired of her, what had once been jest would become
fact. Because once ruined she could never again have
to do with her brothers and sisters, and that was not to
be thought on. She loved them far too well to allow
temptation in the form of Lord Huntingdon to separate
them forever.

But could she avoid him once they were installed at
his home? On the other hand, would he defile his home
by seducing her there under his own roof?

Surely not. The thought lightened her fears to say
nothing of her playing, and she segued from a rather
ponderous piece into a more lilting one.

Surely Lord Huntingdon would cease his pursuit of her, such as it was, once he was in his own home. Surely it was only boredom that led him, on occasion, to look at her in that especially warm fashion that made her heart beat harder and a trembly feeling weaken her limbs. Feelings she couldn't understand, which she felt were exceedingly odd, since, in the past, all she had felt was disgust when other men looked at her in that particular way.

But home where he had duties, where he could entertain friends living in the neighborhood, surely there he would not bother her, and she could make a far firmer effort to rid her heart and mind of impossible dreams.

She played a rather loud and clamorous chord. How, in any case, had it come about that at her advanced age, she had begun dreaming such dreams?

So utterly pointless. And so very melancholy making, to say nothing of rather contemptible. If, for some reason, she wished for a man in her life, then she should pin her hopes on the vicar. Or perhaps the curate was a better prospect. Assuming she *wished* to wed, of course. Who was she to raise her eyes to an *earl*, for heaven's sake!

No one, was the only possible response to that. A *nothing*. She hadn't so much as tuppence for a dowry, which meant, she suddenly realized, that even the curate would find her unacceptable. With that morose realization she went back to playing more dismal music. Obviously she had reached an age of foolishness, and she must work hard to pluck all folly from mind and heart.

Which meant she was right back to the question of whether she could do so if she were to live under his lordship's roof.

Eventually, the question still unanswered, Lydia went to bed. Once settled against her pillows it occurred to

her that since she had no choice but to attend the children, who were to go to the Chase, the question was
rather irrelevant.

She would just have to do the best she could.

After a midday stop the second day of their journey
to Huntingdon Chase, Lord Huntingdon settled Margaret and Mary beside Roger in his curricle, left the
boys to be driven by his own groom in his own curricle,
and climbed into the carriage with Miss Easten, Miss
Cottrell, the twins and little Alice. He had noticed how
frazzled Miss Cottrell looked when they had arrived at
the inn. Miss Easten had seemed somewhat ragged
around the edges as well. And he wondered why the
toddler wasn't in the large baggage carriage provided
by Roger where she was supposed to ride with the maids
and valets. He asked.

"She'll not remain so long with the nursery maid.
She wants me."

"And you persist in indulging her wishes so that she
will not learn that she cannot always have you?" he
asked gently. "That you are not always available to her
every demand?"

The twins, recognizing anger when they heard it even
when spoken softly, looked at each other. Very quietly
and very carefully they settled back in their seat, folding
their hands in their laps. There would be, they knew,
no more nonsense on their parts. Not if they had the
least little bit of sense! Lord Huntingdon had not yet
asked about their behavior, but he very well might. And
they, too, had not behaved so well as they ought. Lord
Huntingdon was not one on whom one might impose
merely out of boredom.

Eunice, recognizing exactly what ran through the
twins' minds, smiled sardonically. "Little Alice isn't

spoiled, my lord. At the moment she is upset by the change in her routine. She will settle down again once we've arrived and she realizes her days will be much as they have been before all this upset."

"But will they? Continue in the old routine, I mean. I have decided that the girls will have a holiday from their studies." He grinned at the suddenly hopeful look the twins cast him. "It will, of course, also give Miss Cottrell a holiday from the necessity of supervising them."

"I have no need of a holiday," said Lydia, hugging Alice a little too firmly for the child's comfort. "Oh, dear." She turned the baby so she could look at her. "I'm sorry, my love. Did I pinch you?"

Alice nodded, put her finger in her mouth and leaned back against Lydia.

"Tell us more of the story," demanded Felicia. At least Lydia thought it was Felicia.

"You said you would once we were on the road again," said Fenella.

"It would not be fair to Margaret and Mary," demurred Lydia, not at all happy with the thought of telling tales while Lord Huntingdon listened.

"They won't care," insisted Felicia. If it was Felicia.

"Besides, they are having a treat we won't have," sighed Fenella.

"That isn't fair to us," finished the other.

"If Miss Cottrell is tired of telling tales, perhaps I might tell one," suggested Lord Huntingdon, leaning back in his corner.

"You . . . ?" Felicia looked at Fenella and Fenella looked back.

"Can you?" asked Fenella. Her doubt was obvious.

"I can only try," said Huntingdon, chuckling. "Have you heard about the Minotaur?"

"Of course."

"But we like it," said the other twin, poking her sister with her elbow.

"Yes. It's a good story. Please tell it," said the first speaker.

So Huntingdon did, wondering at the frowns he saw on the girls' faces at various points.

"Thank you, my lord," said one child when he finished.

"Yes, thank you—but why did you change it from Liddy's story?"

Lydia, blushing for her charges' manners, said, "There are many different ways of telling a story, child. Lord Huntingdon simply told you a bit more of the tale than I have ever done. That is all."

"More?" asked Rafe.

"I have started the story a trifle later than you and did not discuss the necessity of the Athenians sending off their young each year."

"Hmm. I see. And what do the girls know of Athens?"

"It is in the eastern Mediterranean, my lord. It is ruled by the Turks," said one twin.

"It was from Athens Lord Elgin stole the Marbles which are now displayed in London for the interested viewer," said the other carefully, obviously quoting someone or something. "Except it is also said he did not steal them."

"That was in an article in a copy of the *Edinburgh Review* the vicar loaned us," said Miss Easten, scowling at the twins. "I was not aware you girls perused it."

Felicia grinned pertly. "Sometimes."

Fenella scowled. "When there is nothing else to do."

"We take it to one of our special places."

"Where we will *not* be bothered."

"And when we have questions, then we ask Liddy," finished Felicia.

"I can imagine the questions!" Lord Huntingdon

grinned at Lydia, who blushed. "The vicar has a subscription, then?"

"I believe it must be so. Or someone gives it to him."

Lord Huntingdon sighed. It appeared Miss Cottrell was still at outs with him, and he still had not discovered why. Giving it up for the moment, he took a small travel chess board from his pocket and asked if the twins knew how to play. They did not. Rafe spent most of the next three hours helping them learn the basics and was rather startled by how quickly they picked up the nuances.

They arrived at the Chase as the shadows were drawing out, the sun behind them as they drove up the long drive. Lord Huntingdon descended from the Easten carriage and helped the others down.

"Welcome," he said, "to my home." His gaze connected with Lydia's and managed to hold her look for a long moment. And then his aunt's voice, also welcoming, forced him to turn away.

Eunice looked rather shocked. "Milly?" she asked hesitantly.

An equally shocked reply rang out. *"Uny?"*

The two women fell into each other's arms. Lydia, who had never seen Miss Eunice so demonstrative, found her mouth hanging open and closed it with a snap. The twins looked from their aunt to their sister and jerked at Lydia's arm.

"Liddy!"

"Who is she?"

"An old friend, obviously," said Lydia, not looking away from Eunice, who was walking off with Lady Freward.

"When and where," asked Rafe softly, "do you suppose they met?"

"At school?" asked Lydia hesitantly. She didn't think Eunice had been sent away to school.

"Perhaps during a London Season?" suggested Rafe.

"I can't recall that Eunice has ever mentioned joining the season."

"Then, at a house party, perhaps?"

"Would they develop such a close relationship at a house party? I assumed such times were inappropriate to . . . to getting to know one another to such a degree."

"It depends how the hostess has planned to occupy her guests. Such a party can, occasionally, allow the growth of great intimacy." He shrugged. "But it is a mystery we may solve on another occasion. Will you come now to inspect the nursery floor and see that all is as you'd wish it?"

"Surely you do not suggest I'd demand changes!"

"If something is not to your liking, then yes you should ask that it be altered to suit."

"Nonsense. We are guests in your home. It would be outside of enough if I were to do such a thing."

"These children are my wards, Miss Cottrell," said Rafe with a touch of severity. "They are not my children, but they *are* the next thing to it. I want everything done as it should be for their care and comfort."

Lydia was silent for a long moment. "I have been reprimanded quite nicely, have I not?"

"I didn't mean it that way," said Rafe, on the defensive.

Lydia sighed. "No, of course you did not. Nevertheless, I understand your wishes and will act accordingly."

This attitude didn't please Rafe either, but he didn't know what he could say or do to change the situation. Especially when the twins stood there, hand-in-hand, looking from one to the other with an expression of interest on their identical faces.

"Let us go up, then," said Rafe, turning away.

The nursery floor was nearly all anyone could wish.

A trifle drab, it was in need of fresh paint. It had, however, been thoroughly cleaned, the toys sorted and,
those which did not need repair, set out for the children's pleasure. A bookcase held books of varying tastes
and difficulty, and there were two maids detailed to aid
the Easten nursery maid and an elderly nurse who took
to little Alice in an instant.

Alice, not always easy to please, was obliging enough
to be equally happy with the nurse.

What there was *not* was a suite Eunice and Lydia
might occupy. Lydia felt rising panic and pushed it
down.

"You will, of course, be housed on the guest floor,"
responded Rafe when she bluntly asked where she was
to sleep.

"I will be too far from the children. It will not do."

"It will do very well. There are enough women here
to care for your brothers and sisters. You will not be
needed every instant. And someone will send for you
if it happens you *are* needed."

"I do not like it."

"You, my friend, have had the responsibility for them
forced upon your shoulders for many years now. It is
time you recognized that you no longer bear the full
weight of that responsibility."

Lydia felt her skin pale. "I am to be removed from
their care?"

Huntingdon growled. "Why do you always put the
very worst possible interpretation on anything I say or
do? Of course you will be needed. And once you return—" Rafe silently added a caveat to the effect they
might *not* return, none of them, "—to Easten Meadows,
then you may take up your duties as the girls' governess.
But for now you will behave as any guest would do and
enjoy yourself!"

"Is that an order, my lord?"

"That you enjoy yourself?"

Lydia nodded, her lips compressed.

"And if it is?" he asked after a moment.

"Arf arf, my lord."

He laughed. "Am I behaving tyrannically again? I do not mean to. It is merely that you will not accept that you are no longer the children's sole support and mentor. There are others who are to see to their daily needs. And still others who love them and wish them only the best. And some who feel you have been put upon to an extraordinary extent and wish, very much, to lighten your burden. And don't," he added when she opened her mouth, "say it has not been a burden! I am aware you have shouldered your duty and carried it out without becoming bitter or taking the children in aversion. But the burden is no longer so great that on occasion you may not enjoy yourself. Have I made myself plain at last?"

"I . . . don't know that I know how to enjoy myself."

"You do not dance?"

She blushed. "I have never learned. I have, actually, worried about how I am to teach the girls. Margaret in particular, given her age."

"That is something with which we must deal, is it not? I will see to it. To continue, do you not play cards?"

"Never."

His brows arched.

"My mother did not approve. Please do not offer to teach me that skill!"

"Hmm. Well, you may learn if you wish or not. As you decide. Do you paint? Do needlework?" The brow which had lowered reared up again. "Read novels, perhaps?"

She chuckled. "I paint well enough to teach the girls the basics. I do not do fine needlework. At least, no more than is necessary to teach the stitches. And, finally,

I do *not* enjoy reading novels." She cast him a look of mischief he had not seen since their first acquaintance. "So, my lord," she challenged, "just how do you suggest I go about enjoying myself, as you insist I am to do?"

"I must think about it, must I not?" He took her arm and led her from the room which the younger children were exploring.

Mary was already involved in a book, curled up in a window seat. Margaret had brought along some needlework at which she was surprisingly capable given Lydia's lack of interest.

Lydia looked around, wondered where the boys had gotten to, decided their tutor would see they did nothing too outrageous, and allowed herself to be led away. She was guided by a maid to her room which she discovered was next to Eunice's, connected to it through doors in a shared dressing room. Already her small wardrobe was hung or on shelves.

The maid asked if she would like hot water or a bath.

"Water for my hands would be appreciated, thank you. I will, however, want a bath this evening. Before I change for dinner."

Lydia spoke absently, giving the order naturally and without thinking. The maid was prone to approve her manner. She would inform the others that Miss was obviously one who knew how to go on, and if it were true, as rumored, that she would become the next Lady Huntingdon, why she would do very well—even if the poor lady were destitute as a church mouse, which her gowns revealed her to be.

Lydia didn't notice the maid's approval. Her mind was fully occupied elsewhere: it had only just occurred to her that her wardrobe was not at all suitable for a sojourn in a home of the size and quality of Huntingdon Chase. Once again she wished she were housed on the nursery floor and had nothing to do all day but take care of the children. Her beloved siblings.

That, it occurred to her, would in itself be a holiday. No responsibility *but* the children? *What bliss.*

And then she put her mind to choosing between her ruche-trimmed black and her flounced black for that evening's dinner which, she had been informed, would be served at the exceedingly late hour of six o'clock.

Lydia had no way of knowing that Lady Freward felt it an uncomfortably *early* hour when she had set it in accordance with country habits. She had known she must do so, and so she did and would suffer accordingly. How she disliked living in the country and how very glad she would be to return to London.

On the other hand, there was Uny! Dear, dear Uny who had come to her rescue in that long-ago and nearly forgotten foolishness of their grass time! Saving her from a foolish elopement and seeing, young as she had been, that there was no scandal.

Where would she be if it were not for Uny? Certainly not living comfortably just off Grovesner Square in a comfortable house and with a more than adequate widow's mite. *That* was certain if nothing else were. So she would endure the days at the Chase with good will and not complain.

Not even at dining so unconscionably early!

Ten

Lady Millicent Freward, who had looked at no one but Uny when the coach arrived, now took one look at Lydia Cottrell and, pale as a ghost, was as near to fainting as she had ever been. *And a good thing it would be, too,* she thought. "What have I done?" she muttered.

She glanced once more at her young guest, shook her head, and walked out of the room without a word. Lydia stared after her. "What was that all about?" she asked Eunice, who had been about to make the introduction.

"Blessed if I know."

Eunice had reveled in rediscovering an old friend in the woman who she had assumed would be a skitter-witted social matron of the worst sort. Now she revised her first good impression of Lady Freward's maturity and decided she had been correct in the first instance and tricked into complacency by her surprise in meeting an old acquaintance.

"Addlepated female!" she exclaimed, irritated with herself.

Lydia stared at the closed door. "I know I am not notably socially adept, Eunice, but I cannot think of an occasion where I've done nothing at all and frightened my hostess out of her wits."

"Frightened?" Eunice screwed up her forehead.

"Now I think about it, there may have been a touch of fear to begin with. But only to begin with. In the end, I am certain she was merely irritated."

"My gown, perhaps?" asked Lydia after a moment. She brushed her hands lightly down the skirt, grabbed a handful and shook out the flounce. "It isn't particularly stylish, but I hadn't thought it that bad."

"She didn't look at your gown. She looked at your face."

"Then, perhaps that explains it. She saw my mother in it."

"Ah, yes! If she knew your mother?"

Lydia nodded. "Lord Huntingdon told me she did."

"I didn't know. Well, you are like enough to her that it could very well have been a shock to Lady Freward."

Eunice, happy to have solved the mystery and once again free to be pleased with her old friend, moved toward the armless sewing chairs pulled in an arc around a small fire. She settled herself and took from her oversized reticule a shirt she was sewing for James.

"Come sit yourself down, Lydia. You know I detest hoverers. And if you have no work by you, then you may thread a needle and gather that other sleeve for the cuff."

While Eunice organized Lydia, Lady Freward demanded of Rafe's butler where she would find her nephew and, the information forthcoming, stalked down the side hall to the small library in which Rafe toiled over his accounts. She threw open the door.

"I said—" Rafe didn't look up from his work, "—that I was *not* to be disturbed."

"You will just have to forget all that nonsense—" Lady Freward waved a hand at his desk, "—and attend to me. Disaster is about to strike and it is all my fault and you must do something. Instantly."

Rafe glanced up, and a splotch of ink fell to mar the ledger page. "It is *your* fault and *I* must do something?"

"Rafe, she is as like her mother was at that age as two peas in a pod!"

"She?"

"Your Miss Cottrell. I don't know what to do."

"Aunt, I have never seen you wring your hands. In fact—" Rafe settled back in his chair and looked thoughtful,"—I don't believe I have seen anyone do it, excepting actresses on the stage. Take a deep breath and begin from the beginning."

Lady Freward took an agitated turn about the room and returned to stand before him, her hands flat on his desk and her weight leaning into them. "Rafe, I have done a very stupid thing. I invited Charingham to dinner."

"Here?" Rafe rose to his feet as if pulled by strings.

"He is a near neighbor," she said as she, too, stood erect.

"Tonight?" His brow looked thunderous.

"Tomorrow." Lady Freward looked simultaneously contrite and full of mischief. "Don't stare at me as if I were a two-headed lamb. I told you it was disaster. But, Rafe, how was I to know the chit was the image of her mother?"

Rafe dropped back into his chair. "Aunt, sit yourself down and tell me about Charingham and his daughter. I have yet to hear the full story."

"Maggie was as lovely as Miss Cottrell. She was also, well—" Lady Freward searched her mind for a kind way to say stubborn, "—a trifle headstrong?"

"Her daughter has inherited something of that trait as well as her looks," said Rafe dryly.

"Oh, dear. They both got it from Charingham, who

is, I fear, one of the most stubborn men I have ever known."

"Hmm. Go on."

"Well, during her first season Maggie met a certain young man. He wasn't ineligible in the usual sense, Rafe. You mustn't think that. In fact, he was such a serious old sober-sides no one could understand what she saw in him. A younger son, Rafe. Destined for the *clergy!*"

"No question of a fortune hunter?"

"If you'd seen them together, you'd have known it wasn't that."

"So," said Rafe when she didn't go on, "they fell in love, but Charingham forbade the banns?"

"It wasn't quite so bad as that. Lady Charingham was alive then. She talked him into merely insisting the couple wait a year. Maggie was very young, you see."

"And our very-much-in-love couple agreed?"

Lady Freward sighed. "Maggie didn't want to. But young Cottrell talked her into it, insisting that obedience to one's parents was proper and important." She sighed again. "Worst of all, they were not to communicate during the year."

"The idea being that young Maggie would forget her unsuitable young man and obediently and properly wed someone worthy. Someone approved by Charingham?"

"Yes."

"So?"

"So Maggie fretted and fretted and lost weight and became so morose Charingham grew quite frightened for her health."

"He relented?"

"No. He took her off to Italy."

Rafe wiped the ink from his pen and carefully laid it aside. "Aunt, you are making a very long tale of this."

"They returned for the season, and I hardly knew

Maggie. She looked as if a million pounds had been spent on her wardrobe, true, but she was changed in far less obvious ways as well. She wouldn't dance, for instance, and she wouldn't play cards and she read improving books and, for a time, joined a bluestocking circle, but soon dropped out because she decided her dear Cottrell wouldn't approve.''

"*Aunt.* Cut line.''

"The long and short of it is that Cottrell returned to town exactly a year to the day after they had been parted. He entered Charingham's door just as Maggie came down the stairs. Lord Charingham happened to be there as well, and he saw his Maggie's face the instant she saw Cottrell. He knew he'd lost.'' Lady Freward sighed. "Charingham, as you know, hates losing.''

"But he agreed to the marriage?''

"Not exactly. He told her that if she insisted on wedding her nobody, she'd cease to be his daughter. Cottrell explained to her how serious it was for a daughter to become estranged from her family. She asked him if that meant he was no longer willing to marry her. He said that of course he wished to wed her, but not if she would regret it. They were wed, and so far as I know, Maggie never regretted a moment of it. Not while Cottrell lived.''

"But Cottrell died?''

"Scarlet fever got into the village.'' Lady Freward sighed. "He sent Maggie and young Lydia to his mother's, but insisted he must stay to care for his flock. Of course he caught the fever.''

"So Mrs. Cottrell was widowed with a young girl on her hands and no way of supporting herself since her father had repudiated her.''

"Yes. She and I still wrote at that time. Occasionally. She accepted Easten's proposal because she felt herself a burden on her in-laws, who had a large family and were not all that well off. Cottrell's mother did what she could for Lydia; but she, too, died when the girl was ten or twelve, and after that I'd no more word of either of them."

"Now, my dearly beloved aunt, explain why you were so impudent as to invite Lord Charingham here for dinner?"

Lady Freward frowned. "I don't know if I can. An impulse, of course. The Charinghams are our nearest neighbors. I loved Maggie like a sister and should not have lost track of her; but my own family was growing up, and I was busy entertaining for Lord Freward and well—" she grimaced, "—perhaps I felt guilty? I was determined to set things to rights, I think. So stupidly reckless of me!" She rose to her feet and paced the room. "Rafe, I didn't know the chit would look so exactly like Maggie! I don't know what to do."

"Charingham knows I am guardian to the Easten children," said Rafe slowly. "Do you think there is a possibility he accepted, is coming here expecting to discover what he can about his granddaughter? About all his grandchildren, come to that?"

"Perhaps," said Lady Freward and continued with equal deliberateness. "But did he know *his grandchildren* were coming? I think it unlikely he meant to do more than gently feel out what he could in a rather general sort of way. Pick up bits and pieces about Miss Cottrell from your conversation about your wards."

"You did not tell him I'd he bringing the family here."

"Of course not." She couldn't help looking a trifle guilty. "Why would I do that?"

"You say he hates to lose. Does that also mean he hates to admit he's wrong?"

"Of course. How could it be otherwise?"

"Aunt," said Rafe, grinning wolfishly, "it is my considered opinion *you* have a problem."

"Don't tease, Rafe."

"But you do. Have a problem, I mean. The problem of how to word a note to his lordship explaining you were unaware I would bring my wards and Miss Cottrell home with me and that you wish to inform him the company at dinner will include my wards' aunt, who is sister to the late baronet, and Miss Cottrell, of course."

"And?"

"And what?"

"Do I suggest he might prefer to stop at home?"

"Of course not," said Rafe, pretending to be shocked. "How could you possibly be so impolite? You are, my dearest of aunts, merely informing him of the company, as is correct. Oh, I suppose you'd better add that the Marquis of Maythorn is also my guest."

Lady Freward brightened. "*That* will bring him. He is looking for support in the Lords for a proposal he wishes to make concerning the current rash of divorces. An abomination, he says."

Rafe grinned. "There are rumors, my dearest of aunts, that Prinny himself would divorce his princess in an instant if he could discover a way of doing so."

"If," said his aunt, her voice dripping acid, "it were allowed for *women* to bring a bill against their *husbands,* I have nary a doubt that Princess Caroline would elbow her way to the head of the line and demand divorce in her own right! It would be a very long line, too," she finished a trifle more thoughtfully.

Rafe frowned. "Aunt, surely you haven't thought. You are suggesting women would make of themselves outcasts merely because they are unhappy in their marriage?"

"Yes. Exactly. And not a few of them would be better off!" A conscious look passed over her features. "Oh, dear, you set me off, did you not? It is merely I know a lady who is regularly bea—" She closed her lips tightly. "Never mind that. Do forget I said a word, Rafe. It is not at all proper of me to say such things." She made a sound which was very near a giggle. "Even if I *do* sincerely believe them!"

On that unexpected note, she turned on her heel and left the room, shutting the door with a snap. Rafe, both brows arched high, stared after her. Did she truly believe there were so many desperately unhappy wives in the world?

Rafe ran his mind over the marriages he knew intimately. Remembering one of those marriages, he frowned. Perhaps, he decided, his aunt was more correct in her thinking than he would have thought possible. He tucked the notion into the back of his mind along with another to the effect that if he were lucky enough to win her, he would do nothing to make *his* wife feel that the stigma of divorce would be better than remaining at his side.

The next morning Lydia was walking in the extensive park land with her sisters when Rafe saw them. He reined his gelding away from his route to the stables and joined them, dismounting. When the child asked him, more or less politely, he lifted Mary onto the animal's back.

"You indulge her," said Lydia, not entirely happy with the imperious note she had heard in the child's request.

"The children's ponies will arrive soon, and then they may continue their lessons." He eyed Lydia's gown, remembered the well-worn black she had had on the previous evening, and wondered, again, what she had purchased for herself during their day's shopping in Brighton.

An unexpected thought crossed his mind. A very nearly unbelievable thought: perhaps she had bought *nothing*. But surely she was not so different from the women he knew, any one of which would have quite easily outrun the carpenter, after so long with nothing new for her back.

"You are very quiet," said Lydia, wondering what was running through his mind to make him scowl so.

"Hmm?" Rafe forced himself to put his questions to one side. He would ask his aunt later to discover what she could. "Have you enjoyed your walk?"

Lydia smiled. "Yes, my lord. We discovered a folly and a lake where a very pleasant summer house provided shade and an obliging servant provided lemonade. We have traversed only a small portion of the rides through this wooded area, and we were thinking it quite time we returned to the house. The twins have run on ahead and are determining our route so that we will take the fewest possible steps to reach it."

"Hmm. And, in their exploration, taking a great many extra steps themselves?"

"I suspect it is so, my lord."

They chuckled. "Well, Margaret, do you like my home?"

"Oh, my lord, it is the most wonderful house I have ever been in. A maid took me to the picture gallery, my lord. It was quite wonderful. Would you—" she cast a hesitant look toward Lydia, who nodded permission, "—perhaps sometime when you are not too busy, tell me about the artists?"

"I'd be happy to do so, but you might prefer my aunt as guide. She knows much more than I about the portraits. You see, she grew up here. I did not. My uncle was a bit of a recluse, so I wasn't allowed long visits. In fact—" he smiled, "—there were few enough visits of any sort!"

"I will beg the indulgence of Lady Freward, then."

"You enjoy art?"

"Oh, yes, my lord. I am not very good, but it is such fun to try to put on paper the wonderful things we see."

"You are remiss, Miss Cottrell. You did not show me Miss Easten's sketchbook."

Lydia blinked and then chuckled. "It never occurred to me you'd be interested, but, when you have a moment, you might ask Margaret to show it to you herself." She smiled at her sister. "She has some talent, I think, especially for portraits."

Margaret blushed. "Oh, no. It is only that often, when I've finished my work in the schoolroom, there is nothing to do, so I have practiced on my brothers and sisters, you see. And Liddy, of course," she said and grinned impishly.

"Don't you dare show his lordship that awful cartoon!" scolded Lydia, but she laughed. "So very revealing, I fear."

"You do caricatures?" asked Rafe, curious. This was a side of serious little Margaret he had not seen previously.

"Occasionally. Usually when I am angry with someone. I find it a delightful means of revenge, you see."

"Hmm, if only everyone could feel satisfactorily revenged in such a way, there would be no fights and no wars," said his lordship, only half in jest.

"I doubt it will catch on as a means for keeping the peace between nations," said Lydia, a dry note to her tone. "Ah! There is the house. Now I wonder where the twins have gotten to." She looked around, frowning. "Oh, dear. I hope they haven't lost themselves."

"Felicia and Fenella?" Margaret chuckled. "You are likely to find them inside a hollow tree or, perhaps, up one. Those two couldn't become lost if they tried."

Rafe frowned. He looked back into the woods, then

toward the house. Seeing a young gardener, he called to the lad. The boy was sent off to the stables with Rafe's gelding while Margaret and Mary were told to go, immediately, to the nursery floor and remain there until further notice.

"What is it, my lord?" asked Lydia, suddenly worried.

"I am responsible for the chits, and I have not done my duty by them. I should have had a word with them about the differences between the Chase and the Meadows. While here, they must not go off by themselves for hours at a time as they do at home. I have been led to understand that at the Meadows very often no one knows where it is they have gone?"

"True."

He sighed. "I fear I've been far too lenient since inheriting, so we've a few poachers I've refrained from prosecuting. Also, there is a tribe of gypsies who camp along one of the streams with some regularity. I've heard of no serious problems with either, but the twins would be a powerful stimulus to villainy, would they not? We'd best see if we can track them down. Where, exactly, did you see them last?"

Lydia led him back to where the twins ran off, calling back that they would search out the shortest route to the house. Rafe looked around, wishing he had grown up here so that he would have some notion of what might draw the adventurous twins' attention. Margaret's notion of a hollow tree was fine. All the girls were likely to find there were spiders and cobwebs or the odds and ends of an old nest or perhaps the bones of some small creature who had been dinner for a larger.

The idea the girls might actually have climbed up one of the great trees and be trapped was more worrying. They might fall, be badly hurt . . . *where* would the young idiots have gone? He sighed. He would not turn out his workers to hunt them if he didn't have to, but it might become necessary.

"They like to be alone, together, is that it?"

"Yes. I think they also find it amusing they can hide themselves away where no one is able to find them. Not even James."

"We'll start in that direction. Please follow along behind me and, as much as possible, in my tracks."

"We are well to the side of where they ran off."

"Yes. And, where possible, we'll stay away from where they trod. See? If you look carefully, there are signs of the twins' passage. They bent the grasses as they ran through them. And *there*"—he pointed—"they turned into the woods. Let us follow, but again stay to one side. I am afraid we may have to deal with some briars, and I must watch for nesting birds. It will not do to get on the wrong side of my keeper . . . ah! There. I believe they again changed direction, but they appear to be heading toward the house still."

They worked their way through the heavy undergrowth, Rafe pointing out, here and there, signs of the children's progress. And then, for a distance, he saw absolutely nothing that would indicate they passed this way. They returned to where he had last seen sign of their passage and studied the ground, the thickets and even the one tree that looked as if it might be scalable if the chits helped each other.

"I fear we've lost them . . ."

"No, we haven't!" Lydia had begun a cautious circle of the area. "I've found another footprint. It goes that way."

"*Away from the house*. Have they lost their sense of direction."

"I doubt it. There is another print. We are lucky we've had damp weather, are we not? Even here under the trees, the ground has been softened enough they scuff

up the dead leaves and occasionally even leave a footprint like that one." Lydia pointed yet again.

Continuing, Rafe searched out each slightest clue to
the twins' passage. He felt it lucky they had not attempted to avoid leaving the trail of clues. Finally he
and Lydia were rewarded with still better ground: a gentle stream, the soil next it was damper than elsewhere,
and occasionally there was even a scrape where a small
shoe slid perilously near the water. The footprints
turned upstream which was just as well. The Romany
camp was downstream. Not five minutes later, they saw
the girls lying full-length, one arm of each dangling
into the water, fingers moving lazily.

Rafe stopped Lydia, and they watched. "Tickling fish.
I wonder who taught them that trick," he said softly.

"I haven't a notion. I didn't know what they were
doing. I suppose we'd better let them know we've found
them?"

"Let them play now that we know where they are. We
will sit here on this rock and talk a bit."

Lydia sat stiffly. "Well, my lord?"

"You have yet to tell me why you are angry with me.
And do not," he said, a trifle exasperated, "tell me you
are not, as you were about to do."

She closed her mouth and remained silent.

"I do not like it that we are at odds."

"I have nothing to complain about."

"Then, your anger is irrational? I think not. But I
can think of no reason for you to act as you do."

Lydia drew in a deep breath. "I am worried about—"
She could not do it. "The children," she finished.

"In what way are you worried about them?"

"Seven children, five of them girls." She edged toward the real problem. "A small estate. Jasper will have
his work cut out for him if he is to provide for them
all."

"I am doing my best to see that he will," said Rafe slowly. "I know he will have something of a struggle, but it shouldn't be too bad. You mustn't worry, Miss Cottrell, but if you have specific questions, perhaps you could ask them another time. Because," he finished, looking at the twins, "Fenella has caught a fish. Shall we join them?"

Much later that day Lydia wondered how he had known it was Fenella. Because it *was*. She asked.

"I see it now! You wish to wed her!" Lady Freward's expression revealed she had just come to that happy conclusion. The beaming smile which followed indicated how pleased she was by the notion. "So, why do you not?"

"There are several reasons. In the first place, she will not allow me to show her the least favor. She turns cold as ice if I lightly flirt with her. There are occasions when I wonder if she even likes me."

"I suppose that might put a spoke in your wheel," mused Rafe's aunt. "Why would she dislike you?"

"At one time I wondered if it might not be jealousy," said Rafe, fiddling with his pen. His aunt had again accosted him when he was working on accounts. "She had complete care for the children for so long, you see. Then I come along and make decisions which affect them and without consulting her. I have tried to do better in that regard since it crossed my mind, and I think, on occasion at least, she approves. This morning, for instance."

Lady Freward tipped her head. "What happened this morning?"

"The twins did what they often do at home. I knew of the habit, but it didn't occur to me they'd try the same stunt here. They ran off on their own," he explained when his aunt frowned slightly. "We found them tickling fish in the trout stream. Fenella actually caught one. They were debating whether they dared keep it when we joined them. I allowed them to take it to Cook for their dinner, but told them I would see them in my study once they had washed their hands and put on clean frocks." He grimaced. "I felt Miss Cottrell turn stiff as a plank at that order."

"Why?"

"I allowed the twins to run on ahead of us and asked exactly that." He sighed. "You see, she feared I meant to punish them for disappearing. Punishment," he added when Lady Freward's frown deepened, "at the Meadows involved severe whippings. The children's father occasionally drew blood. Especially on the younger boy, who would not allow himself to show his fear or pain. To make him do so, the old man would beat him still more badly!"

"Oh, dear. Why would he do such a thing?"

"There are, unfortunately, people who enjoy dealing out pain to others. I fear the late baronet was one of that sort."

"I . . . see."

"In any case, it was necessary to soothe Miss Cottrell and convince her I would never do such a thing. On the other hand, I was forced to convince her that some discipline is essential and that the twins cannot be allowed to run off on their own as they have done in the past. I had pointed out possible dangers but did so again and in more detail. She was forced to agree. I told her that if she promised not to interfere, she could sit in the study with us."

"She promised?"

"She didn't wish to do so, but it was the only way I'd have her there. I didn't want the twins thinking she would take their side."

"And how did it go?"

Rafe chuckled. "With difficulty. Have you ever talked to the twins?"

"I don't believe I've had an opportunity to do so."

"Make one. They speak alternately, finish each other's sentences with the first stopping and the second taking over with no break or the least stuttering. One becomes charmed by it and almost forgets there is a serious conversation going on. In any case, I did finally get their attention. I wasn't aware that since their mother died, I am the only person who can tell them apart. When they discovered I could, they suddenly became quite docile, paid me close attention and, in the end, looked at each other for a very long moment. Felicia said, *We understand and—*' at which point Fenella finished, *We won't do it again.*' "

"Did they promise?"

"They did." He grinned. "Individually but simultaneously. I have never before heard them speak as one."

"Well, I am glad that is settled."

"It helped that I promised them a room of their own, each of them having a key to it. Mitten found the keys and ribbons by which they hung them around their little necks. It was a solemn occasion."

Lady Freward chuckled. "I can believe it might be. What room did you give them?"

"One I used as my own on those rare occasions when a child and visiting here. It is a sort of box room in the attics. Not even Miss Cottrell knows where it is. A secret, you see, for the three of us."

"Hmm," mused Lady Freward. "I doubt very much Miss Cottrell appreciates *that.*"

"It was her notion."

Lady Freward's mouth dropped open. She closed it. "Miss Cottrell surprises me by her good sense."

"Yes. Me, too. Aunt, how am I to win her? And what

do I do about this problem with her grandfather? It would be embarrassing to wed her and then discover she would not entertain the old man when he has long been at the head of our guest list!"

"And for him, too. If he could not invite you to his parties. Not that he holds so many anymore, but the principle is there. The solution is quite simple, of course. We just have to reconcile the two."

One of Rafe's brows arched.

Lady Freward smiled, but repeated herself. "Somehow, Rafe, we must reconcile them. It is the only solution."

Eleven

"Lord Charingham," announced Rafe's butler in properly sonorous tones. He stood stiffly just inside the door, waiting for orders, Lord Charingham a few steps into the room before him.

Lydia, sewing the cuff to the sleeve she had previously gathered, stuck her finger and made a soft sound of irritation.

"My lord. How lovely to see you again," gushed Lady Freward, rushing forward with both hands extended.

"Hurumph." His lordship glowered from under bushy brows. His eyes flicked toward the young woman in black, her head bent low over her sewing. He looked back to Lady Freward. "Just stopped in the salon here to say hello, my dear. Came early, meaning to speak to the marquis before dinner. Politics, you know."

"Of course, my lord. Mitten, show his lordship to the library. And, Mitten, remember to ask what their lordships would like as a libation. It is dry work, talking politics."

Her hand on his arm, Lady Freward walked Charingham to the door and, as it shut behind him, sighed softly. She turned back to her guests, noting that Eunice scowled one of her patented scowls and that Miss Cottrell, her cheeks showing signs of embarrassment, still bent over her sewing, her handkerchief wrapped around her finger to prevent blood from spotting the shirt.

"Well." Lady Freward sighed again, this time dramatically. "That went better than I expected."

"You did not inform us you had invited Charingham," said Eunice, enunciating each word clearly.

"No. I thought perhaps if Miss Cottrell acted naturally, then the meeting would go better." Lady Freward frowned. "But, oh dear, of course there is still to be a meeting!"

"But"—Lydia rose to her feet, her little chin firmly in the air—"I do not *wish* to meet the man."

"Your grandfather, child!"

"The man who disowned my mother for choosing to wed the man she loved!"

"But still . . ."

"No," said Lydia firmly. "I will go to my room, Lady Freward. At some point, when the servants are not rushed off their feet with dinner, I would appreciate a light supper on a tray." She turned her back and, treading firmly, in an exceedingly controlled fashion, exited the room.

"But this is disaster!"

"Shouldn't have done it, Milly."

"I worried about Charingham's reaction. It never occurred to me to concern myself about Miss Cottrell's! Will she truly refuse to be introduced to him?"

"She is her mother's daughter."

"You mean she is stubborn as sin!"

"I mean no such thing. I mean her loyalties lie with her mother. She feels the insult to her mother as if it had been to herself."

"Insult . . . ," said Lady Freward slowly, drawing the word out. Even more slowly a smile grew. Then a chuckle. Finally a full-throated, surprisingly deep laugh. "My dear Uny! You have given me the answer!"

"I have?" asked Eunice warily.

"Of course you have. It was so very obvious, and I did not see it. Please excuse me?"

"Of course."

Eunice stared after her hostess, who tripped her way out of the room with the lightness of foot of a much younger woman. Eunice had already wondered how Milly managed to look ten years younger than her true age. Now, dressed for company, maybe so much as fifteen. She herself, she knew, looked older than her years, but she had spent the decades worrying about her brother's antics and fretting over his family's problems and the deterioration of the estate. It was no wonder she looked like an old hag in comparison with her friend.

Eunice, who from one year's end to another, never gave her looks a thought, found she felt just a trifle jealous of Milly. Then, always self-aware, she chuckled at herself for such foolishness and went back to the hole she was working for a button.

Lady Freward had no thought of complexions or hair or anything else of such a trifling nature. Instead she wended her way toward her nephew's library in which Lord Charingham would be lecturing Maythorn about his current obsession. Milly didn't particularly think about how she would approach his lordship. She simply relied on her quick wits and the notion put into her mind by dear Eunice.

Milly turned another corner and smiled at having met Eunice again. Dear Eunice, who had always been such a solemn thing, but with a dry sort of humor which caught one by surprise and made one laugh at the most surprising things. Dear Eunice, who had saved her from disaster and ostracism on that occasion she had been so foolish as to elope with the wrong man. Why had she lost track of Eunice as well as Maggie? Were there more old friends she had misplaced in the years when she had been involved in raising her family and keeping a busy husband happy?

Very likely there were. Once all this was settled, she would think about it. Friends were far too important to one's enjoyment of life to allow them to get lost. She must recover all her old connections.

But not now. Now she must deal with Charingham. For half a moment Lady Freward stared at the library door. Then, drawing in a deep breath, she opened it and strolled in.

"My dear Marquis," she said, brightly, "I dislike disturbing you in this way, but I must inform you a message has come and a messenger awaits your response."

"I'll go at once."

Lady Freward didn't quite smile at the alacrity with which Maythorn rose to his feet. She returned to the door with him where she whispered, "It isn't true. I wished to speak with his lordship, and you are in the way, you see?"

Maythorn winked and softly closed the door behind himself as Lady Freward returned to where Charingham sat, scowling, by the small fire. One foot, she noticed, was resting on a footstool. Was the poor man in the gout?

"Oh, dear, I hope not," she muttered, and then, more loudly, she asked.

"Gout?" His brows arched in surprise. "Oh, no. Lucky soul. Never been bothered with it."

"Excellent news, my lord, because I want words with you."

"You do, do you?" The brows lowered and formed a glower. "Well, I want a few with you, too."

"Ladies first," she said, knowing she was taking advantage of his old-fashioned ways. She smiled when he bowed agreement. "Well," she said, sobering, "I wish to know what you have done which demands an apology before that poor child will come face-to-face with you."

"Ashamed, is she? Well, she should be."

"I see you know exactly to whom I refer. And I believe I now understand why *she* feels so deeply insulted."

"Why should she feel insulted? Never set eyes on the chit!"

"Exactly."

He blinked. "What?"

"You never set eyes on her. And by your own choice. Instead you allowed her mother to suffer in a marriage which must have been hell."

"Been complaining, has she?" He showed his teeth in an unfriendly smile.

"No, she has not. Miss Eunice Easten accidentally let a few things drop into our conversations this afternoon. Actually, I doubt she knows how much she revealed. Then, too, my nephew has been put into a state of outrage by what he found at his wards' home. They were living in squalor, my lord. Old Easten crying poverty when he was nothing but a penny-pinching miser with a small fortune in the three percents! No servants, my lord, and that poor girl doing everything she could to keep up some sort of gentility. And *your fault,* my lord."

"Bah!" But his scowl had grown fiercer during her speech, his thick brows lowering over his deep-set eyes, half hiding them. "Brought it on herself. She knew . . ."

"If you refer to your daughter, as you must be, she certainly didn't know that her beloved Cottrell would die young simply because he was the sort who would do his duty, even when faced by a danger which might well give pause to the men in our intrepid army. Maggie's beloved husband died, as you well know, when her daughter was no more than eight. When Easten offered for her, she believed she'd no choice since she felt it outside of enough to be a further burden to her already burdened in-laws, and besides, there was no one to warn her what an evil little man he was."

"Evil? Nonsense."

"When my nephew arrived at the Meadows to take up his duties, it was some little time after the old man died. The younger boy still had healing strips on his back. How hard must you beat a boy before he bleeds and takes weeks to heal properly?"

"Probably deserved it," muttered Charingham.

"Even the girls received beatings."

His brows flew up, and he stared straight at her. *"My granddaughter?"*

Lady Freward hesitated. "Miss Cottrell? I don't know. I didn't ask."

The brows lowered again. "Don't see why you say it was my fault," he muttered. "Chit knew she'd get nothing of me if she married that prosy boor."

"Because she was deeply in love with a man of whom you did not approve, you cut her off from all contact with yourself. You are angry because her marriage to him was not the failure you predicted. Because she did not feel properly unhappy while suffering the deprivations you forced on her and her husband by refusing her so much as a dowry. And you did it claiming to love her. I do not understand a love which is so selfish! And then later, although you seem to have kept track of her in some furtive fashion, you allowed her to wed a known villain and, I suspect, reveled in her pain and the horror of her life."

"I did not!"

"Did not know what was happening to her, you mean?"

"Well, what if I did know. No worse off than a lot of women."

Lady Freward folded her hands and raised her eyes toward heaven. "Oh, Lord, if only I could pick up on *that* and lecture his fine lordship on why a *woman* should have as much right to divorce as a man has!" Then she dropped the pious pose and stared at her adversary. "If you have any imagination at all, will you think of how a daughter would feel watching her mother fade away to a shadow and finally, after still another successful pregnancy, happily die, certain *her* daughter would not allow the children of her second marriage to suffer more than could be helped."

"You can't know that," he said promptly.

"You did not receive a letter announcing that your daughter had died?" asked Milly, quite certain Miss Cottrell would have written a polite note.

"Is that what it was?" he asked carelessly. "I threw it in the fire."

"Ah. Then, when my nephew arrived, if he'd thrown Miss Cottrell off the property on which she has no call, and she'd been forced to earn her living, you'd have thrown a letter to that effect on the fire as well?"

Red rose up into Charingham's ears. "Deserve it."

Lady Freward cast him a startled look and then laughed. "Nonsense!"

"Sins of the fathers . . ."

"Ah!" Lady Freward triumphantly pointed an accusing finger. *"You admit it!"* she exclaimed. "Admit sin that is in *you,* her mother's father."

She grinned; he glowered, the red in his face still hotter.

"You insulted your daughter," her ladyship continued more gently, "by denigrating her quite proper if not brilliant choice of husband and by disinheriting her and ignoring all the pain and horror of her life since that husband died. Yet you persist in your wrong-headed ways even when you've the opportunity to set all to rights *and* a chance to meet and enjoy the company of a truly delightful young woman who is your first grandchild! Of course, by refusing to apologize to *her* you also deny yourself the company of your *other* grandchildren, one of the nicest group of youngsters I remember meeting."

"Other grandchil—"

Much surprised, Lady Freward was forced to conclude it had never crossed his lordship's mind the Easten children were also his grandchildren.

He glanced away. "Bah!"

"I had forgotten how very stubborn you are. If poor Lydia were not female and were not so much younger than you, then I believe I would urge her to send you a challenge so that she might revenge the insult!" She rose to her feet. "Miss Cottrell asked to have a tray in her room rather than sit at table with the man who insulted her mother. I have decided Miss Easten and I will join her. Good evening, my lord," she said as she exited, her voice icy cold.

Lady Freward found Mitten and informed him that the ladies would dine in the breakfast parlor, that the men would be dining alone.

"If that makes any difficulty, Mitten, we may dine either before or after the gentlemen."

"No problem at all, my lady," said Mitten, bowing low so as to hide the curiosity he felt certain his expression revealed.

Lady Freward then joined Eunice and told her what had happened and, when she had finished, wrote a quick note which she had a footman carry up to Miss Cottrell concerning the dining arrangement and asking that the young woman rejoin her and her aunt in the salon.

Lydia, reading the note, felt guilty for putting the household to so much work, but she felt not the least guilt for insisting she would not sit at table with the monster who left his daughter to the less than tender mercies of the recently deceased baronet!

While Lydia read the note and dithered, Eunice and Milly put their heads together.

"I am so very angry at the man," said Lady Freward.

"Never thought much of him myself," said Eunice gruffly. "Remember how he cut poor Wilberton that time and only because Wilberton disagreed with him on the question of the cut of Prinny's coat?"

"Oh! So long ago! I'd nearly forgotten. But Wilberton, you know, is very like him. Later they were the best of friends when they agreed about the King's choice of bride for Prinny—" she grimaced, "—only to fall out when, once again, they contradicted each other on something else which was, I am sure, equally silly."

The two women shook their heads, in full agreement.

"Men!" said Eunice. "You would suppose they had more sense since they have taken it upon themselves to run this world."

Milly adopted a thoughtful look. "You know, Uny, I sometimes believe it is more that women do not believe it *needs* running. I mean, if everyone simply paid attention to their own little patch in the scheme of things, then everyone would get along just fine, would they not?"

"Only if men did not interfere. My brother was constantly battling with his neighbors about property lines. And they were constantly threatening to sue if he did not keep his fences and hedges in proper condition, which he would *not* do unless forced. Not when it meant he must lay out the least little bit of his blunt!"

"I see exactly what you mean," said Lady Freward.

"But that does not help us decide what to do about Charingham and Miss Cottrell."

"Is it truly necessary to do anything?"

"I doubt if I am revealing secrets when I tell you my nephew wishes to wed her." Lady Freward laughed a delighted little laugh. "I see I am! It is true. He does. But there appear to be problems. The estrangement between Charingham and Miss Cottrell is only one of them. For instance, she treats poor Rafe very coldly. He says if he so much as attempts a mild flirtation with her, she turns into an icicle. Does that make sense to you?"

"Very natural in her."

"But . . . but . . ." Lady Freward stared. "Oh, but surely you mean very *unnatural?*"

"I meant exactly what I said. Despite her beauty, she has had only one offer of marriage and that one totally unacceptable. She has, however, although she will not discuss it, received at least one offer of an entirely different sort!"

"But she is a lady!"

"Her beauty draws men to her. But men she'd find worthy of wedding require a decent dowry before they'll ask." Eunice twisted her lips in a grimace. "At least, before they ask for *marriage!*"

"I see . . ." Lady Freward leaned forward, setting her chin in her hand and staring glumly into the fire. "You would say that she would not expect dear Rafe to be serious in his intentions."

"A London beau stuck in the country with responsibilities for which he did not ask? Possible entertainment right there at hand? Why would he *not* begin a flirtation? She might even suspect he wished to seduce her!"

"Yes, I suppose that is the way a wary young woman might think. One who had suffered from ill-considered attentions from badly brought up young men. Well, *that* may be easily settled. Rafe will just have to tell her he wishes to court her with marriage in mind!"

"Oh, yes, I can see him doing that. *'Miss Cottrell'* he will say. *'I wish to inform you that in future you are not to turn a cold shoulder my way when I flirt with you. I only do it because I wish to wed you,'* and she will respond with utter disbelief and will refuse to have anything more to do with him! Which I would understand entirely, would not you?"

Lady Freward cast her a baffled look. "What *do* you recommend?"

"We must somehow reconcile grandfather and granddaughter," said Eunice, echoing, if she had known, Lady Freward's earlier conclusion. "When we have done that, your nephew may make a proper offer for her hand, and she may then be approached fully in accordance with common practice."

"Oh, yes," exclaimed Milly, sitting back and looking scornful, "and then she will instantly ask if he decided to wed her only because her grandfather will give her a proper dowry!"

"Hmm. You are very likely right in that." It was Miss Easten's turn to lean chin on hand and stare into the fire.

The door opened, and Lydia strolled in. "Why so glum?" she asked.

"We are," said Miss Easten in a grumbling way, "wondering what to do with two stupidly stubborn people who refuse to see sense."

Lydia flushed. "You refer, of course, to my grandfather and myself."

"Yes."

"There is nothing to do."

* * *

The next day Lady Freward took up the discussion all over again. "If he were to apologize?"

"As if he would!" said Lydia. "But even if he did, that will not help my mother."

"Lydia, nothing can help your mother. She made her bed and lay in it with all the grace of which anyone would be capable," said Eunice. "In fact, she is now experiencing a far better world, as she much deserves, and you should not wish her back!"

Lydia had the grace to blush. "Still, I cannot forgive his lordship for putting her in the position she was in. He is a monster."

"No."

"My lady?" Lydia turned to Lady Freward, not certain she had heard correctly.

"Not a monster. Merely stubborn. When he says something unconsidered and the results are not what he expects, he is incapable of backing down." She shrugged. "He said he'd disinherit her, so he had to do so. He was not happy about it."

"How do you know?"

"I have known the family for many years. Your mother and I were dear friends. *She* forgave him, you know. She knew him well and knew he'd be sorry for it but that she could not expect him to change his mind. And she was sorry for the breach between them. Of course, she and her mother kept up a correspondence. To do so, she wrote me, enclosing a letter for her mother, which I would then forward as if from myself."

"I didn't know. When did my grandmother die?"

"I believe it was only a few years after your mother married Easten. I do know your grandmother had begun to suspect something was very wrong. She worried about it, I know, because she wrote asking me if I knew what the difficulty might be. But then she became ill. I believe it was one of those cases where one becomes partially incapacitated and can no longer speak clearly?"

"Oh, dear."

"Your mother asked me to attend the funeral in her stead. We didn't, of course, tell your grandfather that was why I went. But, then, he was far too distraught to care who attended. He loved her very much, you see."

"Perhaps as he loved my mother? Just so long as she agreed with his every dictate?"

"It is unbecoming in you to sneer, child," scolded Lady Freward, tapping her hand with her fan.

Lydia bit her lip.

"Their love became a saga in their own time, my dear," said her ladyship, relenting. "He waited a long time to wed her, and once wedded, I do not believe they were ever parted. I have heard that he spent very long hours in her rooms once she became ill. Day after day he would hold her hand. He read to her, fed her . . ." Once again she looked a trifle stern. "It was a deep and abiding love."

"Then, why was he incapable of understanding that my mother and father had such a love?"

Eunice looked at Lady Freward, who stared back.

"I wonder . . . ," said the one.

"Do you suppose . . . ," said the other.

"We must ask," said Lady Freward. She rose to her feet. "Now. Do come, Uny, I will need your support."

"Very well."

"What are you meaning to do?" asked Lydia, looking from one to the other.

"Why, is it not obvious?" asked Lady Freward.

"Really, Lydia, you are not stupid. But if you do not understand, we refuse to explain," said Eunice gruffly. "Come along, Milly."

Bewildered, Lydia followed them into the hall and heard Lady Freward ask that a carriage be brought

around on the instant. When the older ladies continued
to ignore her, Lydia headed for the stairs, meaning to
go up to the nursery.

But before she could do so, Rafe and Lord Maythorn
appeared, strolling toward her. Rafe hurried forward.
"Miss Cottrell! Well met. We are about to go riding.
Will you change and join us? I've a young gelding in
my stables I think you'll like. I will have him saddled
for you."

Lydia was torn. She hadn't ridden since leaving Easten Meadows, where she had become used to a daily
ride. Riding might also settle her confusion. "I will
change," she decided. Although it meant spending
time with Lord Huntingdon, Lord Maythorn would be
there as well. She would be well enough chaperoned.

But she was not. Lord Maythorn, after no more than
twenty minutes, pulled up. "Rafe," he called.

"Yes?"

"I must return to the stables. The devil's in it, this
animal has thrown a shoe. Oh, excuse me, Miss Cottrell!" he added, blushing slightly at his use of unacceptable language.

"We'll go on," said Rafe.

"Of course. Only meant to inform you."

"I don't think . . . ," began Lydia.

"Don't think," said Rafe softly. "You know you've not
yet had enough of a ride."

It was true. And they were on horseback. She could,
if necessary, ride away from him.

"Besides, I must apologize—" He reached for her
reins and pulled her horse to a walk. "Miss Cottrell, I
am sorry Charingham arrived last night with no warning. My aunt informed me, after the fact, that she'd
hopes of reconciling you to each other." He glanced
sideways at the mulish look that took up residence on

her features. "Neither of you were the least coopera-
tive," he finished, half-amused, half-rueful.

"I will have nothing to do with a man who could not
only insult my father by thinking him unworthy of his
daughter, but then treated my mother so shabbily it led
to her death at far too young an age! The only good
thing from her second marriage are my brothers and
sisters whom I could not wish did not exist. They are all
the family I need now, my lord. I want nothing to do
with Lord Charingham. He may be a blood relative, but
his behavior has been such I cannot like him and—" her
chin rose that revealing notch, "—again I say it, *I will
have nothing to do with him.*"

"Even if he can be brought to apologize?"

"Ha!" She repeated what she had said earlier to his
aunt: "As if he would! But even then I do not know
that I could forgive him. My mother . . . was not treated
well, my lord."

"No, she was not. Charingham asked questions about
you. About the children as well. Before he left last night,
I mean. He'd drunk enough to feel a trifle nostalgic, I
think. And perhaps," Rafe added thoughtfully, *"more*
than a trifle lonely. His beloved wife has been dead
quite a few years now, and they had no children but
your mother. By his own stubborn nature he could not
reconcile with your mother. I think he might with his
grandchildren if you do not forbid it."

Lydia was silent for a long moment. "You think I
should allow the others, at least, to meet him and learn
to treat him as a grandfather?"

Rafe was silent for some time. He sighed. "He is an
elderly man now. Stubborn as an old goat, of course,
but, as I said, lonely. If one avoids personalities, there
remains the fact his personal fortune is extensive. He
might, you see, leave it to Jasper. Or perhaps divide it
among the younger children which would be no bad

thing. Lydia, from something he said, I have the odd notion he'd not thought of the other children as his grandchildren. *You* were his grandchild. No question of that. But somehow it escaped him that the others were also grandchildren!"

"He is more than odd. He is stupid!"

"No. I think it more that having cast off his daughter, it hurt too much to think of her, of what she was doing or how she was faring."

"Well fal-la to *his* pain! Living with Easten hurt *her* far more!"

"Yes."

The simple agreement deflated her anger. She bit her lip, thinking. "You believe," she said finally, "that I should not interfere in the others meeting and dealing with their grandfather."

"From a mercenary standpoint if no other, I do."

Lydia turned her horse so her back was to his lordship. A rigid spine and head held high revealed her emotions. Then she slumped. "Jasper's estate is small. He truly cannot afford decent dowries for five sisters. If their grandfather provided for them, it would not be necessary for him to suffer years of deprivation." She sighed. "I cannot interfere with what may be such a great benefit to all of them." She drew in a deep breath as she twisted in her saddle, turning back toward him. A grim look about her eyes and mouth, she said, "I will not forbid them to have to do with him."

"But you, yourself, will continue to hold aloof?"

"I must." She looked away.

"Well," he said, "I suppose one could say you come by it naturally!"

"By what?"

"Your stubbornness!" He smiled, taking the sting from his words.

She sighed. "I know I am stubborn. I have had to be, I fear."

"Perhaps it is a trait you might try to modify now it is no longer so needful?"

"Perhaps." She rode on for a bit, debating whether to ask him about the earlier scene with his aunt and Miss Easten. It had preyed on her mind. "Lord Huntingdon, Lady Freward, Miss Easten and I were talking about Lord Charingham earlier, and suddenly, I don't quite know why, they decided to visit him. Something was said, but I cannot for the life of me think what. They were determined to ask him . . . whatever."

"So?"

"So . . . oh, I do not know. And I must not object! Because, if they can possibly make the man come to his senses, then the children are likely to benefit. As you were kind enough to point out!" Again she spent a thoughtful moment considering. "For so many years," she said on an aggrieved note, "I have been angry with the man. Your aunt told me my mother forgave him, but I do not understand how she could."

"We may never understand it. But if *she* did—" he spoke very gently, "—do you think it right that you do not?"

"I . . . don't know. I must think about it."

Rafe, with sudden wisdom, remained silent. They rode on for a short distance, and then, coming to a gate, he suggested they take the lane up onto the Downs so that their mounts might enjoy a good run. Lydia readily agreed, not once thinking that she should not go, alone, with a man to such an isolated area.

And nothing occurred to make her consider it either, which fact, later, convinced her she had been correct in thinking Lord Huntingdon had attempted to flirt with her at the Meadows out of boredom.

She didn't want to think about why she went to her

bed that evening far from content and feeling decidedly unhappy. Perhaps it was because they had been invited to Lord Charingham's for dinner the following evening, and Eunice had informed her she was to attend. No arguments and no excuses.

Surely *that* explained why she was not happy.

Twelve

Lydia looked at the flounced gown, at the ruched one and back again. She sighed. She was so tired of them. "Mama?" she said softly. "I love you very much."

There was no answer of course. Not that she expected one. But, oh, how she would love to possess a lovely new gown. In a dusky reddish brown, perhaps, which would set off her pale hair. In silk. *Real* silk.

Have some sense, she told herself fiercely. She pushed the flounced gown aside and carried the other into her room where a bath awaited her. She had, earlier, found her undergarments and was now ready to undress and sink into the lovely warm water, ready to soak away the worries and the idiotic fancies that kept her mind in turmoil.

The water was just as relaxing as she had expected.

That is, it was until the door opened and Margaret walked in. She was followed by Jasper, James, Mary and the twins. Much to Lydia's relief, Baby Alice did *not* appear. Alice liked, all too well, to play in water and would have had her little hands dabbling in among the soap suds in an instant.

"We are sorry, Lydia, that we did not knock," said Jasper, his face reddening. He turned his back, turning James, too, so that both looked at the door.

"But we must speak with you," said Mary, a stern tone to her voice. "And we must do so at once."

"Liddy, please?" asked Margaret more softly. "It *is* important."

"Liddy?" said one twin.

"Please?" said the other on a plaintive note.

Lydia sighed. "If you all go back out into the hall and wait until I've clothed myself, you may return and we will have this important discussion. I will *not* discuss *anything at all* while sitting in this tub!"

The children put their heads together for a moment. Then, as spokesman, Mary turned back. "We will wait. But you must promise you will take no longer than necessary. Someone might come along and send us all back to the nursery, and we can't have that. It was too much trouble getting away in the first place!"

The children stomped out, shutting the door with a snap, and Lydia, sighing, rose from the water. As she did so, the door to the dressing room opened, and Eunice strolled in.

Lydia reached for the towel and hung it before her. "Good heavens! Why is it impossible for one to have peace and quiet even in one's own room? One is not even allowed to take a bath in peace!"

Eunice glared. "I haven't a notion what you are going on about. We must talk."

"After I've had my talk with the children, if you please, which I cannot do until I have dressed."

"So get dressed. We will talk while you do so."

Lydia was unused to robing before an audience and bit her lip. Eunice, noticing, barked a sharp laugh and turned her back.

"There. Is that better?"

"I suppose," said Lydia, feeling almost as sour as she realized she sounded.

"Well, then. We will discuss this evening. I will not

have you embarrassing everyone with behavior unbecoming to your mother's teaching."

"I am well aware of what is required of a guest. I will
embarrass no one." Lydia pulled on her chemise. "So
long, that is, as Lord Charingham has the sense to leave
me alone."

"I feared it."

Lydia tied her petticoats around her slim waist. "My
mother suffered, Eunice. You know she suffered."

"Probably far better than *you* know," muttered Miss
Easten. "Lydia, she is dead. Let the dead be and allow
the living to live."

"Does that make sense?" Lydia's words were muffled,
since she was pulling her gown down over her head.

"You cannot live in the past."

"I've no intention of living in the past. I merely do
not foresee a future which includes Lord Charingham."

"Have you no pity for him?"

"Did he have pity for her?"

"Lydia . . ."

"I will be polite. I will answer when spoken to."

"That is not sufficient."

"It is all I can promise. Oh, Eunice, go away. I have
to deal with the children, who are waiting in the hall."

Eunice went to the door, opened it and glanced at
the circle of faces. Margaret looked worried, James belligerent, and Jasper very nearly as concerned as Margaret. Mary's features might have formed a model for
the epitome of stubbornness. The twins looked warily
passive, but Eunice guessed that behind their mild expressions was a determination to match that of the others. There was something about the firm way they each
held the other's hand.

"What do you want?" she asked.

"We want to speak with Liddy," said Mary. "And we
will."

"Come in, then. She is nearly ready." Eunice ran her eye over the children, who had also been invited to Lord Charingham's dinner party. "I see you have followed orders."

"We wish to speak to Liddy *in private,*" said Mary, the stubborn look still more pronounced, although Eunice would have said that was impossible.

"Are you meaning to upset her?"

"Upset her?" asked Margaret. The children looked at one another. "Maybe," said James, reluctantly.

"She doesn't need upsetting," said Eunice, frowning. "She's upset enough."

"We must speak with her, Aunt," said Jasper, sounding just a trifle desperate. "I assure you, it truly is *necessary.*"

Their aunt looked from one child to the next and back again. "It cannot wait until tomorrow?"

Again the children looked at each other. "I suppose," said one twin, looking at her sister.

"That we *might . . . ,*" went on the other.

". . . wait for morning. But only if . . ." continued the first.

". . . we may come early. Before breakfast."

"*And* if Liddy tells the nursery maid we are allowed to do so," added Margaret, who had, with difficulty, convinced the maid they might, without breaking some unwritten rule, visit their sister before leaving for Lord Charingham's.

"It's *important,*" stated James, glowering. His belligerence had not abated one jot.

"Might I know the subject of this important discussion?" asked Lydia.

"Well, Liddy, you see James was in the stables and—"

"When he was supposed to—" began a twin.

"No." Jasper put one hand gently over Mary's mouth, the other around a twin's neck, covering her mouth as well. "Until we've time to finish our discussion, I don't think we should begin it. Liddy, you *will* tell the nursery we may come to you early tomorrow?"

"I'll send up a note," said Lydia, sighing.

"If you were to write it now," suggested Margaret diffidently, "we might take it back up with us."

Lydia promptly seated herself and wrote a quick note. "There. Now go away so I may finish dressing." She raised her hand to her head. "I haven't brushed my hair!"

"You look very nice," said Jasper, glancing at her. "Even if you haven't yet brushed it. I wouldn't have noticed."

Lydia bit back the words that brothers rarely noticed their sisters' looks. "Leave me, children. A footman will come for you when it is time to leave for . . . your grandfather's."

"If he is anything like Father was, then I don't know that I want to go." said Mary.

"None of that, my girl," said Eunice, taking Mary firmly by the shoulder and leading her from the room. "We've had quite enough of that sort of nonsense. He is merely an old and lonely man and you *will*—" she scowled fiercely. "Are you listening? You *will* be polite!"

"Liddy once said . . . ," said Mary.

The door closed on the rest, and Lydia, feeling belligerent, hoped Mary might harass Eunice for a change, instead of her. She seated herself at her dressing table and picked up her brush while looking at her reflection . . .

. . . and blushed.

What Jasper had noticed was that the humidity of her bath had curled short wisps of hair about her face in a way that softened her usual severe style. She did look better than usual.

But it wouldn't do. Firmly and with a great deal of energy, Lydia set to putting her hair back into proper order. Which meant every strand was firmly in place and not a single hair allowed the least bit of freedom.

Finally, as ready as she would ever be, Lydia went to the salon where she expected to find Lady Freward. If her ladyship was not there, then she could, perhaps, sew on the second cuff before it was time to leave . . . for her *grandfather's!* Lydia gritted her teeth at the thought.

Dinner was nearly finished when Lord Charingham looked around his table. His heart swelled as he stared, in turn, at the polite youngsters who were his Easten grandchildren. Then he looked at Lydia and winced. She was so very like his beloved Maggie. So very like . . .

Charingham rose to his feet. He waited while the conversation among his guests trailed off, and he stood in the ensuing silence, smiling broadly. "Most of you," he said to his neighbors, "met my grandchildren before we came into dinner. My quite wonderful grandchildren," he said softly, smiling from one bemused child to the next. "But now I want to introduce them formally."

Mary, remembering Lydia's long-ago comments about her grandfather, scowled slightly. Jasper, who had had a talk with Charingham before dinner, smiled shyly. James looked to Lydia and then at his plate. The twins reached out and held hands tightly, and Margaret, not at all certain what was to come, shrank back into her chair, trying very hard to become invisible.

Lord Charingham introduced each in turn, urging the child to stand when called upon, a footman behind them pulling the chair away from the table. He hesitated slightly when he came to Lydia. "My eldest grand-child, Miss Lydia Cottrell," he said firmly.

Lydia stood, her lips compressed and her eyes firmly ahead, staring at nothing at all.

"I mean to see to the needs of each and every one of them, but my eldest is most urgently in need. I'd like to inform her now that she will be as well dowered as my granddaughter would be expected to be dowered. She is not to worry about her future in any way. And that"—Lord Charingham swallowed hard—"I am very sorry that I was so very stubborn about her mother's first marriage. It never occurred to me, you see, that anyone could possibly love another as much as I loved her mother, but I am assured that not only was my daughter blessed by such a love, but that her first marriage was idyllic. It is sad it lasted so short a time." His mouth compressed for a moment. "I have also been informed that her second marriage was not so blessed. On the other hand, without it, I would not be blessed with this wonderful young family of grandchildren."

He glanced at his silent neighbors who, although they didn't actually gape at him, obviously felt like doing so. At what he read in their expressions, Lord Charingham continued a trifle more sardonically. "Thank you all for your patience. The ladies will now adjourn to the salon, and we gentlemen will join you there shortly. I hope—" once again he hesitated, "—my eldest granddaughter will be agreeable to playing for our enjoyment. I am informed she has a wonderful touch on the pianoforte, and I have heard no really good music since her mother last played for me . . ."

Lydia turned a glare of outrage his direction, and his voice trailed off.

He sighed. "We will not, of course, insist."

Lydia was glad Lady Freward moved away from the table. She followed. How dare the man request a favor from her? How dare he try to bribe her with a more than adequate dowry? How dare he try to bribe the other children, for that matter, buying their affection?

She discovered she was stalking, rather than walking, down the hall, and knowing her emotions were unlikely to settle to the point she might behave in a properly polite fashion among strange women in the salon, she quietly asked a footman where she would find the lady's retiring room.

It took her most of half an hour before she felt calm enough to rejoin the company. She thanked the maid who had brushed her hair and opened the door. Leaning against the wall across from it, arms crossed and an exceedingly patient look on his face, was Lord Huntingdon.

Lydia sighed. "My lord."

"Miss Cottrell?" He offered his arm.

Lydia, wishing he were not there but abiding by her decision she would, hell or high water, be properly polite for the remainder of the evening, laid her fingers on it. It wasn't until they passed the stairs returning them to the first floor she realized they were not returning, immediately, to the salon.

"My lord!"

"I have permission to speak to you, Lydia."

"You have permiss—" Her voice broke on a squeak.

"It is expected that we have a few minutes alone."

"No." She halted, refusing to move when he laid his hand over hers and tugged. "No. Don't do this."

"I have wished to do it for some time. Hear me out, Lydia. It is, after all, the proper thing to do, and you have, have you not, determined you would do the proper thing this evening?"

"I don't know how you know that, but my decision did not include . . . this."

"Fifteen minutes."

He paused outside a door and opened it. Lydia could see a long, narrow room, windows along one side and pictures along the other. "His lordship's gallery?" she asked.

"Yes. Family portraits going back forever." He paused between a pair of rather crude portraits. "These are the earliest. Your ever so many great grandparents. Someday you must ask his lordship's housekeeper to tell you the history of each. She knows it as well as anyone. People stop and wish to see the house, and Lord Charingham doesn't like to be bothered; so Mrs. Humber does the honors. It would make her very happy to do so for you and the other children."

"You say that with just a hint of . . . something, my lord," said Lydia bitterly. "Are you urging me to ask or *ordering* me to ask that woman for a tour?"

"Lydia, you are doing it again."

"Doing what?"

"You are once again thinking the worst of me when you've no reason to do so."

"But you always lay yourself open to my thinking the worst."

"You will also think the worst when I tell you I love you and wish very much to wed you?"

"I will think you have decided to ask me now you've heard I'll bring you a proper dowry."

"Lydia!"

"What else can I think? We all heard Lord Charingham at table this evening, doing his best to bribe his way into our affections! How dare he embarrass us that way?"

"How dare he open his emotions before all his neighbors and do something he has never before done?"

Lydia frowned.

"How dare he," Rafe asked sternly, "for the first time

in his life, admit publicly that he was in the wrong? Have you any notion just how hard that was for him?"

Lydia turned away.

"You are not so lacking in sensitivity, Lydia. Nor are you short of a loving heart. I do not believe you can long continue to hate the man now you have met him. You will see that he is merely a very human man who made a terrible mistake which he now wishes to put right."

"Bah."

Rafe sighed loudly. "Bitterness does not become you, Lydia."

She turned, her skirts swinging. "You have no notion of the years of terror through which we lived."

"Terror?"

"All right, then. I'll admit there were long periods when Jasper's father was merely an old grouch. But when his temper was roused, and you never knew what would set it off, he was an animal. A beast wilder than any tiger."

"I see. But, Lydia," said Rafe after a long moment, "your mother forgave your grandfather. Can you do less?"

"I . . . don't know. I have resented him for so long. He allowed my mother to *sacrifice* herself when he might have—"

Rafe, desperate to change the subject back to themselves, stopped her words in the traditional way for a man who knows not what else to do: he kissed her. When he raised his head and looked down at her bemused expression, he smiled slightly and pulled her head against his chest, just holding her close.

"Lydia, we will be wed, if you do not object, in the Huntingdon chapel just as soon as the banns may be called—" He grasped her wrist as she twirled away from his gentle embrace. *"Lydia."*

"I have not said I'll wed you. I will *not* wed you. I will not marry a man who only asks me because he finds I am, after all, an acceptable *parti.*" She pulled against his grasp and then, when he didn't release her, pried at his fingers. "Let me go."

"I love you."

"Do you?" She cast him a contemptuous look. "Cream pot love," she said with all the scorn she could manage, covering the hurt she felt. How dare the man do this to her? Why were men so . . . so . . . oh, she didn't know. "Lord Huntingdon, release me this instant."

He looked down to where his fingers were still tightly around her wrist. Almost as if he had been burnt, he let her go. And then he reached for her hand, lifting her arm to look at the red marks his grip left there. "Lydia . . ."

"It is all of a piece. A man doesn't instantly get what he wants and he reverts to force."

"Don't, Lydia. Please . . ."

"Don't tell the truth?"

"The truth as you see it is distorted."

"Is it?" She studied her arm. "How does one distort *that?*" She held it out for his inspection.

"I . . . don't know." Rafe's mouth compressed tightly, forming little lines raying out around it. "I just know I love you and want to marry you and you are behaving as if I were a monster for wanting to do so." He sighed. "I know I am not, but I don't know how to convince you."

"You weren't listening, were you, Lord Huntingdon? I would never think a man a monster for loving a woman and wishing to wed her. It is only when he wants to wed her simply because she is, financially, a boon to him that makes him a monster in my eyes. Good-bye, my lord. Much to my regret, I cannot leave your roof tonight, but tomorrow I will find some means of removing to the Meadows." She exited on the words.

"Lydia . . ." The door slammed. "Blast and be damned to all women!"

Lord Maythorn eased himself from the window seat in which he had been hidden. "You must admit she has a point."

"What?" Rafe turned so fast he nearly lost his balance. "Blast you, Roger! How dare you eavesdrop on us that way?"

"I was napping. By the time I was enough awake to know what was going forward, it seemed better to remain hidden."

Rafe tacitly admitted that was likely true. "What am I to do, Roger?"

"Woo her. You haven't, you know."

"You are recommending I court her? You? You who have been suspicious of her from the beginning now think I should pursue her with all the trappings of a lover?"

"Yes."

Rafe studied his friend. "Why?"

"Because I think you've finally met your match. Because I have watched the two of you. You *do* love her and it isn't cream pot love or whatever she believes. But your love alone wouldn't be enough to force me to give you encouragement. The important thing is, *she* loves you."

"What?" Rafe stared at his friend. "But . . ." He frowned. "Roger, why, then, did she say me nay?"

"Because, as she said, she thinks it cream pot love with you. You have shown no sign you wished to wed her until suddenly she has a grandfather willing to dower her."

"Dammit, Roger, I've tried to get close to her. She has not allowed it."

"I know nothing about that. I just know this proposal came out of nowhere to her way of thinking. And don't ask what you should do, because I haven't a notion."

"I won't lose her," said Rafe stubbornly.

"Oh, in the end, I doubt you'll lose her. But you may have to develop what is, in you, an underdeveloped trait."

"What trait?" asked Rafe, suspicious.

Roger grinned. "Patience, Rafe. Patience." He clapped his friend on the back and urged him out the door. "We should, I fear, rejoin the rest. With any luck at all your Miss Cottrell will be in such a state of agitation she will play for the company merely to get her hands on a piano. I have noticed, since arriving at the Chase, that she tends to work out her emotions on the piano. Given the roiling state they were in when she left here, she should put on an impressive performance." He chuckled. "If she will play, that is. Her grandfather tends to put his foot in his mouth to almost the degree you do, my old friend!"

"What do you mean by that?"

"You weren't watching her at table when he asked her to play for his guests? And mentioned her mother's playing?"

"I don't mean her," said Rafe, waving his hand. "I mean how did *I* put my foot wrong?"

"You ask her to wed you not five minutes after learning she'd be well dowered and you need me to tell you how you made an ass of yourself? Rafe, boy, you aren't feeling well!"

Rafe groaned softly. "You are quite correct. I am not feeling well."

Strains of a piano reached their ears.

"Aha!" Roger picked up his pace. "Come along, Rafe. We may at the very least enjoy her playing."

Rafe didn't respond; but he was first through the

door, and he took up a stance near the piano, leaning against the wall and, arms crossed, stared at her the whole time she played. There was a bit of gossip whispering around the room about that, but soon everyone was silent, listening raptly. Even those who had thought themselves not particularly musical were enthralled.

He had seated himself well into a shadow so that no one noticed the tears running down Lord Charingham's face. Except Mary. Mary, not entirely certain she was doing the right thing, edged nearer the old gentleman and, hesitantly, gently, patted his hand. When he turned his palm up, she put her little hand into it, and they held hands through the rest of Lydia's wild but wonderful performance.

The next morning, early, Lydia awoke to a rustling and soft whispers. She had forgotten the children were to visit her. In fact, she had spent so long crying, going over and over the preceding evening's events, it had been late, indeed, when she dropped into a dream-agitated sleep. In fact, she remembered hearing the first soft morning chirps of birds before drifting off.

Bleary-eyed, she stared at the children spread out around her bed. This time little Alice was among them, held against Margaret's shoulder. Seeing her oldest sister was awake, Alice leaned dangerously forward, and Margaret was forced to drop her onto the bed. Alice scrambled up to the pillows and into Lydia's waiting arms.

"Are you awake now?" asked James.

The most practical of the children, Mary poured her sister a cup of chocolate from the small pot waiting on a tray at her bedside. She very carefully held the cup and saucer so as not to spill it.

"Put pillows behind Liddy, Jasper, so she may drink this," she ordered sternly. "Then she'll be awake."

Jasper hurried to do so. The children then waited as patiently as their various natures allowed while Lydia shared her chocolate with Alice, who would grimace at each bitter taste and then want another. When the cup was empty and back on its tray, Lydia settled the toddler comfortably beside her and, slightly less bleary, asked that the children open their budget.

"We are afraid you'll marry Lord Huntingdon and leave us," blurted Mary.

"We don't want to go home without you," said Fenella, and for once, her twin, with nothing to add, merely nodded agreement.

"The girls will need you," said Jasper gruffly. Then, when Lydia looked at him, he reddened and added, "I know James and I need you, too, Liddy, but we will be away at school. We could write you here as well as there, you see."

"I see. Why do you think I might wed Lord Huntingdon?"

"James heard him."

"James—" She stared hard at her younger brother. "Heard him?" When? *"Yesterday?"* Her heart pounded. "Where? What did he say?"

"I was in the stables, Lydia. Actually it was a couple of days ago." He dug his toe into the fine carpet covering the bedroom floor. "Wasn't supposed to be there," he mumbled.

"In the stables." Her clutch on little Alice tightened to the point the child squirmed to free herself. "So. What did he say?"

"Lord Maythorn was there, too."

"Yes. I see. What did he say?"

"They were talking. About you."

"What did he say?"

James pouted. "I'm getting to that, Lydia. If you would just be a trifle patient?"

Lydia heard her own voice in his words and forced herself to relax. "Yes, dear. Now, please, if you would"—she lost control—*"tell-me-what-he-said."*

"They were talking about Rafe wanting to marry you and you not being nice to him. And Lord Maythorn said Rafe would just have to ask you and take his chances . . ."

". . . and we don't want . . ."

". . . you to . . ."

". . . marry him. You'll *leave* us."

As each child spoke, Lydia looked from one to another. Their expressions were identical ones of deep concern. Fear, even. She cuddled Alice closer. "I won't leave you as long as you need me. You should know that. You are my brothers and sisters. I am *not* your mother, but I feel the same need to be near you as a mother would." Again she looked from one to another. "You do know that, do you not?"

There were sighs of relief. The children looked at each other. "So," asked Mary, "we don't need to worry that you'll marry him and leave us to a stranger?"

"No, of course you needn't worry that I'd ever leave you to a stranger's care. What a foolish notion!"

"That's all right, then," said Mary. "Come, Alice. We'll breakfast now." She took the child, who waved over the sturdy girl's shoulder before putting a finger in her mouth.

The children were no more than gone, the door shut behind them, when it struck Lydia that Rafe had spoken of wedding her *before* he knew of the dowry.

"Why," she asked herself outloud, "did he not say so?"

Would you have believed him? asked an inner voice.

"Of course," said Lydia.

Really?

Lydia slid off her pillows and back down under the covers which she pulled up to her neck. "I don't suppose I would," she whispered.

You must apologize to him.

"He'll think I only want him to ask again."

You do wish he'd ask again. But even if he does, you must turn him down, so what does it matter?

"Of course. The children . . ." Lydia thought she had cried every tear in her the night before. She discovered she was wrong.

Lydia remained in her room for some hours. Finally, certain she had her emotions well in hand, she descended to the lower floor. It took some doing, but she finally found Mitten and quietly requested directions to where she would find his lordship.

"He is in his study, miss. This way, please." The butler led her down a long hall she had not previously traversed. He knocked on a door, opened it, and announced, "Miss Cottrell."

Backing slowly, the butler watched as Lord Huntingdon's scowl faded into a wary sort of welcoming look. Very gently, Mitten closed the door. And then, reprehensibly, he leaned an ear against it. He was quite miffed he could hear no more than a murmur of voices and took himself off in something of a huff, and just to make himself feel more the thing, he informed the youngest footman he was *not* giving the silver anything like a proper polish.

Inside the study, Lydia stood before Lord Huntingdon, her hands folded before her. "I've come to apologize."

"Apologize."

"Hmm. I should not have accused you of . . . of cream pot love."

"No. You should not have done that."

Her lips compressed, then relaxed. "You've no intention of making this easy for me, have you?"

"I don't quite know what *this* is."

"An apology."

"I see."

Rafe stood up and came around his desk to lean against it. His new position put him far nearer to Lydia than she quite liked.

"So," he said, "if I were to ask again if you would wed me, you would not bite off my head?"

She turned away. "Please don't, my lord. It cannot be, you see. The children . . ."

"The children?" he asked softly when her voice trailed away.

"They came to me this morning." She turned back. "You see, they feared we might wed." When his brows arched high on his forehead, she blushed. "James. He overheard . . . something. In any case, I've promised them I'll not marry and leave them, so don't, please, ask again."

"Because you might be tempted to say me yea?" he asked softly and, secretly, breathed a sigh of relief at her rosy color. "You *would.*"

"No," she said overly quickly. "No, of course I would not."

"Not so long as the children need you."

"You understand."

"I understand you are all a family of ninnies! Do you truly think I'd ask you to leave them? Make them return to the Meadows without you?"

Lydia frowned.

"My ridiculous love, they would remain here with us. Oh, it will be necessary to spend a certain amount of time at the Meadows. The boys' vacations from school, perhaps. Jasper must learn his responsibilities, and his people need an opportunity to know him."

Lydia's frown faded into a look of hope.

"But don't think I'd make *no* demands on you, my love. We would go to London for the season each year and very likely for the little season. We would travel on other occasions as well. To house parties, among other things, and sometimes the children would *not* be welcome and would be left behind. It is true they'd have less of you than they do now."

The look of hope became a conflict of hope and worry and something Rafe couldn't quite determine.

"Lydia?" He placed his hands gently on her shoulders. *"Will* you wed me?"

"I . . . I admit I would like to." She drew in a deep breath. "Rafe, do you think we might discuss this *with* the children? Make them understand how it would be?"

His brows arched. "Get their approval, you mean?"

"Well . . . yes. I guess that is what I mean. In part."

"If they do not approve," he asked with rather cold politeness, "then you would say me nay?"

"I . . . don't know."

"Are you quite certain there isn't a stray dragon you'd prefer me to slay?" he asked, still polite. "Or a tower from which I might rescue you? Mary, you know, can be quite frightening." He adopted a thoughtful look. "I think, on the whole, I'd prefer facing the dragon."

Lydia smiled at this whimsy. "I want to wed you, Lord Huntingdon. Very much."

"Then we will go, immediately, to the nursery where I will do battle with dragons. I will win you, Lydia, with all the vigor and courage of one of those ancient knights who did, we are told, slay the beasts."

Mary persisted with her questions until she had determined exactly when each year and for how long Lord Huntingdon meant to steal their beloved sister from them. The children, once they were reassured they would not lose Lydia altogether, agreed that if Lydia wished to wed his lordship, then it was likely the proper thing for her to do.

"Besides, then we will have . . . ," began one of the twins.

". . . nieces and nephews!" finished the other.

Lydia blushed rosily, but Rafe, putting his hand on one twin's shoulder, shook her gently. "Fenella," he said, "you are embarrassing Lydia."

"Rafe," asked Lydia, embarrassment lost in her curiosity, "how do you know that is Fenella. If it *is* Fenella, of course."

"Of course I'm Fenella," said the child.

"But how do you know?" Lydia repeated her question to Rafe.

"It is obvious." He smiled down at Fenella.

"It is not obvious," objected Lydia, frowning.

"Oh, *one* particular clue *is*. Fenella always begins talking for the two of them."

Fenella and Felicia looked one at the other. They grinned. Lord Huntingdon thought he had discovered their secret, did he? They knew it *wasn't* always the case. Just almost always.

"*I* think," said Felicia, a cat-eating-cream smile tipping her lips as she spoke.

". . . that you might . . . ," said Fenella, her smile equally sly.

". . . sometimes be wrong," said Felicia.

"Ah! But it isn't the *only* way I tell and"—he frowned, staring at Lydia—"frankly, I cannot explain it. It is a mystery to me, too!"

Everyone laughed, and then everyone went, together, to find Eunice and Lady Freward, who were delighted at the news and immediately put their heads together to begin planning the wedding.

". . . at St. James . . ." heard Rafe.

He instantly interrupted. "I mean to get a special license and we will wed here in the chapel just as soon as may be. You may, if you will, plan a reception for us instead . . ."

The two ladies stared at him, recognized there would be no arguing the point, and their heads instantly went back together.

". . . for *after*—" he spoke loudly and firmly—"the bridal trip which will take us to the lake district. Roger has had a letter from his mother which says the whole region is delightful and in which she praises one particular inn to the skies. I will write at once that rooms be reserved for us and we will stay there."

"There is one small problem," said Eunice, staring at Lydia, who blushed if anyone so much as looked at her. "I will not allow the child to be wed in that dress. Or in any of those hanging in her wardrobe! I forbid the banns, my lord, until she may be properly gowned!"

"But there will be no banns. The license . . . ," Rafe argued, but on this point, he lost.

The last stitch was taken in a truly lovely gown, and the wedding took place as scheduled one month later. It was attended by everyone who could squeeze into the chapel. The remaining guests waited beyond the open doors, bathed by the sunshine with which the day was blessed. And everyone followed the wedding party back to the Chase where a truly lovely wedding breakfast awaited them.

Rafe, seeing his bride in her new gown, was almost reconciled to the wait. He didn't yet know it, of course, but there were quite a few new gowns in Lydia's portmanteau . . . along with an exceedingly beautiful night-

gown and lace-trimmed robe which were Lady Freward's wedding gift to her.

It was quite lovely, but, as he insisted many times in
succeeding years, he would just as happily have wed her
in her shift if that was all she had owned.

Dear Reader,

There are lots of children in *A Love for Lydia*. My next, *Taming Lord Renwick* (December, 1999) has only one: A royal brat is sent from India to Lord Renwick for training in English ways. A charming boy, but a bit of a pain and more of a problem. You see, Lord Renwick was blinded some years earlier protecting the prince from a man-eating tiger and the boy fears nothing but Renwick's pet, a fully grown white tiger—the man-eater's cub!

Our blind hero hears a woman's voice and compares it to that of an angel. His aunt, who would do anything to help him, "tricks" the girl into visiting. Eustacia Coleson has problems, too, so her ladyship's suggestion "her friend's daughter" come for a long visit is accepted—even though Lady Blackburne could never have been a friend of Eustacia's long deceased mother!

Despite deceit on both sides, the women join forces to make Lord Renwick's life happier. It would help, of course, if they agreed on how to go about it.

The book after *Taming Lord Renwick* involves one of Renwick's friends. Ian McMurrey weds a young lady against her wishes. Not that McMurrey is aware of that until after the wedding: Lady Serena greets him on their wedding night with a knife in her hand!

I love hearing from my readers and can be reached at PO Box 81771, Rochester, MI 48308. I'd appreciate an enclosed self-addressed stamped envelope for my reply. Alternatively, I can be reached via E-mail at:

JeanneSavery@Juno.com

Cheerfully,
Jeanne Savery

BOOK YOUR PLACE ON OUR WEBSITE AND MAKE THE READING CONNECTION!

We've created a customized website just for our very special readers, where you can get the inside scoop on everything that's going on with Zebra, Pinnacle and Kensington books.

When you come online, you'll have the exciting opportunity to:

- View covers of upcoming books
- Read sample chapters
- Learn about our future publishing schedule (listed by publication month *and author*)
- Find out when your favorite authors will be visiting a city near you
- Search for and order backlist books from our online catalog
- Check out author bios and background information
- Send e-mail to your favorite authors
- Meet the Kensington staff online
- Join us in weekly chats with authors, readers and other guests
- Get writing guidelines
- AND MUCH MORE!

**Visit our website at
http://www.zebrabooks.com**

More Zebra Regency Romances